Merlin's Chosen

BOOK 1

Rise Of The Wyvern

Victoria Kaer

Cover art by Cory McMahon

Author photo by Altenburg Studio

ISBN: 0578071924
ISBN 13: 9780578071923

Deep Dish Publishing

Las Vegas, Nevada

Acknowledgments

For my daughter first and foremost, without whom this story would never have begun. This is for you, Monkey, keep reading.

To my husband for putting up with the endless hours I've spent hiding in the office, for the endless takeout dinners, and for his constant love, support, and encouraging words when everything seemed darkest.

Thanks go out to you, Dad and Mom, for everything you have done to get me here. I couldn't have asked for any better in-laws. You are the best ever, period.

To our good friend Alan for your help, advice, support, and putting up with my endless e-mails to you because "If Alan doesn't know the answer, no one does."

To my awesome friend Kris, for the help, advice, and letting me pick her brain.

Finally, to all my Warriors—thanks, guys, for getting me started. If it hadn't been for those first few nudges from all of you, we wouldn't be here; you all know who you are. You gave me the courage to put my story to paper and get it out there for everyone to see. Thanks for letting me bounce ideas and stories off you at all hours of the day and night. For reading, revising, and helping me through it all. You will all remain forever my Warriors.

And always, always remember: Mouse in a Blender!

Contents

PROLOGUE

The Nightmare Is Born

Theryn stared across the room at the squat little magic maker. He didn't know why the man had brought him here. Nor why the sorcerer felt he had to bind him here with a spell. Dragons had always worked with sorcerers; all the magic maker had to do was ask Theryn for what he wanted, and he would gladly give it. Instead, the squat, ugly little man had brought him here to his dirty little hut and bound him with a spell. Theryn tried to break free, but he was bound tight by magical means. He could neither move nor speak, and his fire was stuck in his belly, useless. The little man was shuffling around the room, taking jars off shelves and throwing things into a large cauldron hung over a fire.

Soon the little man rubbed his hands together, glanced briefly at Theryn, and began to mumble to himself, raising his hands over his head as he spoke. Theryn's ears perked up. He knew not what the words were, but he recognized them as being of the old tongue. This was bad, very bad indeed; he renewed his struggles for freedom. The sorcerer's words grew louder and sudden pain tore through Theryn's large body. It was almost as if his entire skeleton were trying to rearrange itself into some strange new form. The dragon writhed on the floor; pain wracked his huge body. The spell that held him broke, alas, caught in the depths of this new spell as he was, he took no notice of his sudden freedom.

The sorcerer finished his spell and waited patiently for his greatest work to be completed. There was a flash of brilliant white light, and a creature rose through it. A creature so horrid he feared his own creation—feared it so greatly that he backed away from it, crashing over the pedestal that held his spell book. The thing roared and rose through the air crashing upward, tearing through the roof into the night sky, disappearing.

No! That wasn't supposed to happen! he thought. The sorcerer scrambled through the debris on the floor, searching desperately for his spell book. When he found it, he began flipping through it, searching for the spell, tearing some of the delicate pages in his frantic search. Here it was. His finger ran down the list of ingredients. He had done it perfectly; he flipped the page, then another, and he found his mistake immediately. In his haste to complete the incantation, he had flipped the pages too quickly. He hung his head, letting it fall forward to rest on the pages of the spell book. The pages had stuck together; he had mixed two spells together, a deadly mistake only a novice would make. He was no novice.

Suddenly, he stood and began grabbing items, tossing them into a ragged-looking satchel; whatever he touched was flung carelessly into the bag. He must hurry; he had to leave now before anyone found out. He looked at the spell book sadly and tossed it into the fire in the hearth, briefly watching as the pages began to peel at the edges, eaten by the hungry flames of the fire. He grabbed a large log and set the end in the fire, leaving the rest dangling out onto the floor. His eyes swept the room, falling on the bed; he grabbed the ragged bed covering, feeding it to the growing flames, and then fled out the door.

Leaving his home to burn, he ran across the open field. No one must find out what he had done—no one. There was only one creature; surely, it would die out on its own, surely. He continued to run on in darkness.

In the distance, the creature roared in rage, and a village screamed in terror.

CHAPTER 1

My Mom's Car Gets A Moon Roof

I turned and looked over my shoulder—nothing, just the wind. I still felt there was *something* there. I shook my head to clear it. Just the darkness making me think that I was being followed, that's all—nothing more. *The dark of night did that to you, didn't it?* I continued walking down the dimly lit road. Looking over my shoulder every now and then, hoping that it was only my imagination playing games with me. Then a noise, definitely a noise, off to my left. *A kind of scraping metal noise, like giant claws, on what, a car? Where had that errant thought come from?* I began walking a bit faster, wanting to get home before whatever had made that horrid sound caught up to me. There was a sudden flash of something to my right. *Impossible; the sound had been off to my left. Hadn't it?* No answer to that silent question, there was just empty darkness and my own nagging fear.

I sped up, moving even faster, rounding the corner to my block, knowing my house was only five off the corner. *Just a few more houses!* I encouraged myself. *You can make it!* Swish. I felt a breeze pass over me. *What was that?* I didn't dare look. *Faster, I had to move faster!* I broke into a run. My house—I could see it now. The lights were on. Mom always left them on when I was out past dark. I ran up the front steps, jammed my key into the lock, nearly snapping it off in my haste to open the door. I slammed it shut behind me and bolted it. I ran and peeked out through the front curtains and saw … nothing. Blackness and a deserted street.

"Chandra, what in heaven's name are you doing?" I nearly hit the ceiling when I heard my mother's stern voice behind me.

"*Mooom* ... jeez, you freaked me out! Don't do that!" I jumped off the couch and headed to my room to dump my backpack and get ready for dinner. She followed me down the hall.

"Chandra, you slam into the house like a pack of wild boars and go peeking through the curtains, spying on the neighbors. What's going on?" I rolled my eyes—when her back was turned, of course.

What was I supposed to tell her? *Well, Mom, I think some creature with giant metal shredding claws was following me home from the library. So I sprinted home and slammed the door shut to keep it out!* Yeah, I didn't think that was such a great idea. Instead, I just shrugged and asked how long till dinner was ready. She rolled her eyes at me and mumbled her usual bit about teenage girls and how she never would have acted like that when she was my age, and then she took herself off to the kitchen. It was times like this that I was glad I would be eighteen next year, a senior, and soon after that I would be off to college, and then I wouldn't have to listen to her "when I was a girl speeches" anymore. Still, I wondered what had been following me. I couldn't shake the feeling that something *had been* there, just behind me. I wasn't sure I really wanted to find out what it was. Then again, I had a feeling that it was something important, too.

The next few days made that night of fear fade; actually, I totally forgot about it all together. With my schoolwork and my few friends I hung out with, it was easy to forget. My birthday came around; it was a small celebration. It was just me, my mom, and a couple of my friends. We didn't have much money for a big bash, so Mom just took us out to dinner. It had always been just me and Mom. Mom teaching, she was a high school teacher— thank God, not at my school. Me growing up and making her life, well, as interesting as a kid can. My dad had died in a car wreck when I was only a month old. Mom had never even looked at another guy since Dad died. I told her that she could date, it was fine by me; but she never did. I don't even remember my dad. She would give me a sad smile and just shake her head whenever I asked about him. I guessed that she just loved him so much that she wouldn't even consider another guy in her life. I always wondered what that would be like, to love a guy so much you wouldn't even consider ever being with anyone else. I wasn't much interested in any of the guys in our little town. They were just what they looked like, small-town guys. Not that I hadn't tried dating any of them. They just weren't very interesting to me.

I slumped in my seat at the restaurant while the waitresses sang happy birthday. My friend Shina was grinning at me, and she was singing the loudest; her birthday was next week.

"So, Chandra, how does it feel to be seventeen?" I shrugged; it didn't feel so very different from sixteen, really. I yawned; I was really tired for some reason. I just wanted to go home and go to bed. I didn't feel well at all. Great, sick on my birthday—story of my life! After dinner, we dropped my friends off and drove home. Mom was pulling in the drive when she frowned at me.

"Honey, are you all right? You don't look so good." Leave it to my mom to notice the obvious.

"Actually, Mom, I don't feel good. I'm really tired, and hot. I feel like I'm on fire." She felt my forehead and leaned away, her face looking worried.

"Chandra, honey, I think we had better get you to the hospital." She looked scared, which didn't bode well for me. My mom didn't scare easily. If she was scared, it was a big deal, so I slumped down in my seat.

"I don't want to go to the hospital, Mom; I just wanna go to bed!" She frowned at me in that *don't argue with me, young lady* way of hers. I wanted to cross my arms and give her a stubborn teenager look, but I simply didn't have the strength. She backed out of the driveway and headed down the street, eventually turning off on to River Mt. Trail Road, which would eventually take us to highway 93, into town and the hospital. I hated River Mt. Trail; it was long and twisty and led through a bit of forest, which, I'd always thought was just odd since we lived in the desert. I mean a forest in the desert? Come on! I never could figure out how those trees survived; it was like magic or something. It was just *way* creepy at night, and it always freaked me out.

As we drove, I suddenly had that strange feeling again that something was following me. I dragged myself up in my seat and looked in the side mirror. I saw a flash—nothing solid, really, just *something.*

"*Mooom* … something is following us." She frowned over at me.

"Chandra, honey, stop that. No one is following us; there are no headlights in my mirror." I kept my eyes glued to the mirror on my side of the car; I was sure I had seen something. There was no way I was going to miss it again, no matter how crappy I felt. I waited, trying hard not to blink. My eyes were drier than my cat Legend's litter box, but I didn't blink.

"Come on." I muttered under my breath. As badly as I *didn't* want something to be there, I *did* want it to be there, to prove I was not going insane. Suddenly the car did a 180; Mom slammed on the brakes and the tires locked and squealed.

"What in the hell was that?!" That was about as close to swearing as my mother ever came. She threw off her seat belt with every intention of getting out of the car and checking to see if she had hit some poor furry little animal. That's when I saw it. I grabbed her arm and yanked her toward me.

"Mom, I don't think you should get out just now." It was huge, whatever it was. The shadow loomed out of the night sky, flying straight toward the car. I wanted to scream, but somehow it never made it out of my throat. I heard the sound of claws scraping metal. The same sound I had heard that night as I walked home from the library. It had to be the same creature that had been following me home that night. The car rocked as claws ripped through the roof. I shrank down in my seat, watching those claws slip through the metal of the roof as if it were nothing at all, just mere tissue paper, leaving huge gashes behind. The creature flew off, probably to turn and make another pass at the car. What was that thing?

"Chandra, come on, we have to get out of here before it comes back!" I turned and stared at my mother. Had she lost her mind? How could we outrun that thing? It could fly! "Chandra, let's go, now! We have to hurry." She latched on to my arm, dragging me out of the car and into the woods on the side of the road. We crashed through the trees. The creature roared in frustration when it realized its prey had fled the scene. Great, now we had ticked it off! I suddenly realized one very important detail: My mother was completely unfazed by the fact that a large flying creature had just totaled our car. The sound of large wings beating the air distracted me from my thoughts. I tried to look up and locate the beast through the canopy of trees. It was too hard to run and look up at the same time. I nearly collided with a tree the size of a VW bug—okay, maybe not that big, but in the dark, it sure as heck seemed like it!

"Mom, we can't outrun that thing!" I knew we were probably gonna die any second. I was still burning up, and running through the woods wasn't helping any. I wasn't about to remind my mother I was sick. She was trying to dial her cell and run at the same time. Not easy in the dark of an overgrown forest with some winged beast chasing you down like you were tonight's blue-plate special. I wondered who exactly she was trying to call; the cops weren't exactly going to be much help. What would she tell them? Puff the Magic Dragon was trying to eat us. She tripped; I grabbed her arm to keep her from going down and sprawling on the forest floor. She nodded at me in thanks; we ducked down behind a large group of fallen trees, and she finally got the phone dialed. She waited for an answer and immediately began shouting into the phone when she got one.

"Fredrick, thank goodness! Yes, I know you said not to call unless it was an emergency. Well, it's an emergency! No, no! Listen, will you? They've come for her! Yes, right now! No, when did you think? We're in the forest off River Mt. Trail Road. Yes, on foot. It destroyed the car! We had no choice! Okay, yes, I will. No, I won't. Of course, I have it with me! Yes, she has. Yes, yes, I understand. What, that long?! No, no, no! Fine." She hung up the phone. I decided that that had to be the strangest conversation I had ever witnessed in my entire seventeen years of life. I sat there and stared at my mom.

"Mom, who was that?" I asked. She fumbled with her phone as she stuffed it back into her purse, which, somehow she had managed to bring with her from the car, despite our hasty departure. She didn't bother to answer me. Instead, she pulled a small sphere out of her purse. It was about the size of one of those super bouncy balls that you used to love as a kid, but it was clear and appeared to be made of glass. She turned to me and held it out.

"What?" I asked, staring at the little sphere sitting in her palm.

She rolled her eyes at me like I was supposed to know what to do with the thing. "You have to do it, Chandra. My body temperature isn't high enough to light it, but yours is now." I stared at her. Light it? What in God's name was she talking about?

"Just take it in your hand and squeeze it; when it glows, that means it's lit. It's a signal. So he can find us, before the wyvern figures out a way to get to us."

I stared at her, my eyes wide. She knew what that thing was called! Who was this woman? She couldn't be *my mother*. I snatched the little glass ball—it was warm despite the cool night air—and squeezed it. The orb glowed a faint orange color as soon as it lit. She took it back and put it in her purse.

We sat there for what seemed like hours, but what could have really only been twenty or thirty minutes. That thing—I couldn't begin to remember what she'd called it—was circling overhead and roaring down at us. It couldn't seem to figure out how to get to us through the trees, which was, in my opinion, a good thing. Suddenly, there was an answering roar. I froze—oh, great, it had friends! Mom stood up, a huge smile on her face.

"He's here to get us." How did she know that was our ride and not that thing's buddies? Then the second thing roared again. I listened hard to the roars above us, and I understood what she meant; it was a little different. I couldn't exactly explain how it was different. I just knew it was, somehow. Mom took my hand, and we began to walk back toward the road. She was still smiling brightly.

"We have to get to an open area; they can't get through the trees any more than the wyvern can. Not without destroying half the forest, anyway." I wondered what exactly a wyvern was. I also wondered what exactly our ride was and who the "he" was that came with it. I figured now wasn't the time for a game of twenty questions. We made it to the edge of the forest, stayed just inside the tree line, and waited. We heard a lot of roaring and large wings beating the air. Were the creatures fighting? I wondered, just a little worried about maybe ending up in the middle of a war of battling creatures of immense size.

A short time later, a large crimson dragon landed on the road in front of us, followed closely by a smaller emerald dragon. No kidding—dragons, honest-to-goodness dragons. This night had gotten seriously strange. I brushed a hand across my forehead. I was still hot; I wanted to tell my mom. She only had eyes for the dragons in the road. I turned back to see what was so interesting. A man climbed down off the crimson dragon, patting the dragon and saying something to it before walking toward where we stood. The man was the last thing I saw before I passed out.

CHAPTER 2

We Move To A Cave With A View

I awoke to the sound of hushed voices close by. They were trying not to wake me, I guessed. I was lying on what felt like a soft bed. I wondered where the man with the dragons had brought us. The thought occurred to me that maybe the fever I had could have made me have a really bad dream, and *maybe* I had imagined everything that had happened after dinner. I rolled slowly on to my side and cracked one eye open. I nearly fell off the bed when I saw exactly where I was. Mom came running to my side when she saw I was finally awake.

"Chandra, honey, are you okay?" I stared at her, shocked. How could I be okay? We were in a freaking cave, for God's sake! I looked around again just to be sure. Rock walls check; rock floor, check, rock ceiling, and check. Yep, it was a cave, all right. Except for the fact that it was fully furnished, it was most definitely a cave. The man I had seen earlier was standing on the far side of the cave. He walked to my mother's side.

"Let her be, Mere, it's been a long day." I frowned at him. Who was this guy? How did he know my mother, and why was she letting him call her *Mere?* Mom *never* let anyone call her Mere. Her name was Meredith, and that was that. At least, that's what she always told everyone. Chandra really had had enough weirdness for today. When did I start referring to myself in the third person? The dragon guy was definitely right; it had been a long day! I sat up and pushed my mom away, coming to my feet beside the bed.

I was miffed—I wanted to know what was going on, and I wanted to know now.

"Okay, I want some explanations, and I want them now, this second, not later. Now!" I stared at both adults; they just stared back at me in silence. I crossed my arms over my chest and waited, deciding I could wait them out if I had to. I began tapping my foot impatiently on the cave floor. Honestly, a cave—we were living in a cave! This was most definitely a step down as far as I was concerned. If my friends at school found out about this, I was going to be at the bottom of the lists for any future social events. Not that I had been at the top of any of those lists to begin with.

Both adults exchanged looks, and my mom held out her hands in a gesture that I could only interpret to mean she didn't know exactly what to say. This was the first time in my life I had ever seen my mother look helpless. She had always known what to do in every situation. Jeez, she had just run through a forest and saved us from a—whatever it was! The dragon guy put his hand on her arm and spoke instead. I still didn't like him, just because he knew my mom and I didn't have a clue how. Was he an old boyfriend or something? That thought made me like him even less.

"Chandra, you have a right to be upset. We should have told you a long time ago something like this might happen. We just hoped that it wouldn't." It was just about the least helpful thing he could've said at that moment.

"What kind of explanation is that? *Gee, we hoped it wouldn't happen, but it did?* You hoped what wouldn't happen? That I wouldn't get eaten by some giant flying whatever it was!" My voice had gone high pitched by the end. I figured only dogs could've heard me at that point. I sat down on the edge of the bed; I felt hot enough to set the whole place ablaze. I took a deep breath, trying to calm down, fanning myself with my hand.

"You'll get used to the temperature change in a few months. I should've warned your mother about the fever." I raised my head, frowning at him.

"Get used to it in a few months?" I was sure I sounded disbelieving. How was I supposed to get used to being hot and sweaty 24-7? In addition, *why* would I have to get used to it? He sighed and sat down next to me. I scooted away from him, and he sighed again.

"It all depends on how quickly you learn to control your powers. We should have prepared you for this, Chandra, but we never thought you would be the one. The chance was very small that you would be the Chosen." I stared at this man who was a total stranger, yet seemed to be dead set on giving me advice on my life. What was he saying? Powers? Chosen? Chosen for what? To do what? To be what? I looked at my mom; however, she had turned away and was staring out of the mouth of the little cave into the room beyond. I could hear sounds coming from out there, but I didn't want to try to identify them. I was afraid I knew what they were, though. I returned my gaze to the man.

"Chandra, your mother and I met, and we fell in love. She knew from the start what might happen if we stayed together," He hesitated. "If we had a child." I jumped up and streaked across the room to where my mother stood. I stood close to my mother, so different from me, with her wavy, tawny blond hair and green-blue eyes. I look nothing like her. She had always told me I look like my father.

"No! My father died in a car accident a month after I was born! Tell him, Mother, tell him!" She didn't turn around to look at me even though I was shrieking at her. She shook her head. "Mother, *tell him!*"

"No, Chandra, he didn't. Fredrick is your father. We came up with that story when the wyvern showed up after you were born. Somehow, they knew Fredrick had had a child. We couldn't ..." She broke off, unable to continue, waving a hand in Fredrick's direction. I faced Fredrick again. This stranger, whom it seemed, was my father.

"When the wyvern showed up, your mother and I thought it was for the best that I *die,* and she and you start a new life somewhere else. So my car drove off a bridge. My body was never found, assumed lost in the river. Your mother took you and moved away, too distraught to stay in the house that held so many memories for her. When she moved to the new town, she became a widow looking for a new start. A few spells kept the two of you hidden. I left and came here." That damned impossible forest in the desert—that's what was supposed to keep us hidden. Is that what he meant by spells? I looked from one to the other. They made it sound so simple and easy. My whole life was a lie. Who was I, exactly?

"Chandra, come here and sit down; there's a lot more I need to explain to you." Did he seriously think I wanted to listen to some more of his explanations?

I turned and stomped out of the cave, across the small hallway, and into the outer chamber, which turned out to be a huge mistake. I stopped dead in my tracks as soon as I made it out of the smaller cave and across the narrow hallway into the larger chamber. Besides the outer chamber being colossal in size, it was also largely occupied by dragons. About fifteen of them, in fact, of varying colors and sizes, which explained all the sounds I had heard out there.

They were talking and moving around, going about whatever business dragons do in their spare time. Several looked up at me, curious, I supposed, about the new arrival. I very slowly backed up toward the safety of the little cave where my mom was. I turned and ran the last few steps and dove under the covers on the bed.

"I think she took that rather well, Mere, don't you?" I heard laughter in his voice when he spoke. I really was liking him less and less the more I got to know him. I didn't care if he was my dad.

"So, are you ready to listen now, Chandra?" I peeked out from under the covers to look—yes, he was definitely laughing at me. His eyes were all crinkled at the corners, and he had a large smile on his face. I had to admit I could see what my mom saw in him, if I looked at it objectively. I crawled out from under the covers and sat rather mutinously on the edge of the mattress.

Fredrick was handsome even if he was my dad, so I could cut Mom some slack for falling for him. He was the tall, kinda dark, handsome type, I guessed. His hair was dark brown just like mine, just as straight, with barely a trace of a curl, too. He could be called handsome. He was somewhere around six feet tall. He was certainly in shape, not some middle-aged guy with a spare tire. No wonder my mom had never wanted to date; Dad had been here waiting for her the whole time. I would listen to what he had to say, but then I was out of here. I had had enough fairy-tale theater for one day.

"I assume you saw enough out there to want to listen to the whole story?" he asked, and I nodded. "The creature that was chasing you and your mother earlier was called a wyvern." I nodded again. "Do you know the difference between a dragon and a wyvern?" I stared at him, dumbfounded; before tonight, I hadn't known a real dragon existed. As for the other thing, I had never heard of it! I shook my head at him. "Okay, I'll give you the short version for now. Dragons are the noble, intelligent ones. They prefer knowledge and peace."

I held up a hand and stopped him. "Aren't dragons the ones who lock damsels in towers and eat the knights in shining armor?" I asked.

He chuckled and shook his head. "Those are fairy-tale stories for children, Chandra. Most are misconceptions and started because of the wyvern. Let me finish. Dragons are old creatures, older than most creatures on earth. They used to live in peace with man—until the wyvern appeared. No one knows where they came from or exactly how they were born. There are some that say they were an experiment by a sorcerer gone wrong. That he'd been trying to control a dragon, take away his free will, and enslave him. However they were born, it never should have come to be. They are horrible creatures. The wyvern are aggressive and will attack just about anything in sight. They stand on two legs and have true wings, wings more like a bat's with claw-like hands at the end, claws that can rip and tear you to pieces. A barbed stinger at the tip of their tail that can easily kill, that stinger carries a deadly poison with it. The poison usually kills instantly. The wyvern breathe no fire."

I shuddered involuntarily as he finished. That's what had been following me in the street as I'd walked home from the library and what had attacked our car. A wyvern, the enemy of the dragons out in the cavern; now it would seem they were my enemies as well, for whatever reason.

The wyvern sounded like horrible creatures, I didn't ever want to meet one face-to-face. I stared at Fredrick, waiting for the rest. There had to be more, right?

"What about me? Where do I fit into all of this mess of creatures?" I asked him, a little reluctantly.

He nodded and continued. "I'm not as old as the dragons or the wyvern. But I'm still old." I rolled my eyes. I never understood why adults seemed to enjoy making fun of how old they were. "I'm a lot older than I look, Chandra. A couple of hundred years, if you wish to be exact, I don't really keep track anymore; I stopped right around when I turned a hundred and fifty." I stared at him; he had to be kidding. A glance at my mother told me he wasn't. She'd taken a seat in an armchair across the room near the entrance to the little cave. She smiled at me encouragingly.

"I'm a sorcerer born many years ago; in England, if you wish to know. I've traveled all over the world in my fight against the wyvern. I've been fighting on the side of the dragons for a very long time. The wyvern have been growing stronger and stronger. The dragons are losing, to put it simply. Merlin made a prophecy many years ago." I stared at him in awe. Was he serious? Like Merlin, Knights of the Round Table Merlin, King Arthur Merlin? I'm not sure what the look on my face told him, but it must have been something pretty good because his eyes had gone all crinkly at the edges again.

"Yes, Chandra, *that* Merlin. Do you want to hear the prophecy or not?" I could only nod; words had escaped me for the moment.

"*A child will be born of magic blood, a chosen child with powers beyond those we can imagine; this child will save all of dragon-kind and destroy the wyvern.* I am pretty sure I just might be the last sorcerer, Chandra. The wyvern have been hunting down our kind since Merlin made that prophecy. I haven't seen another sorcerer in many years. Many of us went into hiding, stopped practicing openly. When you were born, I had hoped you would be the Chosen, but I also feared it as well. I knew they would come for you, to kill you. The fever is the first sign that your powers are growing. Most sorcerers gain the use of their full powers on their eighteenth year."

He fell silent, and I saw tears in his eyes. This man was my father. I knew it now; I could see it in his face. I had his eyes, hazel, ever changing from brown to gray and back, depending on my mood. His were doing that now. Maybe it was a sorcerer thing, the eyes. On impulse, I jumped forward and wrapped my arms around him, giving him a hug.

"Thanks for coming for us in the forest, Dad." I didn't know what else to say. It sounded lame when I said it out loud, but he smiled back at me. He seemed relieved that I had called him Dad.

"Why don't you get some sleep for now? We can talk about things some more later. I need to get your mom back to the house while things are quiet, so she can get both of you some of your things before the wyvern come back." I nodded and curled up on the bed. Getting under the covers was out of the question; I was way too hot. At least it was cool in the cave. I yawned and called out to my mom as they walked out of my little cave room.

"Don't forget to get Legend, Mom. She would freak if we left her behind." I wondered how my cat was going to do around a bunch of dragons as I smiled and drifted off to sleep.

15

CHAPTER 3

I Shower With Dragons

I woke up feeling just as hot and sweaty as I had last night. I grumbled and rolled out of bed. I looked around; it hadn't been a dream, and everything was real. I poked at my brain to see how it felt about it all. I was a sorceress. It felt odd to think that. My dad was alive, an even odder thought. Nevertheless, a good one.

I wondered where the light in the cave came from—magic, probably. I looked around my little room; it was nicely furnished. I wondered if Fredrick—Dad, I corrected myself—had furnished it just for me in the expectation that I would one day live there. That thought made me smile. He had wanted me to come and live here—well, Mom, too, I guessed.

I felt clammy and utterly gross; suddenly, I wondered if there was such a thing as a bathroom with a shower in this cave of wonders. I decided to go in search of my dad and find out. Before I left my room, I rummaged in the drawers of the dresser, which was against the wall across from the entrance to my room. Mom had been in and put my things away that she'd gotten from the house the night before. I must have slept like the dead because I never heard her. I found my favorite pair of jeans and an old worn T-shirt. A sound behind me made me jump and turn. Legend was purring from the armchair near the entrance to my room. I smiled at her. It felt good to have her there, something familiar in this whole mass of weirdness. I patted her on the head and smiled when her purring rumbled louder.

I set out in search of my dad. It still felt a little odd to think that, Dad, after a whole life of not having a dad. I peeked out into the main chamber; most of the dragons were curled up on top of their piles of treasure, still asleep. Apparently, that part of the fairy tales was true. Dragons liked to hoard treasure.

"Looking for me, perhaps?" I really was going to have a heart attack eventually if he kept sneaking up on me like that. I turned on my dad, ready to give him a good teenage fit for scaring me, until I remembered I really wanted a shower. Therefore, I figured I had better be nice if I wanted him to tell me if there was one someplace around there. I nodded instead, not trusting myself to actually speak instead of yell. He smiled as if he knew exactly what I was thinking.

"What can I do for you this morning, Chandra?"

I sighed and took a deep breath before I spoke. "Is there a shower in this place?" I shuffled my feet a bit, feeling suddenly silly asking for something as stupid as a shower after everything he had told me about the wyvern and the dragons last night. A shower in the middle of a war sounded kinda selfish. He only smiled and nodded.

"Come on, I'll show you where it is—it's just down the hallway." He pointed back the way I had just come, toward my room. We stopped so I could get my things on the way back. We walked back down the hall past a few more empty caves—there seemed to be a lot of them, of varying sizes. I frowned.

"Do you expect a lot more people to come and live here?" I asked as we continued down the widening hallway. He shook his head as we turned down a narrower passageway. "Then why all the extra caves?" I wondered out loud.

He sighed and smiled at me. "We were prepared for anything, Chandra. However, we didn't exactly expect anyone else, no." He pointed to the curtained entrance in front of us and smiled at me. "Your spa, madam." I had the distinct impression he was laughing at me again. I chose to ignore it and pulled back the curtain instead.

The cave was a tiny bathroom with a white tiled floor, a toilet, a tub/shower combo, and an old-fashioned pedestal sink with a mirror above it. I was beginning to really love magic. It looked so normal that I very nearly cried. I turned to tell my dad thank you, but he had vanished. I wondered if he had a habit of doing that—also appearing out of thin air when he wished to. I was going to have to ask him to teach me how to do that someday. Right now, all I cared about was a hot—no a cold, I corrected myself—shower. I let the curtain fall back into place behind me. When I looked back over my shoulder, from the inside, it looked just like a plain old bathroom door, painted a deep forest green, wooden and solid. I went to work getting myself back to human cleanliness.

I felt better when I was all clean again, except for the nonhuman temperature. I gathered up my things and lifted the curtain door. I really wasn't all that surprised to find my dad lurking outside, leaning against the wall, his hands thrust into the pockets of his khakis.

"Ready for the grand tour?" he asked, pushing himself away from the wall. He didn't strike me as an old man, certainly not anywhere near one hundred and fifty—or rather over that, since he had stopped counting at that point. He moved with the ease of a young man. I nodded at him, and we started off back down the hall. We stopped in my room to dump off my things. I noticed that Legend had vanished from her spot on the chair, probably off ridding the caves of mice, I thought. He showed me the slightly larger cave he and Mom shared just down the way from mine. Strangely enough, it was furnished just like Mom's room at home.

Dad told me that Mom had picked out the furnishings for the rooms here when they had found out that Mom was pregnant with me. They knew that there was a possibility the wyvern would come after me someday. Eventually, it could have become necessary for Dad to leave us; he would have to go into hiding. I couldn't believe that my mother had actually helped set up this place.

"You should see the massive amount of extra furnishings she stuffed back into one of the other caves." He said it with a little laugh. I stared at my father. Then I remembered my mother's love of garage sales and penchant for constant redecorating, and I grinned. The extra furniture was no surprise, I supposed. We went into the large outer chamber where the dragons were. Most were up by now, chatting, it would seem, with one another.

I saw Mom perched on top of one of the treasure piles, calmly talking with a smaller violet dragon. Funny, but it looked completely natural at this point to see my mother sitting on a pile of gold and jewels, talking with a dragon and waving at me. I waved back. Dad continued on, weaving his way around the various piles of treasure. He seemed to be headed in a certain direction.

"Dad? Does each dragon have their own pile of treasure?" I asked curiously.

He nodded absently. "Each dragon guards his or her own hoard; no dragon would ever consider stealing from another, especially here in their own clan. It would be against their code of honor. If that code were broken, it would make the offender no better than a wyvern in the eyes of the other dragons."

"I always thought dragons were solitary creatures. That they lived alone in little caves."

He chuckled. "More fairy tales, Chandra. We humans tend to make up stories about things we don't understand. The dragons live in clans; they were much larger in years past. They can protect one another better in larger groups; hunt better. It works best for everyone. Some sorcerers even lived with the dragons, but that was centuries ago. Our kind is extinct now, I believe. Even the dragons outnumber our kind." He gave me a grim smile.

I considered everything he'd told me as we walked on. Dad stopped just then in front of a ledge, which held the largest pile of treasure. Sitting atop it was also the largest dragon. Dad cleared his throat, and the dragon stirred, uncurling and raising its massive head. It was a deep golden color. I thought if any dragon embodied the legends of old, *this* was that dragon. I was in awe of it as it rose before me, so different from my father's description of the wyvern.

I could see that the dragons stood on four legs, instead of two, as the wyvern did. Their wings sprouted from their rib cage just behind their front legs, though the wings appeared just as bat-like as the wyverns. The only difference was the hand-like extensions the wyvern had at the ends; the dragons had no "hands" at the ends of their wings. I watched as the dragon pulled itself up and stretched, and then turned to face us fully. The dragon had a set of horns crowning its head. I wondered if the wyvern had horns, too. I also knew that the dragons could breathe fire and the wyvern couldn't.

"Fredrick, is that you I smell?" I realized with a start that the dragon was blind. I saw its eyes were milky white, blinded by cataracts. How old could this dragon possibly be?

"Yes, Queebo, it is," my father answered.

Queebo? I thought with a small chuckle; it didn't seem like a very dignified name for a dragon to me. My father nudged me with his elbow; he obviously knew I was trying hard not to laugh. I tried harder. The dragon swung its head in my direction, the nostrils flaring briefly as it sought to know my scent.

"Your daughter, I presume, Fredrick?" The dragon drew its head back and rested it on its front paws.

"Yes, Queebo, this is Chandra. I brought her to meet you. I thought it was about time. Chandra, this is Queebo. She is the leader of the clan."

I turned to the dragon. "It's very nice to meet you, ma'am." What else were you supposed to say to a dragon? She chuckled, a deep, gravelly sound, and smoke came out her nostrils. I looked at my father for a clue as to what to do next, but he was watching Queebo.

"Fredrick, her temperature is high." My father nodded, but said nothing.

"Dad?"

Queebo answered instead of my dad. "You see, child, in most cases when a sorcerer comes into his or her powers, as you are now, the higher their temperature, usually the greater their powers. Yours is the highest I have ever seen, my dear." She reminded me of someone's elderly grandmother. Except for the scales, wings, and fiery breath. My father shifted uncomfortably beside me.

"That's not always the case, Queebo. You know, sometimes it can be a false indicator; it has happened before. Let's not get her hopes up to high, shall we?" I wondered who had gotten disappointed before. Was it someone he knew?

Queebo only nodded. "Well, Fredrick, I hope you will start instructing her immediately anyway." It didn't sound like a question. He nodded again, and Queebo put her face close to mine. I wondered if she even knew he was nodding, agreeing with her. "I think we can expect some surprising things from you, my dear, yes."

I smiled, feeling warmed by her confidence in me. I didn't even mind her calling me child earlier; it had been done in such a gentle voice, even for so large a creature. I reached out and put my hand on top of her snout, closing my eyes as I did. I'm not exactly sure what compelled me to do that, but it turned out to be a life-changing moment.

When I opened my eyes, I stood on a hill above a large valley. It was dark, with evil-looking clouds roiling overhead. Lightning flashed and struck the ground, lighting up the valley below, charring the grass where it struck. What I saw terrified me. I wanted to turn and run; my feet seemed fixed to the spot where I stood. Wyvern swarmed the valley below. They were attacking a clan of dragons, who were bravely fighting back but were horribly outnumbered by the wyvern. A shadow flew over my head; I shrank back, trying to hide, until I realized it was a dragon, not a wyvern.

The dragon flew down into the valley, circling and blowing a stream of fire into a cluster of wyvern that had brought down a much smaller dragon. They scattered, running from the fire, terrified by the bright flames snaking toward them. It took me a few minutes to realize who the large dragon was. Queebo! She was leading her clan in to save the outnumbered dragons!

Out of the trees across the valley came the largest of the wyvern I had yet seen; at his side was a woman. She looked tiny compared with the massive form of the wyvern. Gripped in one hand she carried a staff; I doubted it was to assist in her movement. I could see her clearly, even from where I stood atop the hill overlooking the valley. The sight of her sent chills down my spine. She was evil; somehow, I could just tell. She was shouting orders to the wyvern. She lifted the staff aloft; its shaft was pitch-black. At the top was a grapefruit-sized globe glowing faintly red, held in place by a claw. I gasped. It wasn't just any claw—it was a small dragon's claw! The woman must be a sorceress, in league with the wyvern, helping them against the dragons. I wondered if my father knew they had a sorceress on their side. Would he know this woman, if he saw her? I tried to memorize her face.

She was casting a spell; the red glow at the end of the staff had grown brighter. She took aim with the staff. I tried desperately to scream a warning, but nothing came out. My voice seemed trapped somewhere near my bellybutton; fear held it down. Fear of that woman with the evil-looking staff.

A bright red bolt shot from the end of the staff, striking Queebo. The great golden dragon fell from the sky, spiraling downward and hitting the ground with a sickening thud. The others from her clan surrounded the fallen dragon, flames bursting forth from them, consuming the sorceress.

I wanted to run to Queebo; tears were streaming down my face. The dragons were now carrying Queebo away.

The massive black wyvern that had been standing next to the sorceress was roaring in anger. He hastened to his mistress's side, accidentally stomping on her in his rush to aid her. I winced, what a way to go. Flambéed by dragons, and then stomped on by your own lieutenant. The large wyvern roared again, blowing out a long breath over the sorceress. The flames surrounding her sputtered and died. I was stunned to see that she yet lived.

I now found myself standing in the valley next to the dying woman. The large wyvern was nudging her gently and making a sort of purring sound. Such a gentle sound for such a large creature, I thought. The woman reached up and put her hand to its cheek.

"Theryn … my staff … fetch … my staff." Her voice was weak, barely a whisper. She was going to die; what did she want her staff for? Surely it couldn't save her now? Still, I watched, my eyes glued to the horrific scene playing out before me. The wyvern fetched the staff and brought it to his mistress. The globe at the top had been shattered. Broken off, the ends were left stuck up in sick little spikes; the half of the glass globe was like a hollowed-out grapefruit. She took the staff in her hand, the wyvern still holding it in his jaw.

"Theryn … you must … lead the others now. You m—m—must … continue w—w—without me." It was hard for her to speak, her words coming in gasps and stutters. The beast made a whimpering sound but did not release the staff. It was as if he knew, no matter what, he had to hold on to it. She began to mutter something. I knew it was a spell of some sort. I looked around, but the dragons had all gone; no one was here to witness the spell except the wyvern army. I wanted to yell, to scream, for anyone to come and put a stop to this. The broken globe at the end of the staff crackled and glowed red briefly, and then died. The woman's hand fell, making a small, sickening slap on the grassy ground as it slipped from the staff's shaft.

"My powers … are yours now. Theryn … lead them … well." Her eyes closed and did not reopen. The wyvern dropped the staff by her side. He let out a pain-filled roar that echoed around the dark valley. Lightning flashed again, thunder boomed, and the wyvern roared once more. I closed my eyes tight, not wanting to see any more.

When I opened them, again I was standing in front of Queebo, my hand still resting on her snout, staring into her sightless eyes. Her vision was taken by that spell, not by age. I *knew* I could give it back to her. I put both hands on the great dragon's snout and shut my eyes tightly, concentrating on her vision and the spell that had taken it. From somewhere far off, I thought I heard my dad's voice shouting my name. I ignored it, Queebo was more important.

Fredrick frowned the minute Chandra placed her hand on Queebo's snout; he knew something wasn't right. They both grew very still and quiet for a long time. When Chandra finally opened her eyes, they were wide, and she looked stunned. Almost like she had just found out something she hadn't known before, something gravely important. Suddenly, she grabbed Queebo's snout with both hands and closed her eyes again. Fredrick yelled her name and closed the short gap between them. He wasn't sure what was happening, but he wasn't going to let it continue. He reached forward and grabbed Chandra's shoulder, intending to break her contact with Queebo.

When he opened his eyes next, he was fifty feet away, lying flat on his back on the cave floor, with Meredith leaning over him, screaming his name. He sat up dazed; what had happened? Chandra was still standing with her hands on Queebo's snout as if nothing had changed.

"Fredrick! Fredrick, are you okay? What happened?" Meredith was looking toward Chandra as if she wasn't sure exactly what had taken place. Frankly, he wasn't exactly sure what had happened at all. This had never happened before, at least not to him.

"Mere, what did you see? When I touched Chandra, what happened?" He had to know exactly what she had done to him. It may have just been a reflexive action. He hoped his own daughter had not intended to hurt him.

Her forehead crinkled as she tried to remember. "You reached out and touched her shoulder; there was a sound like … like … a … thunder … rumble … and you just flew across the room! What happened? Why did she do that?" She sounded distraught. He patted her shoulder. He had a feeling that whatever Chandra had done, she hadn't done so on purpose. He crept closer to his daughter and simply waited.

I knew that the only way to undo the spell was to concentrate *really* hard. I couldn't let anything interrupt me. I tried hard to block out any noise from around me and think only about Queebo and her sight. After what seemed an eternity, I opened my eyes and looked into hers. They were clear, bright, and staring straight at me. A bright gold, to match her deep golden hide. I stepped back, releasing her snout, stumbling. I would have fallen if my dad hadn't been there to catch me. He righted me, and I leaned back against Queebo's ledge.

"Sorry," I muttered. "I'm just a little dizzy." Dad frowned at me; I'm not sure he bought that. I listened as he spoke with Queebo.

"What happened, Queebo?" He sounded angry. I frowned; why was he mad? Couldn't he see that she could *see*?

"Fredrick, she restored my sight! It's marvelous! Look at everything, everyone!" I felt her swoosh over my head as she took off, dipping and weaving around the cavern. I guessed she was happy about it. She finally landed after doing several passes around the cavern. "Chandra, how can I thank you for returning my sight to me?"

I looked up at her and smiled. "No thanks needed, Queebo. I was happy to do it." I just wanted to go to sleep right now. I didn't think I could get to my room by myself, so I stayed right where I was. Dad still looked ticked off, so I tried not to look at him too closely. He came and sat down next to me.

"Chandra, how did you know how to reverse that spell?" I shrugged, not looking up at him. I knew eventually I was going to have to tell them about what I had seen when I was standing up there, holding on to Queebo. "Do you know what happened while you were *healing* Queebo?" I frowned at him. What was he talking about? "I tried to touch your shoulder; I was thrown fifty feet across the room." I stared at him in horror. I had done that to him? He frowned back at me. "You didn't do that consciously?" I shook my head at him vigorously. He nodded, deep in thought. "If you didn't do it consciously, I can only guess it's a defense of some kind against anyone harming you while you're healing or whatever it was you were doing."

I frowned, wondering about what he had just told me; did that mean I could heal anyone or only those affected by a spell? If I could heal anyone, that would come in handy during the war.

"That's an interesting thought. I suppose we'll have to find a way to test your powers out." My head snapped up; I knew I hadn't spoken out loud.

"*Daaad* ..." He turned and looked at me questioningly. "I didn't say that out loud."

"Are you sure?"

I rolled my eyes at him. "Yeah, I think I know the difference between when I have a thought inside my head and when I speak out loud!"

He gave me the *don't take that tone with me, young lady* look. "Your powers are developing faster than expected. Your ability to heal Queebo was amazing. No sorcerer in the history of magic has ever been able to heal a dragon. Though, I'm not sure if what you did qualifies as healing or reversing a spell. Either way, it was amazing; you reversed a spell without knowing its origin."

I frowned; it was confession time, I supposed. "I did know its origin, sorta." Before he could ask how, I told him exactly what I had seen when I first touched Queebo's snout. His eyes got wider and wider as I told the story. Queebo was leaning close to us as well, wanting to hear everything. I could feel her warm breath fanning the back of my neck. She jerked back when I said the name Theryn.

"Chandra, are you sure that's the name she said—Theryn?" I nodded, not knowing what was important about that name. Queebo frowned and shook her head. "This is bad, Fredrick, very bad. If what Chandra saw is the truth, then the origins of the wyvern may have been found."

My father was frowning now, too. "I'm not sure I understand, Queebo."

She hung her head, turned, and settled on her nest of gold and jewels. "Theryn was one of the first dragons, the great black dragon, one of the most powerful clan leaders of our past. He disappeared without a trace one summer day. It has always been thought that a rival killed him and had not wanted to admit that the fight wasn't fair." She looked at us both sadly. "Now it would appear that that is untrue. It would seem that Theryn was used to birth the first of the wyvern. The battle Chandra witnessed was one of the very first, near the start of the war. Had I only known that was him. We didn't know that beast was Theryn, never heard him referred to by name. The other beasts don't speak English, and he never spoke in front of any of us." She shook her great head in sadness. I doubted there was anything she could've done to save him, even if she had known it was Theryn. Dad put his hand on my shoulder. I turned to look at him.

"Chandra, the woman you saw, did she create the wyvern?" I shook my head and shrugged my shoulders; I didn't know. "Queebo, if Theryn has her magic it would explain why they've been able to beat us time and again. It would also explain how they were able to track me after Chandra was born. All they would need was a simple spell to see if any new magic had been born. As soon as it was, they would've known."

I gave up on my quest to regain my strength. "Dad, I need to rest. I feel really weak." I had tried to just sit there and collect myself, but I wasn't feeling any better. Fixing Queebo's sight had sapped my strength. He helped me up and walked me to my room; Mom hovered right behind us the whole way. I slumped down on the bed; I felt like I had been totally wrung out. Dad looked worried, but he didn't say anything, just shuffled Mom out of the room and left me to rest.

I slept badly, my rest disturbed by phantoms and visions I couldn't explain. Actually, I didn't want to explain them. I knew most of what I saw was brought on by my experience with Queebo. The sight of the wyvern army, Theryn their leader, and the sorceress had been an experience I didn't want to repeat. My mind seemed to enjoy torturing me, showing me snapshots of the scenes from Queebo's mind.

CHAPTER 4

I Become A Legend

"Chandra, wake up."

I groaned and pulled the covers up over my head. I had slept so badly I certainly didn't want to get up, not now, not ever.

"Chandra, come on, don't you want to learn anything today?" That got my attention. I peeked out from under the covers at my dad.

"Learn anything, like what?" I asked a little skeptically. I wondered if this was a trick; after all, I'd missed several days of school since coming to the dragons' cave.

He chuckled. "Like some spells, maybe."

I probably hadn't gotten out of bed that fast since I was six on Christmas morning. He was laughing at me again. I didn't care; I seriously wanted to find out what he was going to teach me. I showered and dressed in record time for a teenage girl. Dad was waiting for me by the tunnel entrance to the larger cave where the dragons stayed.

"We're going outside?" I asked in surprise. I knew that once we were outside, there was more of a chance the wyvern would be able to find me, what with me being a heat beacon and all. Dad had said Theryn could track us—well, not us so much as our magic. Especially mine because I was just coming into my powers. Mine were haywire right now, spiking and flaring. Until I learned to control them, it would be child's play for him to find me. I followed my father down the entrance tunnel.

"We're not going far from the cave entrance; you'll see why."

We stepped outside. We were standing on a large ledge overlooking a canyon. The ledge was perhaps big enough for two or three of the dragons to sit on comfortably. Sort of like standing on the dragons' front porch. I frowned; there was something distinctly familiar about the size and shape of the long wide canyon. I just couldn't put my finger on what it was. It didn't help that it was still dark out. He was smiling again. "Welcome to one of the seven natural wonders of the world, Chandra."

I smacked myself on the forehead. Stupid. No wonder it looked familiar—Mom had shown me pictures of it a million times! The Grand Canyon! No wonder she was always showing it to me. *Duh*, because Dad was here the whole time. That's why she turned me down every time I said we should just go there to see it in person, instead of looking at all the pictures in those books of hers. She never could've come here and been so close to him without actually seeing him in person.

"Are you ready for your first lesson, Chandra?"

I nodded eager to learn some sorcery.

"Okay, first thing we're going to learn is a simple spell that will help you relieve some of that heat you're carrying around. It also comes in handy for defense." He did this twisty thing with his hand. When he held his palm up, he was holding a ball of fire the size of a baseball in the palm of his hand.

"That is *so cool!*" I was amazed by the trick. I wanted to be able to do that. To be honest, what I was thinking was this: If a boy ever tried anything he shouldn't on a date, it would come in handy. I could set him on fire.

He chuckled. "It is *cool*, isn't it?" He tossed the fireball at a target he had set up in front of us at the edge of the ledge. He hit it dead center. I wanted to learn this spell very badly.

"I wanna try, Dad!"

He smiled a wide grin, showing all of his perfectly straight, white teeth. "It's an easy spell to perform. Watch me, okay? All you have to do is think the word *incendiarius* and twist your wrist the way I did. I'll do it slower this time so you can see it, okay?"

I nodded. Then I asked him to repeat the word slower so I could get it.

"I-n-c-e-n-d-i-a-r-i-u-s. It's Latin. Basically, it means to raise a flame, roughly translated," he explained. He did the spell very slowly this time so I could see it. He had to do it a bunch more times before I could finally copy the wrist movement properly. I practiced for what seemed like forever. I seriously thought Apollo was going to make an appearance, dragging the sun into view with his almighty chariot, before I got the hang of the spell and even produced a tiny spark!

All of a sudden, a tiny little ball of fire appeared in my palm! It was barely enough to be called a ball of fire, but it was there. I got so excited; I immediately dropped it and set my shoelaces on fire. Luckily, Dad knew a spell for water and put me out. We practiced for a while longer until I was good enough to produce a real ball of fire and lob it at the target. It was a lot of fun. I was glad Dad had thought ahead and put a magical barrier around the edge of our little practice space because I managed to miss the target as many times as I hit it. I didn't want to start a giant wildfire in a national park.

We had a few days of practice on the fireballs, and then he decided we could take a break from that since I had gotten pretty good at it. My next lesson was shape-shifting. I was just as excited about that as the fire spell.

"I was never very good at shape-shifting, so bear with me here." I was surprised. I thought he was good at everything. He immediately shifted into an oak tree. I stood there with my mouth hanging wide open. Wasn't good at it? He sure looked like a tree to me. Then I noticed something odd about said tree and burst out laughing. The *tree* had a hand up at the end of one of the higher branches. He transformed back into himself. I was laughing so hard I couldn't even talk. He waited for me to wind down before he said anything.

"I told you I wasn't any good at it." He didn't look mad, even though I was wiping tears from my eyes. "That's why I don't depend on shape-shifting as a means of escape when running from nasty creatures or angry mobs."

I started laughing full force again as I pictured an angry mob from an old horror movie, complete with pitchforks and torches. He rolled his eyes. He could pick up my thoughts if I didn't guard what I was thinking. It was annoying, but it did save me the trouble of explaining things sometimes.

"Okay, okay, I'm done now, really. But you have to admit, it was funny, right?"

He shook his head at me. "Chandra, just concentrate, okay? Think *transformis* and concentrate hard on what it is you want to transform into. Think the same thing to transform back to yourself."

I nodded and closed my eyes. At least transformis was easy to remember—it had transform right in the word. I picked something simple. A rock, a nice little rock. Legend walked out onto the ledge, apparently interested in what was going on, and meowed at us.

I wasn't aware that she had shifted the focus of my thoughts until I opened my eyes and looked up at my dad. He smiled down at me.

"Well, that was quite good for your first try. I never would've tried something that ambitious on my first try."

Ambitious? A rock was ambitious? "Dad, really, you must not know many sorceresses then, because I really wouldn't call a rock all that ambitious!" It was after the words came out of my mouth that I realized; rocks don't have mouths, so how could I have said that to him? Something had gone wrong. I looked around as Legend padded up to me. She purred right in my face and licked my nose. I raised my paw to wipe it off. Wait, *paw?* I looked down at myself. *I was a cat!*

"Chandra, you are the spitting image of Legend right now. You could be her twin, actually."

I immediately thought myself back to being me.

Dad was still chuckling an hour later when he told Mom about it as we sat and ate breakfast in the cave's magical kitchen. I doubted he would ever get sick of telling everyone he could about the look on my face when I realized I had transformed myself into a replica of my cat.

We spent the rest of the week working on my transformation spell. I also spent any of my own free time, which was a lot, working on the fire spell. Dad spent a lot of time with Queebo and Echo, the crimson dragon, who I now knew was dad's fighting partner when they went into battle, discussing strategies for fighting the wyvern now that we knew about Theryn having his own magic. I was worried that we were going to lose no matter what strategies they managed to come up with. The wyvern weren't going to just sit around and wait till I turned eighteen and had my full powers to come and attack us. Theryn didn't seem the type to sit back and wait for us to come to him. The days were ticking by, one by one. How long would the wyvern wait to renew their assault on the dragons?

I started wondering, one evening as I sat out on the ledge, if maybe there were other dragon clans out there in hiding, just like Queebo and her clan. I hid my thoughts from everyone, since they had a random way of popping up here and there for everyone to *hear*. I had to be careful about that. I wanted to ask Queebo about other clans, but my dad always seemed to be around. I doubted he would ever agree to such a plan; going to look for other clans would be out of the question. Once we were out of the safety of the cavern, the wyvern could track me too easily. Dad would never allow me to go dragon hunting in a million years, even if he was by my side the whole way.

I knew that our small band wouldn't stand a chance against the wyvern if it came down to it. We would need help. Dad had been telling me lots about the wyvern, stories about battles, more stories about legends—some true, some not—so I could get a better understanding of the history I had been thrust into. It was clear that the wyvern were strong, and the dragons were outnumbered. We needed help, badly.

I trained hard every day. I really wanted to be able to prove to Dad that I could do this. Fighting the wyvern and helping Queebo and her clan was important to me. If someone had told me just a week ago I was going to help fight a war alongside a bunch of dragons, I would've been looking for the TV host and the hidden cameras. Now it seemed like the most natural thing in the world for me to be doing with my time. Dad wanted me to concentrate on the two basic spells he had taught me for right now. He didn't want to tax my strength. He was worried about what had happened after I had healed Queebo's sight. He didn't want a repeat of how I had felt afterward, fearing that healing Queebo had been a mistake. He didn't want me to try it again—as if there were a bunch of injured or spelled dragons hanging about for me to test it on. He thought that my powers weren't strong enough yet to try it again. Maybe after I turned eighteen, he decided. Magically healing a dragon was not something normal, even for a sorcerer. I think it scared the life out of him that I could do it.

That's the real reason why he didn't want me to do it again—at least, I thought so.

CHAPTER 5

I Jump Off A Cliff

After a week of practicing the fireballs and my transforming, Dad decided I deserved a reward for all my hard work. He took Mom and me out for dinner to one of the touristy restaurants out on the rim of the canyon. I was excited about having what I deemed "real" food. The magical kitchen in the dragon lair made good food, but it just wasn't the same somehow.

Dad figured a short trip out of the cave would be okay since he would be with us.

I ordered a cheeseburger, fries, and a giant Coke. I was in teenage junk food heaven. Mom and Dad were making goo-goo eyes at each other like they were on their first date. I was trying really hard not to look at them too much; they were embarrassing. We were halfway through dinner when suddenly the hairs on the back of my neck got all tingly.

I looked around, trying to be inconspicuous. Then again, if a big, ugly, winged beast were watching me, with its big snout pressed against the window of the restaurant, that would be pretty attention getting. I turned and looked over my shoulder and found myself staring straight into the eyes of a teenage boy about my age sitting a couple of booths away from us. A really cute boy. I immediately turned scarlet and whirled back around in my seat. I really wished Dad had taught me how to turn invisible right about then. I felt kinda stupid thinking that a wyvern had been responsible for the prickly feeling I had. I may be a sorceress and able to produce flames instantaneously, but I still couldn't talk to a boy if my life depended on it. Especially one that cute. Suddenly, I wasn't very hungry anymore.

"I'm finished. I'll wait for you guys outside. I'm gonna check out the … um, scenery." I mumbled. I made a quick getaway before they could protest. My cheeks felt super hot, and it wasn't from my sorceress-like temperature, either. I could feel the boy's eyes on my back as I made a dash for the door. I only had a brief moment to wonder why he was still watching me. He probably thought I was a major dork, since I was running away from him. Or maybe it was just because I was—and always had been—just plain old Chandra Strandon. Perhaps he felt he had to study the strange, plain Jane girl as she fled from him.

God, how embarrassing. I wanted to get out of the restaurant and away from him, fast.

I was glad to get outside; it was a little bit cooler, anyway. I stood near the rim looking out over the canyon. I liked the spot. It was one of the few where there was no railing, so you could walk right up to the edge and look straight down into the canyon. It was dark and quiet; most of the tourists had all gone for the day. I shivered despite the heat coursing through my veins.

"Dinner with the parents is the pits, isn't it?"

I spun around, prepared to fight whoever had taken me by surprise. It was a good thing that I noticed it was the boy from the restaurant right away, before I was able to produce a fireball. That would have been embarrassing, as well as hard to explain.

"Uh, yeah, they're acting all lovey-dovey and stuff," I mumbled.

He kinda rolled his eyes and smiled. I tried not to stare at him too much. It was really hard not to do, because he was extremely good-looking. He was taller than my boring average height of five-foot-four, which would put him at right about six-foot. I was taking a guess—he was standing close, but not too close—since I had to tilt my head a bit to look up at him. I figured it was a good guess. His eyes were this gorgeous blue-gray color. I thought of Legend with a small grin. She's a Russian Blue; his eyes reminded me of her soft fur. I felt like an idiot as soon as I made the comparison. His pitch-black hair was perfect, honest, like a magazine cover model or something—not a single hair out of place. It gave me this urge to reach up and pat at my outdated tresses. *Wait, who says tresses anymore?* I shook my head. This guy was making my mind go all funny.

He was still smiling at me. It made me a little uncomfortable. I knew I couldn't begin to compare to him. Which brings me back to my imperfect hair; it's so old-fashioned. That's how all my friends continuously describe it. It's straight, barely a trace of a curl, and waist-length. Sorta a boring dark brown color, nothing to write home about. I refuse to go with every trend that comes along. Still, I like my hair the way it is—at least, that's what I have always told my friends. But standing there looking at Mr. Perfect Hair, suddenly, I wanted to run out and have it cut, dyed, and fried, whatever the very trendy fashion cover models were doing this month. That is, until he spoke again.

"Hey, I hope this isn't, like, weird or anything, me following you out here and all. I saw you in the restaurant, and I kinda wanted to talk to you. You seem … different than the rest of the girls around here." If only he knew how different, I thought! He stopped and smiled at me again. That perfect smile of his went so well with the supermodel hair. He looked like he had run out of things to say; he glanced at my hair. I wanted to groan out loud. Why did he have to notice my hair! I wanted to run and hide.

"I, uh … I really like your hair. It's different. Every other girl just, you know, tries to be exactly like whatever actress is hot at the moment; you have your own look. It's kinda cool." It was my turn to smile at him. I really liked him a lot already. Then something occurred to me. I wasn't exactly available to just go out on a date. Dad would have a cow, and not just a *daddy's little girl is growing up and dating* cow. More along the lines of a *daddy's little girl is out on a date and is gonna get killed by a wyvern* cow. Besides that little problem, how would I explain to a guy about dragons, wyvern, and the fact that I was a sorceress? I turned back toward the canyon, now more than a bit uncomfortable with the situation. I was going to have to tell Mr. Perfect Hair good-bye. Permanently.

It wasn't just his hair and his eyes that were attractive, either; he was just downright gorgeous. He must spend hours at the gym working out because he was definitely all muscle. He had to be a football player, wrestler, or something. The type who normally wouldn't give me the time of day. I wasn't exactly in the popular clique at school. I didn't hang with the cheer squad and the football players. But I wasn't in chess club, either.

I was just somewhere in the middle with the normal kids. This guy was definitely with the popular kids. His clothes had to be designer everything, not that I would know. He wore jeans, a black T-shirt with some sort of design I couldn't begin to fathom on it, and a black leather jacket; they all suited him to perfection, which is what made me think designer, fitting his muscular frame perfectly—I mean *perfectly*. I wondered if he would flee if I reached out to touch one of those perfectly muscled arms. He interrupted my thoughts when he introduced himself. I was sure my cheeks turned a flaming red at that point.

"I'm Chase Ivers, by the way." He smiled again. He was clearly waiting for me to introduce myself. I shouldn't—after all, we could never be anything together. But he was *sooo* cute. I simply couldn't resist it.

"I'm Chandra Strandon." He was still smiling. I knew I was fully in love with that smile already. He held out his hand; thinking nothing of it, I reached out and took his hand in mine. The second our hands touched, it felt like a million volts went through my body. My eyes locked with his; a thousand thoughts raced through my head. Uppermost on the list: None of this could be good.

The only thing I knew for certain at that moment, was that I wished my father were outside standing next to me instead of sitting in the restaurant with my mother. I tried desperately to yank my hand out of his inflexible grip.

"Let go of my hand, or I'll scream," I hissed through my clenched teeth.

His smile had changed somehow, becoming icy. Less friendly. "I highly doubt you'll do that, Chandra. You wouldn't want some innocent mortal to get injured, would you?"

My eyes widened; his voice had changed now, too. No longer light, flirting, and friendly, it was deadly serious. It was different, scary. His hands, I realized belatedly, were as warm as mine. Which could only mean one thing: He was a sorcerer.

He pulled me closer, now smiling that too-sexy smile of his. Now that we were standing much closer, I had to tilt my head way back to look up at him. This probably put him closer to about six-foot-two. I didn't much like where this whole situation was going.

"You do realize that you are a complication we can't afford? As beautiful as you are, you are going to have to die."

This was definitely bad. Wait, did he say *we*? Wait, did he say *beautiful*? I shook my head—no time for that now!

"Who exactly is the 'we' part?" I asked, trying to ignore the fact that the boy, who a moment ago I had thought was drop-dead gorgeous, seemed to now be my enemy. He smiled that smile, which I still loved, despite the fact that things were *definitely* not going well.

"Silly little girl—the wyvern, of course, who else? The dragons must die, Chandra. We will not let you stand in our way." *Little girl? Did he just call me little girl?* I thought as he released my hand. Before I could react to the fact that I was free, he grabbed me around the waist, turned, and flung me over the rim of the canyon. The last thought that tottered through my brain as his face disappeared from view was, *Why does evil have to have perfect hair?*

I hit the rocks and bounced off; pain burned through my shoulder and side. I had to concentrate, or the wyvern would get their wish, and I would indeed die. I decided at that moment the last thing Chase Ivers would hear from me before he left the lip of the canyon would be a scream of utter and complete terror, so he could report to his evil scaly masters that he had done what he had come to do.

A grin of satisfaction spread across Chase's lips as he heard Chandra's terrified scream. He spun around when he heard Fredrick yell Chandra's name. Something inside Chase's mind faltered—two distinct voices warring for control. One the leader of the wyvern, the other Chase himself. Theryn won, and Chase fled before Fredrick saw him standing in the shadows near the rim of the canyon.

Theryn growled. Chase would pay for his moment of disloyalty.

Fredrick raced to the canyon rim. He and Meredith had just been exiting the restaurant when he heard Chandra scream. *Where is she?* he thought as he searched for her. A shadow flashed by his face; he followed it upward. An eagle landed in front of him and quickly transformed into Chandra. Relief enveloped him. Despite the injuries he could clearly see, she was alive.

"Chandra, what happened? How on earth did you fall?"

I collapsed to the ground, looking around for Chase, but like all good villains, he and his perfect hair had fled the scene. I explained what had happened to my parents. My whole right side burned where I had hit the rocks before I could transform. Dad was frowning while he performed a healing spell on my injuries.

"I don't like this; it isn't good. If it's true that he's about the same age as you are, then we need to find the boy." Was he insane? *That boy* had just flung me off a cliff!

"He's working with the wyvern, Dad! He just tossed me over a cliff! He tried to kill me!"

"Chandra, there's a possibility he didn't do that of his own accord. It may be possible Theryn had something to do with that. If it's true Theryn has powers of his own, he may be controlling the boy. Forcing him to do these things. We can't know for sure unless we can talk to him. For all we know, Theryn may have nabbed him because he believes the boy may be the Chosen. From the way you described his behavior, it leads me to believe Theryn may be controlling the boy. I just don't like it. I don't trust Theryn."

I was still frowning at my father, despite the possibility of Chase being the Chosen instead of me; after all, he had just tried to kill me.

I wasn't going to like Chase after what he had just done, perfect hair and body or not.

I looked at the calendar that I had sort of improvised and hung up in my room, ticking off the days since I had arrived at my new home. It had been two months since I'd come to the dragon cave. I frowned; time was running out. Well, okay, we still had ten more months till I turned eighteen. Again, I told myself, the wyvern weren't going to wait around forever to attack us, especially if they thought Chase had been successful in his attempt to toss me into the canyon. I still wavered between hatred for Chase and worry for him. I currently hated him. I'd decided this week that he was evil and that was that.

Dad truly believed that Theryn was controlling Chase's mind. He and Echo had spent some time searching the canyon for Theryn's lair, to no avail. I hoped Chase was suffering, wherever he was. It simply wasn't fair that he could toss me off a cliff and get away with it. I wondered how evil Chase managed to keep his hair so perfect; perhaps next time I saw him, I should just mess his hair up … that would tick him off. Maybe I'd gone off the deep end where he was concerned, but I didn't care very much. I was angry, and rationality didn't go hand-in-hand with anger.

Dad delighted in teasing me at every turn because he had picked up on a few of my thoughts when I was in one of my more charitable moods toward Chase. My only ally was Hertha, the ice-blue dragon. Queebo had introduced me to Hertha after the cliff incident. She told me that when the war against the wyvern started up again in earnest, Hertha and I would battle together. We had become fast friends; she was a younger dragon, although that still meant she was, of course, much older than I was. She was on my side when I confided in her about my idea to search for other dragon clans that might be out there. That maybe they could help us fight the wyvern. She also sympathized with me about Chase, whether I liked him that week or hated him. She knew how frustrating males could be. She loved Davaintae with all her heart, but the blue-violet dragon didn't seem to notice she existed, much to her despair. I offered to help her catch his eye, but she refused, replying, "That if he was too hardheaded to notice her on his own, he could rot". I had laughed; I couldn't help it. Hertha's pride would be her undoing one day.

Chase was indeed suffering at the moment. Theryn was making sure of it. Every inch of him hurt terribly. He tried to get comfortable on the thin mattress inside his cage. It was next to impossible. He gave up and tried to lie very still instead. He hated Theryn, had hated the wyvern from the moment he had set eyes on him two years ago.

Chase had come to the Grand Canyon with his family on vacation. That's all, a simple family vacation; his mom had been so happy about it, too. It was the first one they'd taken in a long time. He smiled, remembering how happy she'd been, but of course he and his sister had fought, like always. So he'd gone for a walk, just to get out for a while and cool off. That's when they had taken him. One minute he was walking along the canyon, the next a wyvern had scooped him up and carried him off. He had been so terrified, he hadn't even screamed. He wondered if his parents were even still looking for him. He actually missed his sister, and his annoying little brother, too.

Theryn had interrogated him about his entire life. Chase had told him he had no idea what Theryn was talking about, he wasn't a sorcerer and neither were his parents; he had been adopted when he was a baby. He had no clue who his real parents were. Every one of his answers had only made Theryn angry and the beast had created this cage for Chase, and that's where he'd spent most of his days ever since. Theryn had interrogated him more as time passed about Fredrick and Chandra Strandon. Chase hadn't known who they were.

As the days went by, Theryn had figured out how to use Chase to find Chandra. It hadn't been easy; Chase had hated having Theryn in his mind. He had fought the monster every step of the way, but Theryn was too strong. Eventually, they had found her. Chase had followed her home one evening, found her house, the exact street where she lived. When it seemed they would finally have her, she had slipped through Theryn's claws with Fredrick's help. Theryn had blamed Chase for the loss, of course. They had to wait again for their chance at her, and when Fredrick and Chandra had appeared in that restaurant, it seemed that it had finally come. Chase had sat there watching her, with Theryn growling orders inside his head the entire time. Chase wished only to be free of the wyvern, knowing in the end what the monster would make him do to the beautiful girl sitting there so innocently with her parents in the restaurant, unaware that he was there to murder her.

Yet, he couldn't have stayed away from Chandra even had he been able to break free of Theryn's hold on his mind. In the short time he had to study Chandra, she had captured his interest. Now he didn't want to think about Chandra, to think about the look on her face when she had realized what he was going to do to her. To hear again her terrified scream as she disappeared into the canyon below.

He squeezed his eyes shut. She'd been terrified of him. Chase had wanted to scream when Theryn had told Chandra she was beautiful. He didn't like hearing those words when he knew they were coming from the wyvern. When Fredrick had come out of the restaurant, Chase had wanted to call out to him. To tell him how sorry he was for what Theryn had made him do.

He had tried to fight Theryn, but the beast had won control of his mind and body; Chase had lost his battle for freedom once again. Theryn always won, something that made Chase even angrier.

He forced himself to sit up, despite the pain, and lean against the wall of his prison. Theryn had punished him for trying to break free. Chase didn't care; he would rather Theryn just killed him. Theryn wasn't that stupid; he knew Chase still had some usefulness. Chase had disobeyed Theryn in the past. He had tried to escape many times; he had Theryn's claw marks across his chest to show how Theryn dealt with disobedience. That had been the first time Chase had tried to escape. Theryn hadn't touched Chase since, for some reason, hadn't wanted to touch him again. Theryn didn't need to touch him to cause him pain, however; he had found other ways.

The door to his cage opened, and a wyvern guard motioned him forward; all the wyvern were cautious of him. For some reason only known to them, they seemed to fear him, though Chase still maintained his claim that he wasn't a sorcerer. Not that he didn't believe that it wasn't possible for the impossible to happen. He had been living with Theryn and his ilk for the past two years, hadn't he? He just wouldn't buy into whatever it was Theryn was trying to sell him. He wasn't the Kool-Aid drinking, blind following kind. If Theryn thought he could get Chase to go along with the program if he kept pounding away at him, he was very wrong. Chase would die before that happened.

He stepped forward slowly, wondering what torture Theryn had in store for him today; he hoped it would be over quickly. He hadn't felt well in a while. His seventeenth birthday had passed two months ago, not that the wyvern would care about a human's birthday. Such things wouldn't matter to Theryn; all he cared about was getting his grimy claws on Chandra.

Thoughts of his birthday had his mind returning to his family as he walked to Theryn's throne room. His sister would be nineteen now, probably at college. She had been seventeen when he had gone missing. His little brother would be fifteen, the same age he had been when he had been taken by the wyvern. Life went on; even when you felt like your whole world had ended.

He felt hideous. He thought that maybe he was getting sick, the flu probably; maybe he would die in this horrid cave with no doctor to care for him. He was sore from Theryn's torture, and he had the worst fever he could ever remember having in his life. Theryn had laughed about that, thought it a great joke that Chase was ill.

When he entered the throne room, he took his place in front of Theryn, kneeling before the wyvern master. Not because he wanted to, but because he was too weary and sore to really care anymore. He thought again about Chandra, and he wondered if she had died when he threw her over the rim of the canyon. Could she have lived? He hoped her father could have performed a miracle and saved her. Maybe if the man were really a sorcerer as Theryn had claimed, he could have saved Chandra. If he ever managed to get out of here alive, he would find out, somehow.

"How are you feeling this evening, Chase?"

He wanted to tell Theryn exactly how he felt. In very colorful terms. But he kept his mouth shut.

"What, no wisecracks today, Chase? No anger for me? You disappoint me, boy. I miss our little contests of will."

He kept his eyes on the floor, refusing to rise to Theryn's taunts. He felt to weary for anger tonight.

Theryn had rather enjoyed breaking the boy. Chase hadn't been easy to bend to his will at first. Humans thought they were so strong. Theryn rather enjoyed proving them wrong. When the boy had first come here, his mind had been closed to Theryn. It had taken four long days for Theryn to break into Chase's mind. He had been so sure Chase was the Chosen—at first. However, when he was able to bend the boy to his will and use him to do his bidding, he knew the boy wasn't the right one. It had been yet another disappointment in a long line of so many.

He knew that Chandra Strandon had to be the one; there could be no other. He wished he knew if the girl was dead or not. When Fredrick had come out of the restaurant, Chase had wanted to run and apologize to him for what he had done. The foolish boy had tried to break free, causing Theryn to retreat prematurely from the scene. He couldn't afford to lose control of the boy; he still needed him. They did not know if the girl was dead, all due to the boy's cowardice. Theryn knew the boy had developed feelings for the girl, had seen it in the boy's mind. He could use that to his advantage; humans were so very weak, allowing silly things like emotions to rule them.

"You know that Chandra Strandon must die." Chase flinched at Theryn's words. Theryn smiled; an unpleasant thing on the face of a wyvern. "Your attachment to the girl does not change my plans, Chase. I *will* continue with them. I do not care what you want with the girl." Chase glared up at Theryn then, unable to stare blindly at the floor any longer. Theryn had known he would get a reaction out of the boy eventually. It simply would not have been any fun if he didn't. It was not as violent a reaction as he had wanted, though. The boy was still much to calm.

"I know you want the girl for a mate. Really, Chase, I cannot have that, now can I?"

Chase continued to glare silently up at him from where he knelt on the cold stone, wanting to kill Theryn for the cold way he spoke about Chandra. His fists clenched at his sides, while he willed his temper back. Knowing he was no match for the beast before him.

Theryn would never understand humans. The wyvern didn't know about love; they changed mates frequently, never caring who their mate was or why, never forming any attachment to their mates. The wyvern disgusted Chase, and Theryn knew it.

Theryn wasn't getting the reaction from Chase that he wanted. He wanted the boy to get angry; it was much easier if the boy lost control. Chase didn't know that, of course, and Theryn wasn't going to give that kind of information to the boy. He could do nothing with the boy if he wouldn't let loose of his temper. Today, it would seem Chase would not cooperate. He gestured to the guard to take him away. There was always tomorrow.

Chase wondered what that whole show had been about; he didn't care enough to analyze it too closely. He never tried very hard to figure out Theryn's motives for anything. The monster was evil, and it was that simple. Theryn took joy in the little things that made his prey uncomfortable. He knew everything Chase feared;

had seen it all inside Chase's head. No insecurity could be hidden from him when he had scoured your brain from the inside out. That monster took great delight in twisting your mind and soul to suit his purposes. He would use whatever magic he could muster to do it, too.

He crawled back onto his filthy little mattress and tried to get some sleep. He thought once more about Chandra and prayed that she was all right.

CHAPTER 6

Traveling Sucks

After the whole incident with Chase, I just wanted to concentrate on my training. Dad was happy to oblige. We had started a new lesson, a transport spell called *migro*. It was only good for short-distance travel, up to a couple hundred feet. I figured it would come in handy if I was late for class, and I was on the other side of campus … that is, if I ever got to go back to the real world. We started with a distance of a couple of feet. Then Dad thought I could handle transporting to the top of the ridge above our ledge and back.

"Are you sure, Dad?" I looked up at the top of the cliff. It seemed really high from below.

"Chandra, you can do it. Just try and picture the top of the ridge in your mind. You have to know your destination."

I nodded; it wasn't like I hadn't done the spell before. It was just that I had only gone from one side of the ledge to the cave entrance and back again. This was a whole lot farther and higher. I didn't want to miss the lip of the ledge and plummet back down to the ledge below and my premature death. I closed my eyes and pictured the lip of the canyon high above me. *Migro*, I thought. I opened my eyes.

The first thing I thought was that I had mastered the spell, and my dad was going to be proud of me. The second was that I was going to die, and he would never know. So the first didn't matter much.

Chase stood right in front of me. When my eyes locked with his, I thought I saw a flash of something there. What was it? Pain?

Regret? It was gone so quickly that I couldn't know if I had imagined it there or not. The mocking smile had slipped into place. His gray-blue eyes had turned remotely cold. He was so close to me, I couldn't think. My mind had gone blank, hazy.

"Chandra, we meet again. How ... *nice*." He stepped forward, closing the space between us. I couldn't breathe. My treacherous heart was beating too rapidly. His steps had brought him so close that our breath mingled. I shivered. He slowly smiled, sliding his hands down my arms—his touch feather-light against my skin— and linked his fingers with mine. Chills raced down my spine that had nothing to do with fear.

A voice in my head screamed at me, "*Run!*" My heart sighed and kept my feet firmly planted. I knew this was dangerous; *he* was dangerous.

"What ... how?" I stammered. A slow, seductive grin was his answer, and I shivered again.

"I've been watching you practice, Chandra. You know your father teaches you nothing but parlor tricks. You know you will never defeat the wyvern, or me. I told you that you were a complication we couldn't afford, my dear, yet I find you deliciously enchanting." I wanted to run *to* him, not *away* from him. He found me enchanting. But he wanted me dead ... didn't he? That's why he had thrown me into the canyon, right? I was confused, my mind muddled.

Is this a spell of some sort? I wondered silently.

"I have to leave; I can't be here with you. You tried to kill me." I felt those things had to be said, yet I made no effort to move away from him. Somehow, it seemed I swayed closer to him. He was still smiling at me. For the first time, I noticed the small dimple set deeply into his right cheek. I stared at it dumbly. Why hadn't I noticed it before? I wanted to reach out and trace that dimple with my fingertip, to kiss it.

"We don't have to be enemies, Chandra," he said softly. I shook my head to clear it.

"We don't? How could we be anything else?" I asked stupidly. He emitted a quiet chuckle. He was so close, I wondered if he would kiss me—a dangerous thought for sure. Everything about him seemed dangerous. So why couldn't I seem to walk away from him?

"We could leave right now; you could join me, Chandra. Leave with me, and we could be together ... forever." His voice was a whisper. Quiet and seductive, drawing me closer, I couldn't think. Leave? With him? Be together ... forever? Together, with Chase. Forever. My heart gave a little sigh of deep pleasure at that thought.

My traitor of a heart was telling me to go now, to leave with him quickly! It would only be a few minutes before Dad got worried and came looking for me! *Dad.* That thought brought me screaming back to reality. I wrenched myself away from him, stumbling a bit as I did and backing toward the edge of the rocks. Getting away from Chase was now my only thought. I stumbled over loose rocks as I backed hastily away from him, knowing that distance was the only thing that would keep me safe from him, from myself.

"What did you do to me?" I asked him, my voice shaking. I feared the answer. Feared it because, I in some way knew what the answer was. I knew, somehow, what he would say before he even opened that perfect mouth of his. He hadn't done a thing to me. He smiled yet again, mocking me now because he knew that I already knew his answer.

"Nothing, Chandra. I did *nothing.*" I knew he was telling the truth. I couldn't deny it. It was my own disloyal heart that had wanted me to leave, wanted me to betray my own family for him, to betray my friends.

"Stay away from me, Chase. Just stay away. Don't come near me again. Next time, I won't hesitate; I *will* kill you." I kept insisting he stay away, and he had made no move to get close to me since I had pulled away from him. He just stood there with that damn taunting little smile on his face, his arms at his sides. My voice was shaking so badly that I doubted he believed a word I had said about killing him on sight. I knew I didn't. I twisted around and mumbled the transport spell as I stepped off the edge of the rocks. He let me leave, I don't know why.

I reappeared on the ledge below, dropping to the ground, wrapping my arms around myself. I had almost left with him. I couldn't believe that I had even begun to think about it.

My dad's voice brought me crashing down to earth. "What took you so long? I was about to come looking for you."

"Chase." I mumbled. His eyes got wide, and he immediately vanished, reappearing a second later.

"He's gone, Chandra." I nodded numbly; I knew he would be. He wouldn't hang around waiting to be captured. My dad was crouched next to me, hugging me. I couldn't seem to get warm. I was so cold inside. Chase had done that to me, made me doubt my loyalties.

"What did he say to you, honey? God, you're lucky you were able to get away!" He hugged me again.

"He said that he's been watching us practice, that I can't win against the wyvern." I started crying. I wasn't crying because Chase had said I couldn't win but because I had almost become a deserter, leaving everyone I loved behind for a guy I barely knew, like some woman in a cheap romance novel, running off with the first good-looking guy who smiles at her. Dad helped me up, and we went inside. I could see his eyes scanning the dark sky, looking for Chase as if he would be lurking about. No, Chase wasn't that stupid. He was long gone.

"No more practicing out on the ledge from now on."

I just nodded.

True to Dad's word, we didn't practice outside anymore. Dad moved practice to one of the larger caves near the back of our new home, setting it up as a practice arena. At first, I didn't care; I didn't want to be anywhere near the outside. I didn't want to see Chase again, so there would be no chance for me to betray those I cared about. As the days passed, though, I soon became claustrophobic.

I needed some fresh air, to see the sky, something, anything! Dad and I fought about it, beginning a new squabble every few minutes. I was frustrated—mostly with myself—over the incident. I hadn't told my dad exactly what had happened up there. Hertha was the only one who knew what had really happened. Not revealing what had really happened made me short-tempered with everyone else.

"I'm done for today; I need some fresh air." I turned to walk out of our practice arena, but my dad's voice stopped me.

"Stay inside, Chandra!"

My jaw clenched. "I will, Dad. Jeez, gimme a mark for having a brain, will ya?"

"Chandra, stop snapping at me. I just want you to be safe."

"Safe. Oh, okay. Well, I don't think that's a problem because I'm locked in a cave 24-7!" I turned and stormed out of the room before I said some of the other things flying around my brain. I sat in the cave entrance, staring out at the night sky. I knew Chase was out there somewhere, the perfect-haired menace.

I had had some spats with my dad since coming here, but that one had been the worst so far. Dad had caught some of the words that I hadn't said out loud before I stormed out; it seems the angrier I am, the harder it is for me to control my thoughts. The fight had gotten worse before I could escape. He had wanted to ground me, until I pointed out that there was nothing for him to ground me from. I had no friends to go out with, no TV, no phone, and no computer, and he couldn't stop my lessons because I needed those to defeat the wyvern. He'd only gotten angrier when Mom had shrugged and said that I had a point about the grounding part.

So here I was, staring out at the world from my self-imposed prison, afraid to leave because of a boy.

A stupid, perfect-haired, gorgeous boy.

I hated all males at that moment.

CHAPTER 7

Going On A Dragon Hunt

I woke with a start, twisted up in the covers. I tried to untangle myself and ended up falling off the bed.

"Ow!" Cave floors hurt no matter how thick the area rugs are. I struggled out of my covers and threw them angrily at the bed. I groaned and looked at the clock on the nightstand; it was late. I wasn't ready to get up, but after the dream I'd had, I knew I couldn't go back to sleep. Theryn was still rearing his ugly head in my dreams. I kept seeing the same thing over and over: the battle where Queebo had lost her sight. My dreams were also speckled with brief sightings of Chase, which didn't improve my mood any.

I trudged to the kitchen and made myself a cup of tea. I was sitting there, feeling sorry for myself, when I had a brilliant idea. I could talk to Queebo about the other dragon clans right now. Dad was sleeping, and I wasn't. Except that, I would have to wake Queebo. I chewed my lower lip. How cranky would a dragon be if you woke it up in the middle of the night?

Throwing caution to the wind, I sprinted down the passageway in my pajamas and into the main cavern. I slunk over to where Queebo slept on her nest. Suddenly, I didn't feel quite so brave as I stood there in front of her giant sleeping form in the darkness of the cave.

"If you have something to say, child, spit it out," she said without stirring. I stumbled backward and landed on my butt.

"Sorry, Queebo, I didn't mean to wake you," I apologized.

She raised her head and stretched. "Of course you meant to wake me, or you wouldn't be here."

I had to give her that one. I got up and dusted my rear off, and then climbed up next to her. "I had a couple of question I've been wanting to ask you."

She pinned me with her golden stare. "Questions that couldn't wait until a decent hour?" she asked pointedly.

I ducked my head from her probing golden eyes. "I thought maybe my dad wouldn't want me pestering you."

She chuckled at me, smoke rings rising from her nostrils. "I see your point; go ahead."

"Did there used to be other dragon clans?" I asked.

She didn't seem all that surprised by my question. "Of course, Chandra, dragon legends appear in just about every culture around the world. Though, sadly, some of the legends were the work of the wyvern."

I knew that much, my dad had already told me some of the stories. I moved on to my next question. "Do you think any of the other clans are still out there, in hiding, like you are?"

She looked thoughtful for a moment. "I would very much like to think that they are out there, somewhere."

I perked up at her answer, which was sort of an agreement. "If they're out there, wouldn't it make sense for us to find them then? If the wyvern are going to attack us, then why not find the others? It would be nice to have a larger force to oppose the wyvern with." I had warmed to my subject now, glad to have her agreement.

Queebo was staring at me intently. "You have given this a lot of thought, haven't you?" I nodded eagerly. She smiled at me. "Chandra, we wouldn't even know where to begin looking for the others. It could take years to find them all."

I slumped, felling totally deflated.

"We wouldn't have to search everywhere." We both looked up. Hertha was standing nearby; we hadn't heard her silent approach.

I was glad she had spoken up. In my dejection, I had forgotten all of my prepared arguments for finding the other clans. I looked eagerly back at Queebo.

"That's right. We could just look in the places where the biggest clans *used* to live. They would be the ones most likely to have survived."

Queebo still had a frown on her face, but she nodded slowly. I could see her thinking about it intently. "I will have to discuss this with Echo and Fredrick."

My heart plummeted straight down to my toes. I doubted she would be able to convince my dad. I figured Chase had a better chance of having a bad hair day, than Queebo had of convincing my dad to look for other dragons. I really had to stop thinking about Chase; I was in danger of forgetting he had tossed me off a cliff.

Hertha and I left Queebo to her rest. We spent a few hours plotting the most likely places where the clans might have survived, just in case there was a slim chance of Queebo convincing Echo and my father of going along with the plan. Then we finally called it a night.

When I entered the dragon living room—that's what I had decided to call the main cavern where the dragons stayed— the next morning, I found Queebo and my father engaged in a thunderously loud argument. I immediately swung around and made for the passage back to my room, trying to make a quick getaway before I was noticed.

"CHANDRA MARIE STRANDON, GET OVER HERE THIS INSTANT!!"

My shoulders hunched; I made my way over to where my father stood in front of Queebo.

"I cannot believe you would even suggest leaving the safety of this cave and going on a wild goose chase! Putting yourself in danger, after everything you know about the wyvern! After everything you've seen of them!" I could tell he was trying to control his voice and not yell as loudly as he had the first time, but it was a close thing.

"Dad, I just want us to have a fair chance against them. They've been winning—you said so yourself! If we had more dragons to help—"

He didn't even let me finish, just bulldozed right over me. His temper winning out again. "YOU KNOW PERFECTLY WELL I CAN'T GO WITHOUT YOU! YOU MUST KEEP UP WITH YOUR TRAINING!" He took a deep breath, and I saw a muscle ticking in his jaw. He somehow managed to rein in his temper again. His voice was tight and high, just barely under control. "I know you're a teenager, but you don't have to make it quite so obvious to everyone that you want out of this cave! If you need a reminder of how unsafe it is out there, I can remind you of the two incidents with Chase! It is safest for you inside this cave! I am not going to keep repeating myself for you, Chandra!"

I couldn't believe how unfair he was being. Or that he would remind me of what had happened with Chase. I didn't need any reminding about Chase, not ever. "If that's what you really think of me, then you don't know me very well, *Father!*" I spat the last word at him, and then I ran from the room. I heard my mother calling my name, but I kept running, ignoring her. I ran blindly, not really choosing a direction for my escape in my haste to get away.

My flight ended at the entrance to our home, at the ledge. I was sobbing by the time I reached the end of the tunnel, and belatedly I realized I couldn't even go outside—it was daytime. The ledge and entrance to the cave were secluded from the outside world by a spell. It didn't exist out there, the spell hid the ledge and the cave entrance. If I stepped out onto the ledge, well, it would look pretty strange to a passing tourist helicopter to see a teenage girl standing in midair over the canyon. I dropped down to the floor and leaned against the wall, tears streaming down my face. I refused to go back the way I'd come and walk back past my dad, blubbering like a big baby. I wanted to save the dragons. I knew if the wyvern attacked, many—if not all—of my new friends would die in the upcoming war. I also feared for him as well, I didn't want to lose my dad just when I had found him. Why couldn't he understand?

"Chandra, honey?" He sounded apologetic. I rubbed at my eyes with the sleeve of my shirt before I turned around to face him. I didn't want him to see me all teary-eyed. "I don't want us to fight, I ... just ... you ... and your mother ... and then the whole thing with the cliff." He let out a big breath. "I can't lose you again, Chandra. I had to let you and your mother go once, and then I almost lost you over rim of the canyon. I can't go through any of that again." He looked a little lost. I guess I understood, a little, not a little a lot. He didn't want to lose his little girl and I didn't want to lose my dad. I smiled and hugged him.

"Aww, Dad ..." I didn't know what else I could add to that. We walked back down the passage to the dragon living room silently, but content, we had reached an understanding.

Queebo called a meeting; the whole clan gathered, including my family. Queebo told everyone the idea about looking for the other clans, and it was discussed. It was a long and exhausting meeting. In the end, everyone agreed that it was a good idea, the best—and only—chance we had against the wyvern. We took a vote on where to search for the clans and narrowed it down to four locations from the list that Hertha and I had come up with: China, Scotland, Egypt, and Australia. That was all we thought that we would have time to search, even with magical means to assist us. The search party would leave at the end of the week; it wasn't going to be very big. Dad thought we would have a better chance of going undetected that way, both by the wyvern and regular humans.

I was excited by both the search for more dragons and the traveling. Mom and I had never traveled, for obvious reasons. Now I was going to get to go pretty much around the world. Dad reminded me that I wouldn't have time for sightseeing. I was still excited, though. I couldn't help but wonder if Chase would make an appearance. Even if it was for evil purposes, it was hard not to get my hopes up. Even if he did toss me over a cliff. See, I knew I was going to forgive him eventually. I'm a sentimental nincompoop.

I knew I would have to be careful around that boy. Despite my obvious status as a soft-brained fool whenever he appeared, I would try and be on my guard where Chase was concerned.

The rest of the week went by in a blur of preparations for our departure. Mom spent the week packing things into our already overstuffed packs. Since she wasn't going with us, she was worried sick about us. She kept telling us things like, "Make sure you wear your hat and gloves if it gets cold." We just nodded and humored her. Dad knew enough spells to keep us safe and warm if need be. Not that we needed to keep warm, our body temperatures were warm enough on their own.

Our search party would consist of two dragons, Echo and Hertha, and of course Dad and me. Dad also taught me a new spell he thought might come in handy in case we ran into some trouble. I figured trouble meant Chase, but I didn't say that out loud. It was a protection spell, kinda like my own personal shield. It was pretty neat; only problem was, it lasted only a few minutes. Dad's lasted about two; mine lasted about four. He said variations in time depended on a sorcerer's power. He could only assume since he believed I was the Chosen, mine would last much longer than his would. It took me a bit longer to get the hang of the protection spell at first because of the stupid Latin. The word for the protection spell is *munimentum*, meaning protection, fortification, or defense. Seriously, who invented this language, and why did they make it so hard? I was glad that sorcery was a lot easier than I had expected it to be, though. No long incantations and potions to remember. No wand waving, either. Dad said stuff like that was only for very complicated spells.

CHAPTER 8

We Demolish Yankee Stadium

The day of our departure had arrived at last. I was excited to be setting off in search of the other clans. Mom was spending the final minutes fussing over us.

"Mom, enough, okay?" I shook her off as she tried to fix my hair for the third time. Trust me; there is no fixing it. It just sits there and does nothing.

"Look at you, all grown up already. It seems like I just brought you home from the hospital yesterday."

I rolled my eyes at her. "Jeez, Mom, give it a rest. We'll be back before you know it."

She hugged me tight enough that I thought for sure I was in danger of a few broken bones.

"Okay, Mere, I think you've tortured Chandra enough for today. Let her go before she suffocates." I gave Dad a grateful smile over Mom's shoulder, and then made a quick escape before they got all mushy with their own goodbyes.

Queebo wished us luck as we made our way to the exit tunnel. We waved our final farewell and climbed aboard our rides. Hertha and Echo were anxious to get going; they spread their huge wings and took flight. I looked back only once as we headed into the low-hanging clouds that filled the sky. The night air held a chill. I couldn't help wondering if possibly the clouds were a warning of impending disaster on the horizon. They certainly weren't friendly-looking. Both dragons seemed pleased to have been chosen for the long journey. Other than short hunting trips at night, the dragons didn't get out much. They tended to stay hidden inside, both from humans and from the wyvern. Mostly the wyvern. Hertha did a little dip and loop; I screeched. Hertha mumbled an apology. She'd forgotten I was new to flying aboard a dragon, having only done so once before. Actually, I'd been unconscious that time, so it didn't really count. Dad had carried me the whole way to the cave that first night.

I couldn't see where we were headed since we flew up in the clouds; Dad was using a directional spell to guide us. Hertha just had to follow Echo. Dad was also using a traveling spell to speed us up. He had tried to explain how it worked; I stopped him when he started using words like space, time, and dimensions. I had never been a very good student—not that my grades were hopeless or anything; I did have mostly B's, well, maybe a few C's, too. Mom had always smiled and said my head was in the clouds. I was a dreamer, not a thinker. I preferred reading to arithmetic (yeah, I pretty much sucked at math; it was beyond me). I could get lost in a book for hours. I guess maybe my brain always knew I didn't belong in the "real" world.

So, when Dad tried to get technical, I just said, as long as it worked, it was fine with me. Also, no one saw us flying through the sky on two rather large dragons. We had decided to head east across the U.S., and then out across the Atlantic, hitting Scotland first. I wondered how long the dragons could fly without resting.

"We can fly for many hours before we have to rest. However, we prefer not to if we do have the chance to rest." Hertha had answered my silent question. I still wasn't used to my thoughts being broadcast when I didn't guard them close enough. I thought I saw a smile on my father's face, but it was hard to tell in the darkness that surrounded us.

The night soon grew cool, and I began to wonder where exactly we were when my father took us down out of the clouds.

"Welcome to New York City, Chandra," he said with a sweep of his hand across the city below us. I gazed down at the lights of the city. It was so crowded; so many people in one place, I thought.

"It's beautiful, Dad!" He chuckled at the awed tone of my voice and looked at his watch.

"We have a good four hours before sunrise; we'll set down and have a rest. We can get going again before the sun's fully up." I watched as the dragons snapped a few pigeons out of the air, opting for the quick snack before landing. I made a face. *Ew!* Hertha chuckled at me. I looked back at my dad.

"Where on earth are we going to be able to set down in the middle of New York City?"

"I was thinking Central Park is as good a place as any. There's probably enough weird stuff in there that no one would even notice two dragons." I stared at him. I couldn't tell if he was joking or not. "Honestly, Chandra, do you think I would set down in the middle of a city park? Seriously, Central Park is just an old sorcerer's joke." He rolled his eyes at me, and we began our decent into the city. If we weren't going to Central Park, where were we going? When I saw his destination, at first I thought it was more insane than his park gag.

"Dad, you are kidding again, right?"

"Nope, best place in the world. No one there at night except for a few security guards who can be persuaded to sleep the night away with a simple spell." I really seriously thought he was going to yell April Fools'! or something at the last minute and pull up.

"Dad, this is Yankee Stadium! We can't stay here!" I said, sounding, I'm sure, a little panicked.

"Chandra, stop worrying. Honestly, no one will ever know we were here." He jumped down off of Echo's back as soon as we landed. "I need to go take care of the security guards. I'll find something for us to eat on my way back."

I stood there in the middle of the outfield and watched my dad jog over and touch home plate before he left the field. I slapped my hand to my forehead. What is it with men and sports that even a sorcerer who is over one hundred and fifty years old can't resist touching home plate before leaving the field? I turned away and walked over to where Hertha and Echo had settled down to sleep.

"Do you two need anything?" Echo looked up at me.

"No, Chandra, we are fine." I smiled at Echo as he closed his eyes. Hertha was already snoring softly. I sighed, nothing to do but wait for Dad to get back. The stadium seemed kind of creepy in the semi-darkness. Only a few lights had been left on for security purposes. I strolled over to where my backpack was and rummaged through it till I found my hoodie, deciding to put it on. It was a little chilly even with my high body temperature or maybe I was imagining things in the darkness.

As I turned to walk back and sit by Hertha to wait for Dad, something hit me from behind, sending me sprawling to the ground. I gasped as the air was knocked out of me. A weight was pressing down on my back. I struggled to push it off and get back to my feet, fear and helplessness pushing down on me as effectively as the oppressive weight.

"So nice to see you, Chandra." I froze when I heard Chase's voice so close. His breath fanned the wisps of hair next to my ear, sending chills over my flesh. I realized the weight holding me down was Chase, his knees pressing into my back, his lips close to my ear.

There was a brief moment of stillness, and then the world seemed to go haywire. Wyvern were everywhere. Somehow, I managed to throw Chase off my back, rolling as far from him as I could, which wasn't far enough—he grabbed my ankle as I scrambled away. I twisted my wrist, frantically muttering the fire spell, and flung the fireball back at Chase, not taking the time to aim. It sailed past his perfect hair, missing it by inches. I wondered, briefly, as I ran for my life, if he had enough gel in that perfect hair of his to make it go up in flames.

I had to get somewhere, anywhere, safe. I knew I couldn't fight him. Not because I wasn't good enough, but because I couldn't look him in the eyes and disintegrate him. My boast that I would kill him next time I saw him had been false. I realized I really did like him too much to kill him.

I doubted he felt the same way about me.

I stumbled as Echo shot over my head, followed closely by two wyvern. He pelted toward the upper deck seats. My mind screamed at him to pull up. I shouldn't have been so worried; Echo had battled the wyvern a lot longer than I had. He pulled up at the very last second. The two wyvern weren't as lucky; they smashed headlong into the seats.

So much for nobody knowing we had been here, I thought wryly.

I didn't want to look back to see if Chase was gaining on me. The visitor's dugout was just a few feet ahead of me. I staggered down the first set of steps into the dugout, and then the second, and ended up rushing into the hall that led down to, I guessed, the locker room. I was instantly plunged into total darkness. I never could've guessed that they wouldn't leave some lights on down here for the security guys to patrol around! I felt along the wall as I scooted down the dark hall. I had no idea where I was going, what down this hallway.

"*Chaaandra,* come out, come out, wherever you are." Chase's voice floated after me in the darkness. I kept going, fear uncurling in my stomach. I stumbled, hitting a door. Locked. Now what? There was only one way out. Back the way I had come, back past Chase. This had been a stupid move. I shouldn't have been such a big coward. I should've just faced him out on the field! I was panicked now; I had to confront him. I turned back; I knew I couldn't annihilate him. I just had to get past him, back out to the field. With a flick of my wrist, I produced a small fireball. I had barely a second to toss it. Chase was a lot closer than I had anticipated, his face lit by the flickering flames I held in my hand, making his face eerie, evil, and yet still handsome at the same time.

"Ahh, there you are, Chandra." His seductive voice surrounded me. I lobbed the fire at him. He ducked sideways to avoid the flames; I jumped the opposite way and pelted down the hall, back toward the light of the field, feeling his hand glide over the fabric of my hoodie as he made a grab at me when I flung myself past him. I forced myself to keep going, ignoring the feel of his hand gliding over my arm as he missed latching on to the fabric of my jacket.

I bashed my shins on the steps in my rush to make it back into the dugout. I ran up the second set of steps and back out onto the field, stopping dead in my tracks, forgetting that I was running for my life.

In the short time that I had been gone, they'd destroyed half the stadium!

The scoreboard was tottering dangerously to one side. The glass, to what I could only guess was the skyboxes, had been shattered. I turned a full circle; many seats had been displaced as well. My dad was in the upper deck, throwing every spell he had at a couple of wyvern who were closing in on him. I was about to jump the rail and run to help him when Chase appeared and ruined my plans.

"How nice of you to make this easy for me, Chandra!"

I spun back around to face him, raising my right hand to cast the fire spell. He grabbed my hand, linking his fingers through mine, shaking his head, and bringing our linked hands down to my side.

"We'll have none of that, young lady. We have some unfinished business to attend to, and I won't have you delaying it." I just couldn't believe how reasonable he managed to make his voice sound.

"I don't much care for your definition of *unfinished business.*"

"You seem to enjoy making the job more challenging for me, Chandra."

What did he think I was going to do, lie down and die for him? "Did you really think I was going to make it easier for you, you doughnut?"

He arched a black brow at me. "Doughnut? That's your best insult, Chandra? You disappoint me." His lips lifted into an irritating little grin, complete with dimple. I resisted the urge to stamp my foot like a preschooler. I raised my left hand, which I'd been concealing behind my back. I flung a fireball in his face; he instantly released my right hand, spluttering from the blast of fire I had thrown into his face.

I lurched away from Chase, stumbling a bit as I tried to run. He clutched at me, managing to get a good hold on my jacket—he wrestled me to the ground, pinning me there.

"Honestly, I don't know why you keep resisting. If you just cooperated, this would all be over so much faster, Chandra."

I really was getting tired of him telling me to participate timidly in my own death. A thought meandered into my mind at that instant. If Theryn *was* in Chase's head controlling him, what if I could "heal" him, as I had done with Queebo?

Maybe I could force Theryn out of his mind, like he was a bad spell or something. Chase already had me in his dastardly clutches, so to speak. I was touching him; I felt my cheeks grow hot at that thought. Yeah, I was touching him, all right, pretty much all over.

I closed my eyes and focused on his mind, trying to search out Theryn, attempting to force him out. I hoped that Chase didn't take the closing of my eyes as a sign of surrender. I knew that I was safe from harm while healing. Dad's accidental demonstration when I'd been healing Queebo had proven that already.

I had no clue how wrong that assumption was, until it was far too late. A searing pain tore through my chest. I felt Chase's weight leave me; my eyes snapped open.

Chase was backing away from me, a look of absolute horror on his face—eyes pinned to my chest. He backed up till he reached the rail of the visitor's dugout. His hands gripped the rail, knuckles white with the force of his hold on the metal rail.

I looked down to see the hilt of a small dagger protruding from my chest. Blood oozed out around the blade like some sick little fountain, soaking my shirt, the dagger angling downward, penetrating my heart. I could make out every little detail on the hilt of the dagger, all of it perfectly clear. It was in the shape of a wyvern, with blood-red rubies for eyes. The blade protruded from its open mouth. I rolled to my side. I looked to Chase for; I don't know, help, maybe? He was slowly shaking his head from side to side as if to deny what he'd just done.

He would be no help.

It seemed odd that I was abruptly aware of the cool grass beneath me, the starry sky above. Suddenly, my dad was there by my side. I don't know how he knew to come to me; maybe somehow I'd called him with my mind, and I hadn't been aware of it.

"Chandra, sweetheart, it's okay. It's Dad. I'm here … can you hear me?" I managed to focus on him and nodded to show that I'd heard him. "I'm going to pull the knife out, but you need to concentrate, honey, okay? You need to focus so you can heal the wound. Do you understand? You need to try and heal yourself, sweetie." I nodded again. I wasn't sure if I could do it—darkness was already creeping in around the edges of my vision. It hurt badly, and I could feel my heartbeat slowing already … beat by beat.

Chase had done this; he'd killed me. Stabbed me through the heart. *Chase had killed me.* I thought those words over and over.

My dad was speaking again. He sounded like he was so far away. "Are you ready?" Ready for what? I couldn't remember now. Dad grabbed the dagger and yanked it out in one swift, even, fluid motion, slapping his hand on the wound to staunch the sudden flow of blood.

I wanted to shriek when he pulled the dagger out. I focused on the wound instead, suddenly remembering his instructions to me. I blocked out the sound of his voice; he was shouting at Chase. I had to focus; I didn't want to die—but the pain, God, the pain. It made it hard to focus on anything.

"Chase, get over here. I need your help!" Fredrick frowned at the boy. He had to be in shock. His face was white, and his eyes were unfocused. Fredrick was certain that Theryn had left the boy as soon as the wyvern was certain there was no way Chandra would survive. Theryn must have assumed he would kill the boy, thinking he'd murdered Chandra. Theryn didn't know what Fredrick suspected. Fredrick would deal with Theryn later; he had Chandra to deal with now. He wouldn't give up so easily on his daughter.

"Dammit, Chase, move your butt, boy!" Chase's eyes blinked and he snapped out of his trance, eyes focusing on Fredrick, moving slowly toward him. Fredrick gave a small nod.

"That's better, now get over here. Put your hand right here where mine is. Good, now stay by her side and don't leave her. She needs all the help she can get. Close your eyes and focus, that's right. I'm not sure what help you can give, but try." Fredrick had a sneaking suspicion that Chase wouldn't be affected by Chandra's healing defense, Fredrick had to get his hands off of her before she began healing or he'd be thrown away from her.

Chandra's mind had called to him when she'd been injured. He doubted his daughter knew she had called out to him; she had looked shocked to find him by her side. She had been trying to shove Theryn from Chase's mind, in effect heal him, when Chase had stabbed her. Something that shouldn't have been able to occur. For some reason, Chase was unaffected by the electrical shock that had stung him when he had tried to touch Chandra as she had been healing Queebo. Whether it was because she had been attempting to heal Chase or it was something else, Fredrick didn't know. If it had been because of some small fluke, Chase was about to get a nasty surprise. Chase's eyes snapped back open when Fredrick told him to help Chandra.

Fredrick softened his voice. "Trust me, son, you can do it. Help her. I have to clean up this mess we made, or someone is bound to notice that we were here." He knew the boy was confused, maybe even frightened, but he had to do this. Chase closed his eyes again.

Fredrick looked around. He had a lot of work ahead of him, and not a whole lot of time to do it. He whistled for Echo to join him, climbed aboard. He decided the scoreboard was the best place to start. He left Chase to care for Chandra, trusting that the boy could help her. The boy had to have a lot of power, or Theryn would never have taken him.

I felt sudden warmth spread through my body. I wondered where it had come from; it didn't matter, I had to try to keep my focus. That warmth seemed to help, as the pain seemed to recede some with its appearance. I was able to concentrate more easily on the wound. All too soon, my eyes fluttered open. The sight that greeted me was Chase leaning over me, his beautiful blue-gray eyes looking concerned.

"Dad … where's my dad?"

"He went to go make repairs to the stadium." His voice was soft. I was having a bit of trouble focusing.

"Chase, what are you doing here?" I was woozy and more than a little confused. Why was Chase still here? Had we lost the battle after he'd stabbed me? If we hadn't, why hadn't my dad pulverized him for trying to kill me? And why *had* he been able to stab me in the first place? I was supposed to be protected when I was healing.

"Your dad said I had to sit here by your side to help you."

I wondered how he had helped me. I remembered the sudden spread of warmth through my body and wondered if Chase had anything to do with that.

"Help me sit up." I clipped out at him. He slipped his arm under my shoulders and pushed me up. I looked around for my dad. He was on Echo's back, hovering in the air, still making repairs to some of the upper deck seats. I struggled to my feet, wobbling a little.

Chase grabbed my arm to steady me. "Maybe you should sit down for a while longer." He sounded genuinely concerned.

"I'm fine," I said through gritted teeth. I wasn't, though; I was woozy. I guessed dying did that to you. My shirt was all sticky with blood. I grimaced and pulled at my shirt, wanting it away from my skin. I needed to change, but we would have to get going really soon. I looked around for my backpack so I could go change.

Chase produced my backpack and handed it to me.

"Um, thanks," I muttered. He helped me get to the closest bathroom. I didn't really want his help; however, I had little choice. I was still wobbly after my near-death experience. I changed as quickly as I could, sloshing water on myself to wash off most of the blood. I had a ghastly scar on my chest. I wondered if I concentrated hard enough, could I heal a wound without leaving a scar. Shaking my head, I dropped my bloody shirt onto the floor with the rest of my clothes and pulled on my clean clothes. I eyed my pile of blood-soaked clothes in a heap on the floor.

I yanked a trash bag out of an empty can and stuffed the clothes in it, tying it shut and stuffing it into my pack. I wasn't gonna leave it behind for some overly enthusiastic local cop to find and panic the city into thinking a serial killer was on the loose.

I exited the bathroom. Chase was there, leaning against the wall, hands in his pockets, waiting for me; he'd gone to the bathroom, too. I noticed his hair was wet. It wasn't so perfect anymore; it made me wonder a bit. I had no time to consider the ramifications of Chase's new hairdo; we had to get going.

Just as we made it back to center field, Chase clinging to my arm despite the fact that I'd told him I was fine, Dad finished his repairs and landed next to us. "Ready to go, kids?"

I frowned at him. "How do we know it's safe to bring him with?" I asked, jerking a thumb in Chase's direction. Dad rolled his eyes, jumped down off of Echo, and walked over to him, reaching up to place a hand on his temple.

"May I, Chase?" he asked. Chase nodded. A few minutes passed in silence. "Chase is the only one in there, Chandra. Theryn is gone."

He walked over and climbed back onto Echo's back and gestured for us to do the same with Hertha. I suddenly turned red. I really didn't want to be sitting that close to Chase, embarrassed after everything that had happened.

A glance at his red face told me he was thinking the same thing. I secured my pack and climbed onto Hertha. Chase hesitated a minute, and then climbed up behind me, leaving a wide gap between us. I thought I saw my dad grin and roll his eyes just before the dragons spread their wings and took off.

As Hertha took flight, Chase grabbed at my waist, wrapping his arms securely around me, and held on for dear life. *So much for distance between us,* I thought. We set out over the Atlantic Ocean. Our first stop would be Scotland—the Highlands, to be exact. I yawned. I really hoped I wouldn't fall asleep and plummet to my death, not after surviving a stabbing.

CHAPTER 9

We Have A Tupperware Party

I woke with a stiff neck. I was leaning awkwardly back with my head on Chase's left shoulder. I realized that it wasn't just awkward for me. It was really awkward for him, because it left him with no choice but to either stare straight ahead or off to the right. If he looked anywhere else, he mostly got a view of, well, my chest. I was extremely embarrassed when I figured that one out. I sat up quickly, my face more than a little red. I apologized for falling asleep on him.

He smiled, loosening his arms around my waist. He'd had them wrapped all the way around me, holding on to me, I guessed, so I would feel more secure while I slept, or so I wouldn't fall. It was kind of sweet.

"It's okay, you needed the rest after … um … you know."

I assumed he didn't quite know how to finish that sentence. Ending with, "after I stabbed you" wouldn't exactly sound right. He was probably right about the sleep, but I was still hot with embarrassment over the position I had ended up in. I couldn't believe I'd fallen asleep on him!

"Land ho!" my dad called out, breaking the tension between us.

"That was lame, Dad!" I called back to him, giggling. I heard a deep chuckle from Chase, as well. My dad had a big cheesy grin on his face. We flew inland for a while. Dad knew where the clan used to flourish; he'd mapped our entire trip out before we left.

As dusk fell, we finally landed on a moor dotted with heather. In the distance, there were rocky-looking mountains, and all around were clumps of trees. It was beautiful in a rugged, wild way. I loved it instantly.

Echo stretched his wings, I frowned; he had a large gash on one.

"Echo, do you want me to heal that for you?"

He gave me a small smile. "I would not have you weaken yourself any further, Chandra. I will be fine, thank you."

I frowned; did I really look that bad? "Echo, really, it's no trouble. I'm fine, honest."

"No, Chandra, it is okay. Hertha and I must hunt now, and then rest." With a flap of his giant wings, he was gone.

"He's right, you know."

I turned to my father. "I'm fine; you don't need to baby me!" I stomped over to a large rock and sat down, crossing my arms over my chest, glaring at my dad's back as he walked over to stand near Chase, who was staring broodingly out over the now-dark moor.

"Chase is something wrong?" he asked.

"Don't know, I just feel like something is watching us, waiting," He gave a little shrug and then a half smile to my dad. "Sorry, guess I'm kinda spooked after those years with Theryn getting inside my head." He walked over and perched next to me on the rock. Dad stayed where he was, staring at the same spot Chase had been. Now he frowned, too.

"Chandra, Chase, get some firewood and start a fire. *Now.*" We looked at each other. Something about the way he'd said it had us both jumping up without question and rushing off into the dark, looming trees behind us, in search of suitable firewood.

When we emerged a short time later with the wood, Dad hadn't moved a muscle. We quickly built the fire, keeping an eye on my dad for a clue about what was bothering him. As soon as the fire was roaring, he came over and began rummaging in his backpack. He pulled out a small Tupperware container with a blue lid. He muttered a few words, took a small pinch of powder from the container, and threw it in the fire.

We jumped back a step as the flames momentarily blazed bright blue, and then settled down.

"Uh, Dad?" He looked up from securing the lid on the container. "Since when do sorcerers use Tupperware containers for their potion ingredients?" I'd always imagined potion containers as being some old clay jars, like something out of a movie.

"Since it's more convenient, the lids stay on tightly, and it keeps them fresher longer."

I stared at him in disbelief.

Chase burst out laughing. "So what exactly is the Tupperware powder going to save us from tonight?"

We didn't think he was going to answer Chase's question at first.

"If I'm right, it's a banshee."

Chase and I looked at each other, and then back at him. Chase had a look of complete disbelief on his face.

"*Oookay*, and that means what, exactly? She's gonna scream at us and we, what, die?"

My father looked out across the black expanse of moor. "There are different types of banshee. There are stories of banshee who will wail outside of the home of a person who is about to die, and then there is the banshee who will wander the darkened moors and forests waiting to lure unlucky travelers to their doom."

As I listened to my dad's story, I had a feeling the wandering banshee was the one we had to worry about.

"The banshee's wail doesn't actually kill you. It foretells the death of those who hear it. It means you will die, maybe not right this minute, but soon." He gave us a twisted smile. "Something to look forward to, huh?" He turned to Chase then. "How did you know she was out there, Chase?"

Chase blinked at him and shrugged. "I don't know, I just thought it felt weird like something was staring right at me or something like that." He shrugged again and ran his hand through his hair. As I watched that little gesture, I was kinda glad to see that his hair really was no longer perfect. It lay in rumpled, wavy, curling masses all over his head. It was endearing, I grinned stupidly.

Echo and Hertha returned at that moment. Dad sighed; he didn't look like he wanted to end his conversation with Chase just yet, but he stood anyway.

"Why don't you two set up the tent? I need to tell Echo and Hertha what's happening."

Chase and I rummaged in the packs till we found the tent. That's the problem with magical packing—it's convenient in that you can pack a lot of stuff in a small space, but finding anything is the pits.

When Dad returned from his conversation with the dragons, he sat down next to Chase. "Chase, it's possible that you're a sensitive."

I guessed that we had pretty much perfected our blank looks since Dad's pause lasted only a few seconds, and he didn't wait for us to ask any questions.

"Some sorcerers can pick up on other magical creatures when they're nearby. They know what they are and how close they are. Since you haven't been trained, you were only able to pick up on the fact that *something* was there, however, not *what* that something was. I need a spell and a whole lot of concentration before I can pick up on the fact that anything is watching us, and even then, I can't always tell *what* it is." Dad explained.

Chase shook his head. "After everything I've seen in the past two years, I'm not going to say I don't believe in magic. I'm sorry, I still don't think I'm a sorcerer. Theryn kept telling me I was, but ..." He lifted his shoulders in a half shrug.

Dad sighed and stood. "Come on, Chase, it's time for your first lesson. Besides, like Chandra, your temperature is getting too high."

Chase frowned; I guessed that no one had explained that part to him yet. I grinned; I knew what was coming. I hoped he didn't set anything on fire. Dad showed him how to do the wrist movements, and then taught him the word that went with the spell. Chase looked like he was just going to do all this to humor my dad. I wanted to laugh out loud. Eventually, he would make fire, and then he would have to believe. It took him about as long as it had taken me. I was a little jealous of the fact that he didn't drop his fireball and set his shoes on fire. He was sufficiently surprised that he'd done it at all. He stared at the little ball of fire in his hand for a full minute.

"Well, I'll be damned, I am a sorcerer."

Dad and I both laughed; Chase looked up at us, grinning.

Dad frowned at him now. "Chase, this means one thing, however. Your mother or your father, whichever is the sorcerer in your family, is in danger. I can assume Theryn asked you about that?"

Chase nodded in response to my father's questioning. "I don't know who my real parents are; I was adopted when I was a baby. My mom and my dad told me I was left at a church when I was only five days old. The pastor brought me to the adoption center, where my parents adopted me from," Chase answered.

Dad frowned again. "I wish we knew who your magical parent was. It would be nice to have another sorcerer on our side in the fight." Dad had begun to pace. Chase and I looked at each other.

"Dad, what are you thinking?"

"I'm sure whoever Chase's parents are, they knew the wyvern would come looking for him as soon as they found out who he was. They were trying to hide him for however long they could, hoping maybe he wouldn't have any powers. That he wouldn't be the Chosen." Chase looked between us, the blank look only from him this time. We hadn't explained about the Chosen part. Dad left that to me as he went to talk to the dragons one more time before we turned in for the night.

Chase was thoughtful about the whole Chosen Child thing. He wasn't as freaked out by it as I'd been. I wondered if he'd thought all this time maybe his real parents hadn't loved him, so they'd given him away. Now he knew they'd loved him so much, they *had* to give him away in order to protect him.

As we settled in for the night, Echo and Hertha set themselves up at either end of the camp like sentries and were asleep in moments. I grabbed Dad when he came back; there was a problem

I wanted to discuss before bed. I waited while Chase went into the tent.

"Dad, something's bothering me," I said quietly.

"What is it, honey?" he asked, sitting down. I sat down next to him and stared into the fire. I wasn't sure where to start.

"Dad, what happened back there? Why ... I mean, how? I thought I couldn't be harmed while I was healing? I was trying to push Theryn out of Chase's mind. Why was he able to stab me while I was healing him?" I looked at him now.

Fredrick had been wondering when Chandra would get around to asking about that. It had been bothering him as well. Fredrick wasn't sure exactly why Chase had been able to stab her. Nor why Chase had been able to touch her while she had healed herself, even though he had been somewhat certain beforehand that Chase would have no problem touching her while she healed. He was certain of one thing, however: If Chase hadn't been there, Chandra would have died. Somehow, he knew that in his heart. Without Chase there to help her heal, Chandra never would have lived. The wound had been severe; she had needed some sort of assistance with the healing. Fredrick had suspected that Chase was powerful the moment Chandra had told him about Chase, Theryn never would have taken him in the first place, nor would he have allowed Chase to live, if that weren't a fact. He smiled at her as he answered. "I don't know; there could be thousands of explanations, sweetheart. It could be because he was the one you were healing. That could make him immune to the defense you possess. It could be because Theryn was occupying Chase's mind, or one more of a million other reasons I can't think of."

It wasn't a very helpful answer, but I supposed this was a new thing we were dealing with, so I couldn't expect him to know everything. We stood and went to the tent. Dad—Mom as well—had packed so much extra stuff that Chase was just as comfortable as we were.

It was an uneasy night; it took us a long time to fall asleep. We were all worried about our *friend* that might be watching the camp from a distance out on the moor somewhere.

I awoke right around midnight. *Lovely,* I thought to myself, *it would be me that has to pee at the witching hour.* I struggled out of my sleeping bag and crept out into the darkness.

I scanned the pitch-black night for the lumps rising out of the night that would be the dragons guarding the camp. Seeing them gave me a bit of reassurance. After locating the dragons, I set off into the trees to, uhh, well; you get the idea. I yawned as I made my way back to the tent after finishing my business.

That's when I ran smack into Chase.

"Jeez, you scared the life outta me, Chase!" I said a little breathlessly. He had grabbed my arms to steady me and keep me from falling when I smacked into him.

"Sorry, I woke up, and you were gone. I got worried, so I came looking for you."

I thought that was kinda nice. Romantic, even. "You know the call of nature doesn't care what time it is!" I said, trying to be funny.

He chuckled. "Good one." He turned, releasing my arms as he did, and stood looking up at the stars. "There are so many of them out here. I kinda missed looking at them, you know? Haven't seen them in a long time." He shifted uncomfortably, his hand going to his hair. "Come on, we'd better get back before your dad thinks I've kidnapped you and run off!" He gave me a lopsided grin, showing his dimple. I thought maybe he meant, kidnapped me and dragged me back to Theryn.

"Chase? What was it like? Being with the wyvern, I mean," I asked him curiously.

His whole body went rigid. "I don't want to talk about that. I'd appreciate it if you didn't mention it again." His voice was cold. I frowned. He had to talk about it; he couldn't just bury it away. He turned away from me, his back straight and stiff. I placed a hand on his back, trying to give him what little comfort I could. He flinched when my hand touched him, as if it caused him pain.

"Chase, you need to talk about it sometime. It happened; you can't just pretend it didn't," I said, trying to sound like I knew exactly what I was talking about. He spun back around to face me. I backed away when he spun around so quickly. His hands flashed out, grabbing my arms in a painful grip. "Chase, you're hurting me!" He didn't seem to hear.

"I want to forget that part of my life ever happened. You don't know what it was like—you weren't there! I can't relive that! Don't ever ask me about it!" He was starting to scare me. His eyes were hard and far away. This wasn't the Chase I had come to know in the past few hours.

"Chase, I won't know what it was like unless you tell me! You can't pretend it didn't happen. It won't make it go away; it will always be there!" His hands tightened on my arms even as I spoke to him. I knew I would have bruises there in the morning. I should leave it be, let it go, but something was pushing me to make him talk, even though his change in mood was frightening me.

"They're my nightmares then, aren't they? Nothing to concern your pretty head about, right? Why don't you just leave me alone?" He snarled the words at me. What was he so angry about? I just wanted to help him. I wanted to talk about it and to understand what he went through!

"Chase, I'm just trying to help! You need to talk about it; you can't let it fester in your mind like that. If you try to stamp it down, one day you'll just … just …" My voice caught in my throat; I didn't want to cry, but I knew if I tried to continue, I would. His attitude wasn't helping any, either. I would cry, not just from the pain of his grip on my arms, but from the pain his words were causing me.

"What, Chandra? I'll what, explode? Is that what you're afraid of, huh? I'll explode? You think I'll go off and kill someone?" He let go of one of my arms and held up his hand, fire crackling in it. "I don't need a gun for that, do I? I can just go out and kill, right? Is that what you're afraid of, Chandra?" He repeated again. I stared at him wide-eyed as he crushed out the fire in his hand. This most certainly wasn't the Chase I had come to know since Theryn left him such a short time ago. I was scared down to my toes. This reminded me of the Chase I had seen when Theryn held his mind.

Could Theryn possibly be back?

"Chase, *please* listen to me! What happened to you wasn't your fault! What Theryn did wasn't your fault! You just need to talk about it, get past it." He laughed at my words. A harsh, grating laugh. It cut through the last of my defenses, breaking me down, crushing any resistance I might have had left, driving out any thoughts I had about making him talk about what had happened to him. I felt tears rush into my eyes.

"You could never understand any of it, Chandra!" he sneered at me. "The pain and the torture, how I suffered every day. I'm sure my parents aren't even looking for me anymore; they probably think I'm dead! My whole life is gone. Everything I knew has changed. It. Is. All. Gone. I sat in that cage and had that monster in my head for two years! While you were doing what, Chandra? Huh? Out with your friends? Going to the movies with boys? Stay out of it, Chandra. Leave me and my demons be!" He flung me away and stormed off to the tent.

No, Theryn wasn't back, but it wasn't the same Chase, either. Who was he exactly? Man or monster? He'd gotten so angry, so quickly. Why?

I stood there staring after him. I sank into the soft heather at my feet and wept. It was then that I knew, no matter what happened; I could never get any closer to Chase than I was at this moment. It would only cause more heartbreak for me if he continued to hate me. I realized that I loved him with all my heart, when exactly it had happened I wasn't sure, but it had. I cried even harder. It's why I couldn't harm him during the attack at the stadium. I had loved him for a while now, why hadn't I realized it before?

Hertha came to me, coiling her great body around me, comforting me. She didn't speak, just wrapped herself around me and waited while I cried myself to sleep. I slept there in the heather with Hertha.

CHAPTER 10

Return

I woke to the bright sunshine and voices nearby. I lifted my head from Hertha's tail and looked up. Dad and Echo were near the campfire; studying the map. I sat up and stretched. Hertha uncoiled herself and stretched too. I smiled at her.

"Thank you, Hertha." She only nodded. I guess she knew I didn't really want to talk about what had happened. We both walked over to the campfire.

"Morning, guys." To me, my voice sounded dry and scratchy, from all the crying, I guessed.

Dad didn't seem to notice; he looked up, giving me a bright smile. "Morning, sweetheart! Felt safer sleeping with the fire-breathing guard by your side last night?" he said with a chuckle.

"Something like that." I replied, not wanting to go into detail. I looked around, noting Chase's absence. I wondered if he was still sleeping; I didn't want to ask. If I did, I would probably burst into tears. Dad had made breakfast: eggs, bacon, and coffee; I helped myself.

"By the time you're done, Chandra, Chase should be back. There's a small stream through the trees over there. You can go have a wash, if you want to, before we leave. That's where Chase has gone off to."

I gave a small nod, trying hard not to think of Chase taking a bath. I finished eating and went to fish my things out of my pack. I sat back by the fire, listening to my dad and Echo talking about the best route to take to find the Scottish dragons. I unbraided my hair and brushed it out. I hoped the water was deep enough to wash my hair. I waited and waited; Chase still hadn't come back. I frowned. Really, how long did it take him to wash himself? I gave up, grabbed my stuff, and stalked off through the trees.

I found the stream without any problem; there was no Chase there, either. I wondered where he had wandered off to. I didn't bother to go looking for him. I stripped out of my dirty clothes and waded into the stream; the water was a little chilly, but with my body temperature, I would be fine. In the middle, it was about waist-deep, not too bad—I could wash my hair. I waded back out, grabbed my toiletries bag, and plunged back in. I found a rock protruding out of the water and set my bag of stuff on it, and then got to work. After washing both my hair, and myself I waded back to the shore and got as comfortable as I could on the small pebble beach. Being a vain teenage girl, I just had to shave my legs.

When I was finally done, I got dressed. I was glad we had found the stream; I hadn't gotten to totally clean myself at the stadium. I had just done a quick job before we left. I shuddered; there had still been some blood left. I wanted to wipe out that memory, but I knew it would always be there. Every time I looked at my chest, I would see the ugly scar from the stab wound. Even if Chase was out of my life and the pain I felt now faded, I could never truly forget him. There would always be that reminder staring me in the face.

I sat down and set my chin on my knees, staring at the little stream. I'd thought that now that we were on the same side, we would have a chance to be together. I sighed; no such luck, I guessed. Maybe that was part of the prophecy as well: The Chosen Child wasn't allowed happiness. If it was, it wasn't fair. I knew I should get back to camp. Dad probably wanted to leave soon; we had to start searching. I stayed right where I was, though. I didn't want to face Chase again, not after last night.

"Chandra, where are you? Chandra, come on, we have to go!"

I sighed and hauled myself up. He would have to be the one to come looking for me. I gathered my things and headed back to camp.

I walked past Chase, not stopping, not looking at him. He grabbed my arm; I winced. I had bruises where he'd held my arms last night. He let go immediately, running his hand through his hair. I wondered if he always did that when he was uncomfortable or nervous.

"Chandra, I … um … I wanted to apologize for last night. I shouldn't have yelled at you like that. I know you were trying to help. It's just that that was … um … a … well, I'd rather not talk about it, is all." He shifted his feet and jammed his hands into his jeans pockets. I wondered if I should forgive him or not. He'd hurt me, and I wasn't just talking about my arms—that I could forgive. I guessed in the end I could set him on fire if I had to. But he'd broken my heart, even if he hadn't known it.

I took a deep breath and spoke. "Chase, you need to think about things—I mean, really think. If you're going to be here with us and fight the wyvern, things will come up. Dad is gonna ask you eventually. He and the dragons will want to know a lot about Theryn's defenses. How many of them there are, where he's hiding out, stuff like that. All I wanted to know was what happened to you; they will want information for war. Either way, you're going to have to talk about something." I turned to walk away. I hadn't exactly told him *Yes, I accept your apology.* His voice stopped me.

"Why, Chandra?"

I turned back to him. "Why what?"

"Why do you want to know what I went through? What does it matter to you? You want to fight the wyvern, same as your dad. Why do my feelings matter so much to you?"

I shook my head; were all boys so dumb? "Chase, if you can't figure that part out for yourself, then my explaining it won't help." I turned and walked back to camp, leaving him standing there.

Chase had woken up this morning feeling worse than when he'd gone to sleep. When he'd left the tent, it was to find Chandra curled up with Hertha, who had given him a look of pure evil when he'd walked by the two of them. He doubted Hertha liked him very much right now. Fredrick had gotten up just a few minutes later.

Her father thought Chandra had gotten scared in the middle of the night and gone to sleep with the dragon. Chase didn't bother to enlighten him. They had checked around the immediate area for anything interesting and found a small stream. Chase got a few things out of the packs and decided to go for a bath. He had wanted to try to wash away any memory he had left of being at Theryn's place.

The stream would have been cold to anyone else, he supposed, but it was okay for a sorcerer with a one hundred and ten degree body temperature, it held only a slight chill. He had been shocked to find out what his temperature was, and that it was just fine for a sorcerer, when Fredrick had taken it this morning. Fredrick had seemed a bit stunned as well, mumbling something about Chandra's temperature and his being the same and that he'd never seen anything like it before. Chase wondered exactly what he'd meant by that, but Fredrick had given no further explanation.

After his bath, he didn't feel like going back to camp right away. He had some things to think about, he guessed. He wandered a bit farther from the camp than he intended. He took a deep breath and decided he better head back. When he wandered back into camp, Fredrick asked him to go find Chandra; she had gone to the stream. He was glad they hadn't run into each other. With the way he was beginning to feel about her, he knew seeing her in the stream would have been a bad idea.

He decided he wanted to apologize to her. No matter how small a gesture it was, he would try. He found her after a short walk. She didn't seem interested in his apology.

Chase watched Chandra walk off after his attempted apology. Why did girls always talk in riddles? Did they like it when guys were confused? He wondered what she had meant with her whole comment about if she had to explain it to him, it wouldn't help. How could an explanation *not* help?

I stuffed my things back into my pack when I got back to camp. Dad had already cleared up camp while I had been at the stream. We were ready to go. Chase strolled back into view just then. I wasn't sure how comfortable our ride on Hertha was going to be since our fight. Or since I hadn't exactly accepted his apology.

I patted Hertha's side. She looked back at me; I knew she wanted to know if I was all right. I was able to send her my thoughts to let her know I was fine. Chase and I hadn't exactly made up; still, I was okay. She nodded in acceptance of my answer. I was getting better at directing my thoughts. I'd been practicing with Hertha; when I'd begun sending my thoughts to her, she'd been impressed. A dragon's mind was tough to get to, much like their hides are tough for a weapon to penetrate. The fact that I can send a dragon thoughts is a rare trait in a sorcerer. I had asked my dad about it after Hertha told me; he said the only other sorcerer he knew of who could do it was Merlin. My head swelled after that; I thought it was pretty cool to be up there with Merlin.

I climbed aboard, and Chase climbed up behind me. It wasn't as bad as I thought it would be, I still felt reasonably comfortable sitting with him. My stomach did a little flip when his arms circled my waist. Hertha's huge wings spread wide, and we took off. I wanted to cry again, just knowing that I loved him and he didn't share my feelings. I suppose, he would rather get as far away from me as possible.

The countryside was gorgeous; I enjoyed the view as we headed for the rocky cliffs in the distance, I tried to focus on our search for the dragons rather than my feelings for Chase. Dad hoped the cliffs were where the dragons would be.

The mountains grew larger as we neared them. We lowered our altitude and began searching for any caves that might be large enough to hold a dragon's lair. We hoped to find it before dark. Dad was trying to get Chase to focus and locate any source that might be a magical creature using his ability as a sensitive; this was as much training for him as our search. So far, he hadn't found anything. After dark, it would become much harder. More creatures were out after dark, since they were less likely to encounter humans. Chase had his eyes closed, and his forehead was scrunched up in concentration. I wondered how it worked when he found something. Did he *see* it in his mind or just *feel* where it was? I was kinda jealous of him, even though I could heal (something Dad still wouldn't let me do) and throw my thoughts. Being sensitive to other magical beings was pretty neat. I tried to squash the jealous feeling down. It kept poking at me—a little voice kept asking me if I really was the Chosen or not. Suddenly, Chase cried out; he pointed to a cluster of caves midway down one of the cliffs.

Dad frowned. "Which cave, Chase?"

Chase closed his eyes again, his brow furrowing. When he opened his eyes again, he pointed to a medium-sized cave a little to one side. It wasn't the biggest one, and it wasn't anything special to look at—nothing that screamed, "Hey, dragons hiding in here!"

"There's something in there, and whatever it is, it's *big*." He looked nervous about making the call to check out the cave. Dad nodded, and we headed toward the yawning maw of the cave. There was no ledge to land on like our cave back home; we just flew right in, heading downward into the depths of the earth. I hoped we weren't going to get flames blasted at us the minute we erupted into the main cavern. We did cause a stir among the dragons in there, however. There was an uproar as we settled in the midst of them.

A large rusty-brown dragon came forward at once. "What's the meaning of this intrusion?" he bellowed.

Dad stepped forward once he had dismounted from Echo. The dragon's accent was light. Cultured. Funny, but I'd never imagined dragons as having accents. It reminded me of some actor. I just couldn't remember which one at the moment. The dragon was staring Dad down. Dad wasn't the least bit intimidated.

"We're sorry to intrude on you like this. If time weren't so short, we would've made the proper inquires and requests for an audience." I wondered how one went about making the proper requests for an audience with a dragon ruler. The rust-colored dragon swung his head in my direction, glaring at me. I ducked my head and looked at my toes. Dad continued talking, regaining the dragon's attention.

"Queebo has sent us in search of some of the clans. We fear that the wyvern will soon make their final stand for dominance over the dragons. Our forces are small and we seek help from any who would join the cause. I'm Fredrick Strandon; this is Echo, Hertha, Chase Ivers, and my daughter, Chandra." We walked over to stand next to my father. The dragon surveyed us closely. He was still frowning at me; I wondered why he seemed to have a particular problem with me. He swung his head back to my dad.

"Queebo sent you, you say?"

"Yes, she has."

"It was Queebo who saved my clan from the wyvern in a battle long ago. I owe her much. I am Luag, leader of the Scots dragons. How does Queebo fare these days?"

When he said his name, it sounded strange, like LOO-ak, but with his soft accent, it was nice. I stepped forward to speak.

"Queebo is well—" Before I could finish, Dad cut me off. I'd wanted to tell Luag about her restored sight. I wondered why Dad had cut me off. Luag chuckled and spoke.

"Your daughter has much to say, Fredrick; she's not pleased that you have not allowed her to speak." Dad looked at me; I shrugged back at him. I guess I hadn't shut down my thoughts very well. Luag seemed nice enough to me. I didn't know why Dad didn't want me to tell him about Queebo's sight. Queebo had helped Luag's clan once in a battle. I frowned a bit over that.

"Luag, what battle did Queebo help your clan fight?" I asked curiously. I had a feeling I knew which one. He cocked his head sideways at me, looking curious.

"Why would you know, lass?"

"I have a feeling I already know. I just want to know if I'm right."

Now he frowned at me. I guess he thought I was being a know-it-all.

"Chandra, you aren't talking about what I think you are?"

I nodded for my dad's benefit without taking my eyes off Luag. I knew if we were to convince the leader of the Scots dragons, we had to show him what we knew about the wyvern, about Theryn.

I walked straight up to him and placed my hand on his snout. I could throw thoughts—why not memories, too. I closed my eyes and drudged up the memory I'd seen in Queebo's mind of the battle with Theryn, the sorceress, and the wyvern, and I showed it to Luag. When it was over, he stared at me with a sad expression in his large eyes.

"Yes, that was the battle, lass. I owe Queebo a great deal; she lost much that day." He hung his head, his sadness obvious.

"I restored her sight. Queebo is no longer blind, Luag. If you came to battle alongside us, you could see her again." He lifted his head and studied me for an eternity, and then nodded slowly.

"I will fight alongside you, Chandra, for Queebo."

I smiled back at him, and then turned to my father. He didn't looked as pleased as I thought he would. Luag stood and spoke loudly to his clan.

"My friends, we leave in the morning. We fly for America! We will fight by the sides of our cousins! I pray this will be the final war with the wyvern! A war they will lose, if we have anything to say about it! Lang may yer lum reek!" These last words were shouted by the whole of the clan. Luag came over to us, his eyes bright.

"The same for you, then, lang may yer lum reek. It is a Scot's wish for long life and prosperity. You have others to search for before you return to America?"

We nodded.

"You must rest here tonight; you can set out in the morning. Eat, sleep." Dad nodded, accepting the hospitality of the Scots clan. Luag smiled and set off in search of food that would be appropriate for us humans. Echo and Hertha spent some time chatting with their dragon cousins, joining them for an evening of hunting.

"Chandra, that was risky. You shouldn't have tried what you did; you haven't done it before."

I knew Dad would get around to the lecture sooner or later. "I had a feeling that the battle was the same one I saw in Queebo's memories, Dad. Besides, it worked, didn't it?"

He shook his head. "We won't get that lucky every time."

I shrugged; at least we had this time. Chase still hadn't said a word; he was now sitting quietly with his back tight against the rocky wall of the cave, knees drawn up to his chest. I guessed being around this many dragons was a bit uncomfortable for him, after being around the wyvern. I wasn't about to ask him, though. I'd gone that route before, and it hadn't gone so great. I sat down as far from him as possible and ate my dinner. It wasn't far enough. He didn't bother trying to talk to me; that made me a little sad. Boys—who needed them, anyway!

Dad had noticed our distance from each other. "What's going on with you two?"

I rolled my eyes at his question. Why on earth did he have to take an interest?

"Nothing, Dad, absolutely nothing." I stabbed at my dinner.

He raised an eyebrow. "Judging by the way you're trying to kill your dinner with that fork, I would say it's not just nothing."

I shook my head at him. I didn't want to tell him about the fight I'd had with Chase. I knew he would worry about it too much. He would think Chase was unstable or something. The truth was, that's exactly what I was worried about.

Had Theryn destroyed Chase's sanity?

It worried me more than just a little, even though he'd been acting just fine since last night. Still, he had gotten so angry so quickly and at very little provocation. I took a little peek in his direction; he was eating, staring down at his plate, acting perfectly normal. I sighed, trying hard to bury my thoughts so Dad wouldn't hear them.

Dad shook his head and stood. "I will never, in my life, understand teenagers," he grumbled and walked off, probably to find Echo. I'd discovered my dad felt a bit more comfortable with the dragons than with humans. Or maybe it was just teenagers. I glanced at Chase again; he was still staring blankly down at his plate. I gave up on eating my dinner; setting my plate aside, I just wasn't hungry. I crawled into my sleeping bag and closed my eyes. Surprisingly, it didn't take me long to fall asleep.

Chase could feel Chandra's eyes on him; he knew she kept glancing over at him. He sighed and lifted another forkful of food to his mouth. He didn't feel like eating, not since their fight yesterday.

He knew the minute her dad walked away and she curled into her sleeping bag, even though he kept his eyes on his plate. He gave a sigh of relief; at least she wasn't staring at him anymore. He knew she expected him to do something; he just wasn't sure what he was expected to do. Girls—who needed them! He put his plate down and crawled into his own sleeping bag, stacked his hands behind his head. He didn't know why she couldn't just accept his apology and be done with it. Yes, he'd acted horribly, but she had to understand where he was coming from, even if he wasn't exactly sure where that was.

When he closed his eyes, Chandra's face swam up before him. He gave a small groan, remembering their fight clearly. He'd let his temper get the best of him, something he had tried never to let happen.

He clearly remembered the first time in his life he'd ever lost control of his temper. It had ended badly. That event had clearly shown how important it was for him to control his temper. It had taken place in junior high; he and some other kid had gotten in a stupid fight over something, something he couldn't even remember now. He'd always been bigger and stronger than the other guys. His dad would laugh and say he must have some Scots blood in him somewhere; his adopted dad was a Scotsman. Big and muscular. Chase had nearly killed the kid, beaten him nearly to death in a red haze of blinding temper. It had taken four teachers to pull him off the other kid. After that, he never let his temper get out of control, no matter who provoked him.

Until Theryn, that is. Now it would seem he lost it regularly. Theryn had unhinged something inside his mind. Chase closed his eyes tightly. When Chandra had pushed him about talking, he had simply lost control and let his temper fly. Bad, it had been bad. He couldn't let it happen again.

After he had left Chandra standing there in the dark, he had lain in the tent and listened to her sobs. That had made him angrier with himself because he had upset her. With his emotions in turmoil, he figured it would have been a major mistake for him to go back to her. He knew it could have turned out far worse if he had. Something bad may have happened in the state he had been in after their fight. His emotions were confused: anger, frustration, and passion for her all mixed up ... it could have gone south very quickly. So instead, he had put his pillow over his head and tried to drown out the sounds of her sobs. It hadn't worked; he could still hear her clearly.

Now he worried he would never be able to put things right. He felt like some sort of freak. Even though he knew she and her father were sorcerers, too, having had Theryn in his brain for two years seemed to make him more of a freak somehow. He thought of his family. He could never go home, not now, not ever. What could he possibly say to them? *Hi Mom, Dad, I'm home! By the way, I'm a sorcerer, and some freaky winged monsters are trying to kill me, so anyway, I need to go help these other sorcerers fight a war. I'll be back in, oh, I don't know, a few years, maybe, if I don't die first.* He sighed and went to sleep, trying desperately not to think of Chandra sleeping a few short feet away.

Nightmares followed me into the darkness.

I stood on the ledge outside our cave back home. Hertha stood by my side. Echo came flying toward us out of the night sky, fear etched on his face.

"They're coming—hundreds of them. I must warn the others." He flew past us into the cave entrance. I knew the time to fight had come, time to fight Theryn. I mounted Hertha and prepared to go into battle, knowing death might follow. I heard them coming and looked to the sky; it was inky black, not from the dark of night but with the coming of the wyvern army. Echo was wrong, there weren't hundreds—there were thousands. At their head was Theryn. By his side, a slightly smaller wyvern, and on his back, hair in perfect order was Chase.

I woke screaming. Dad was there in an instant.

"Chandra, honey, it's okay … shhh, it's okay, you're safe, sweetheart." I looked around at the dark cave. It had all seemed so very real. I had looked into Chase's eyes and seen Theryn back in there, staring out at me. That mocking smile had been on his face.

Now, as I looked around, I saw him sitting just a few feet away, a look of concern on his face, like he wanted to be the one comforting me instead of my dad. I buried my face in my dad's shoulder. Had the dream been an omen or just a nightmare? I wasn't sure which it was; that's what frightened me most. I prayed it was just a simple nightmare, nothing more. It took me hours to fall back to sleep. I was frightened the nightmare would return. I feared that the nightmare was more than what it had seemed that it was a warning. A warning that the boy I had given my heart to would destroy all that I had come to love in the end. I prayed that I was wrong.

Chandra's screams jerked Chase into sudden wakefulness. He was halfway out of his sleeping bag when he realized her dad was already by her side.

He turned and watched, concerned over what had frightened her. When she looked at him, he saw raw, stark terror in her eyes.

What could have frightened her so badly? he thought. He lay back down; as he closed his eyes, Theryn's ugly face appeared in the darkness floating behind his eyelids. That would do it, he thought grimly. *Or maybe she remembered you stabbing her;* a little voice prodded him. He grimaced. He couldn't blame her if she had bad dreams about that for the rest of her life. Chase listened to Chandra's harsh breathing nearby. It took her a long time to fall back to sleep; he couldn't blame her.

It took him even longer.

In the morning as we prepared to leave, Luag came to me.

"The future is not set in stone, lass. It is always changing. What you saw is just a possible future, a possible path. He doesn't have to choose that one, you know. He could stay with you if given the chance."

I stared up at him; my heart was torn. I doubted Chase would choose to stay with me if given the chance. He was damaged, perhaps beyond repair. I turned away from Luag.

"If you really believed that, Chandra, you wouldn't love him, would you?"

I wished to God he couldn't see my thoughts so clearly. "Luag, it's not up to me what Chase does. He's his own person."

"The lad is lost. He doesn't know his true family; he is in a new world alone. You are his anchor, Chandra. Don't cut him loose, lass. He doesn't know your mind like the rest of us."

I frowned at him. "What do you mean; *he doesn't know your mind like the rest of us?*"

He chuckled. "The lad shuts himself off from everyone; he defends himself out of fear. I'm not sure he is even aware he is doing it. He can't *hear* your thoughts like the rest of us. I can't tell for how long he has done this, but it's there, lass."

I looked in Chase's direction. He had put up a shield without benefit of a spell, and he wasn't even aware he was doing it—amazing. I tilted my head to one side and thought, *Hello, Chase, over here!* He didn't even look in my direction. Luag chuckled softly. I looked back at the Scots leader.

I shook my head. I supposed I would have to tell Dad. Luag only nodded. I left him and went to Hertha, climbed aboard and prepared to leave.

Egypt would be our next stop. I hoped our luck would hold out when we reached Egypt; time was still slipping away from us and I prayed the time we were taking to gather the clans wouldn't hurt us in the end. I looked back at the Scots clan as they also prepared to leave. They weren't as big as the American clan, but they were prepared to help fight the coming war.

A war I hoped to God we could win.

CHAPTER 11

A Goddess Flirts With My Dad

It wasn't long before Egypt came into view—desert, for the most part. Not as pretty to look at as Scotland. The mountains were few and far between, more like low sandstone ridges and canyons cut through the desert, really. We were definitely going to need Chase to find any dragons around here. The sun was setting when we set down in a small, narrow canyon, the clouds turning the sky a brilliant orange. Chase had sensed something, but he couldn't pinpoint exactly where it was.

"I'm sorry, I just can't tell where it's coming from." He looked dejected.

"It's okay, Chase. We'll try again in the morning; let's all get a good night's sleep," my dad tried to reassure him.

I wondered what was interfering with Chase's ability to locate the dragons. I hoped nothing creepy and monstrous was lurking in the growing shadows, waiting to devour us. I shuddered and reached for my hoodie, more for security than out of need. I wondered if his little shield that he'd erected around himself could be the culprit. I tried again to throw him a few thoughts. No reaction. I considered telling Dad about how Chase was protecting himself, but then decided against it, for now anyway. I was still mad at him for yelling at me. If he wanted to shut himself off, that was his business and if it had to do with Theryn, he wouldn't thank me for bringing it up.

We set up camp, and Dad pulled out the magical Tupperware again; I nearly fell over laughing when I saw it. Each container had a different color lid—his Tupperware potion containers were color-coded. Definitely, a side of my dad I didn't want to know—it looked to be his Susie Homemaker side. I continued to giggle as he tried to do the spells to protect the campsite. He finally told me to go help Chase set up the tent so he could concentrate on the spells. I did so reluctantly, since Chase and I were still not speaking to each other.

By the time we returned to the campfire, Dad had made dinner. I picked at my food, barely eating anything again, and sneaking peeks at Chase the whole time. I wondered what he was thinking. I also wondered how I was going to tell my dad what Luag had said about Chase. I was back to thinking it could be important, but then again, it was also Chase's business what he did with his own mind. Wasn't it? After our fight, I didn't want him to think I was interfering, I figured it would only make him angry again. Confusion over what to do about Chase reigned supreme in my heart and mind. I loved him, and my emotions were in turmoil. I finally stood up and turned to go to the tent.

"I'm finished. I think I'm gonna go to bed early. I'm really tired. Night, guys." I turned to go, but my dad's voice stopped me before I got very far.

"Chandra, I was going to teach you two a new spell since we had some time. Why don't you stay up a little longer?" My dad sounded vaguely upset that I was bailing on them. I didn't want to stay; I felt close to tears. I just shook my head without turning around and continued toward the tent. I kicked off my shoes, crawled into my sleeping bag, and rolled toward the wall, praying they stayed by the fire till I could fall asleep. I didn't want either of them to come in while I was crying. I squeezed my eyes shut as silent tears rolled down my cheeks. I couldn't fathom why it should bother me so much that Theryn had gotten into Chase's mind, had lived inside his head for two years, and I couldn't even get in with a few measly little words.

Fredrick watched Chandra walk stiff-legged back to the tent. He shook his head. He had missed her whole childhood; now he had a teenage daughter he didn't understand. She was upset, and he didn't know the reason why, but he was sure it had something to do with the silent boy sitting to his left. She and Chase had hardly spoken since they'd left Scotland. He figured they had argued; however, he thought they would've gotten over their spat by now. He would never understand teenagers. Not these days, anyway—he had been one in much different times. He glanced back at Chase with a sigh.

"Okay, Chase, I guess it's just us, then. You're behind Chandra anyway, so I suppose we should go over the transformation and the shielding spells."

Chase nodded; he didn't like the thought that Chandra knew more magic than he did. He would prefer to be on even footing with her. Who was he kidding—he wanted to be better than her. Yeah, so he was being chauvinistic—sue him.

"Sure, okay, what do I need to do?" he asked her father.

Fredrick stood, and they walked a few feet away from the fire.

"Let's start with the transformation spell. It's simple; you just need to concentrate and focus." He explained the wording, as well as how to transform back. After several tries, Chase managed to transform himself into a small clump of grass and then a field mouse.

"Great, Chase. You learn just as quickly as Chandra. Shielding spell is next. This one is a bit tricky; it depends more on you than anything else."

"What do you mean, 'it depends more on me?'"

"The shield will last only a few minutes, how long it lasts depends on the sorcerer. The more powerful the magic, the longer lasting the shield," Fredrick explained. Chase frowned and stared at Fredrick. One question went through his mind: How long did Chandra's last? He didn't ask, though.

"So how do I do it?"

Fredrick showed him how to do the spell and told him the word that went with it. "I'm going to throw a little water at you, just so we know your shield is working. You will feel a slight tug when the shield engages and again when it begins to collapse. Don't fight it; let it go. If you try to prolong the spell, it will cause your magic to falter. Kind of like a skip in a record."

Chase nodded and concentrated, wanting to get it right. Fredrick waited a few seconds, and then tossed a small palm full of water at Chase. He flinched slightly, but the water hit the invisible wall and slid down the side harmlessly.

Chase grinned. "That was pretty neat."

Fredrick grinned back and started timing. He called out to Chase when he'd reached about a minute.

"Wow, that's ...." Chase stopped speaking and looked confused for a minute, and then his eyes rolled back into his head. He collapsed onto the ground, unconscious. Fredrick ran to his side, yelling his name.

"Chase! Chase! Wake up ... Chase!" He had told the boy not to fight the spell. Fredrick had never seen anyone pass out before. Momentarily falter, maybe, but the shield would just collapse, not snap back and make a sorcerer lose consciousness! He muttered another water spell and dumped a small palm full of water on Chase's face. Chase spluttered and opened his eyes.

"Wha—what happened?" Chase sat up, wiping off his face. Fredrick was frowning at him like he'd just stolen the last cookie from the cookie jar.

Fredrick stood. "I specifically told you not to fight the shield when it tried to disengage, didn't I?"

Chase nodded.

"Well, what the hell was that, then?"

"I don't know."

"You don't know? You don't know!" Fredrick paced away then back. "Chase, you were fighting it; you had to be!"

Chase stood. He was frowning. "I wasn't—at least, I don't think I was."

Fredrick studied the boy's face. He looked genuinely confused. "Chase, unless we figure out what went wrong, this could have some serious consequences. Your powers could fail when you need them the most, when you're fighting the wyvern." Fredrick began pacing again. He stopped suddenly. "Chase, when you were with

Theryn, did this ever happen? Is that how Theryn got into your head?"

Chase stiffened and turned away. "I told Chandra, I don't want to talk about the wyvern."

Fredrick's frown disappeared at his words. Well, at least now he had an idea of what was wrong between the two of them.

"Chase, unless we figure this out, it could be a big problem. You have to understand that." Fredrick knew the boy had decided he was done talking for now. He wouldn't get anything more out of him tonight. "When you decide you want to figure this thing out, Chase, you let me know. Until then, your training is over. I can't continue until we know what's causing the interference with your powers. Good night." He turned on his heels and walked away, leaving Chase standing alone in the dark. The fire casting dancing shadows on the canyon walls.

Chase went back and sat by the fire. He was angry at Fredrick, at Chandra. It wasn't fair. They had it easy—just do the magic, and that's it. Neither of them had to spend two years locked in a cage, being tortured by Theryn, having that monster in their head. He raked his fingers through his hair, setting the waves on end, and put his face in his hands.

Theryn had wanted Chase's total obedience; anything less was unacceptable. When Chase had struggled against Theryn, fought as hard as he could to resist what Theryn wanted him to do, Theryn had done everything in his power to show Chase how useless it was to fight him. He had changed everything about Chase when he'd occupied his mind; it had only made Chase hate him all the more, which made Theryn all the happier. Chase was glad to be his own person again; he would never want to go back to the way he had been when Theryn had been inside his head. Theryn had made him into something he wasn't, made him act as another person. Something nagged at the back of his mind, something dark, something begging to be remembered. He shut his eyes, shaking it away when he couldn't bring it forth from the back of his mind.

Chase stood; he didn't want to go to the tent. He knew Fredrick would still be up, and he didn't want to risk Chandra being up, either. He practiced the fire spell and the transformation spell. He didn't dare risk the shield spell with no one around. If he passed out again and Fredrick found him lying on the ground in the morning, he would probably kill him himself.

He transformed into the field mouse again and scurried around. It was kinda fun. He wondered if he should go scurry into Chandra's sleeping bag and scare the living daylights out of her. She'd probably just whack him with a shoe.

Suddenly, he felt something magical coming toward the camp. He sat up on his hind legs and looked around. He saw something coming out of the darkness, a sudden burst of fear sent him scurrying toward the tent. He stopped and looked back; his beady little mouse eyes widened. The woman he saw radiated a faint bluish light; she walked straight through the fire. He turned and tried to find a way into the tent, not daring to risk transforming back into himself. He was glad to find that Fredrick hadn't zipped the door all the way closed. Once inside, he transformed back and shook Fredrick awake, whispering to him.

"Fredrick, wake up ... there's, uh ...." He frowned, there's what—a ghost in camp? He wasn't sure what the woman was. He had sensed powerful magic in her, but she definitely wasn't human.

"Chase, what in God's name do you want?" Fredrick grumped at him sleepily.

"Fredrick, there's something out there. I don't know what, exactly. But it's magical, whatever it is."

Fredrick frowned and followed Chase out of the tent and across the camp. Chase saw that the blue lady was inspecting their packs. Not the way a normal human person would—she had just stuck her head straight through the side of one of them. Being transparent had its advantages, he supposed. She suddenly stood, pulling her head out of the backpack, and looked straight at them. Chase backed up a step; he couldn't help it. Her eyes glowed a deep golden color. She smiled at them and spoke.

"I should have known it would be you, Fredrick." She floated forward a few paces, and then stopped and shifted her gaze to Chase. "Your son, Fredrick?" She tilted her head to the side questioningly. Fredrick sighed heavily.

"No, Isis, this is Chase Ivers. Chase, this is Isis. I have a daughter, Isis. She's asleep in the tent." He nodded in the direction of the tent. Isis glided over, stuck her head through the side of the tent to get a look at Chandra, and then returned to where they were standing.

"She's beautiful, Fredrick. Then again, I would expect nothing less from you; you always were so very handsome. Now what brings you here, Fredrick?"

"Isis, you know why I'm here; don't play coy. You would've known we were here the minute we set down. I'm sure you've seen Echo and Hertha already as well."

Isis smiled and made a show of settling down on a nearby rock. She really just hovered several inches above the rock, rather than actually sitting on it. "Why so hostile, Freddy dear? Have a seat. Let's talk, shall we? We haven't seen each other in years." She smiled sweetly, batting her eyelashes at him.

"We haven't seen each other in years because the last time I saw you, Isis, you tried to kill me."

"Oh, come now, Freddy, let the past go. I know I have."

Fredrick was grinding his teeth; Chase could clearly hear it. He wondered what on earth had happened between them.

"Now really, Freddy, you can't blame a girl; I was jealous, after all. So how is your dear Meredith these days?"

Chase was certain he saw Fredrick make a fist. Just as quickly, his hand relaxed.

"I'm not here to relive the past with you, Isis. We're here for the dragons. Where have you hidden them?"

Isis pouted at Fredrick. Chase wondered how a spirit could be so beautiful. She turned and batted her eyelashes at him.

"Aw, come now, Freddy. Even your friend thinks I'm pretty."

"Isis, I grow weary of your games. Tell us where they are or else."

Isis stood and floated gracefully over to them. "Or else what, Freddy? You can't threaten me, you know that. You have nothing to threaten me with, Sorcerer." Fredrick raised an eyebrow. Chase wondered what Isis was, exactly, if she wasn't threatened by a sorcerer.

"I don't know, Isis, what about Osiris?"

She whirled on him, her eyes suddenly blazing red. "You wouldn't dare call on him, Fredrick!"

He raised an eyebrow again. "Try me, Isis! I need to find the dragons; tell me where they are!"

"I am their guardian. It is my job to protect them, Fredrick—you know that!"

"You think I would harm them? I protect the dragons just as you do, Isis!"

"I know of your plan, Fredrick; it is foolish. To fight the wyvern is murder. They will wipe out the dragons. It is better if I keep them hidden."

"If Chandra or Chase is the Chosen Child, we will win, Isis!"

"And if they are not, you will all die, and it will be for naught, Fredrick! I will not let them die for nothing!"

"It should be their choice, shouldn't it, Isis? You are only their guardian, not their jailer. You were appointed by the gods to protect them from the outside world. Not from the wyvern. They should make the decision whether to fight this war or not. That's not up to you."

She glared at Fredrick, finally nodding slowly. "Fine, I will tell them you are here. I will come to get you tomorrow at sundown and take you to them." She turned to Chase, looking at him for a long moment. "You will certainly die, boy, if you do not learn what you can from Freddy." She shook her head. When she placed a pale glowing hand on his chest, it was warm. "Let the pain go, boy, or it will eat you from the inside out. Already it festers and begins to interfere with what he must teach you." She smiled sadly and turned away. "Until tomorrow, then, Freddy dear." She gave an airy wave.

Chase watched her fade into the darkness. "What is she?" he asked in the barest trace of a whisper. He didn't turn away from the dark night where she had disappeared when Fredrick answered.

"Isis, the Egyptian goddess of rebirth and magic, as well as my own personal tormentor."

Chase turned and looked at Fredrick. He wasn't smiling; he was staring into the darkness.

"You two don't like each other very much, do you?" he asked Fredrick. When Fredrick laughed, it wasn't a laugh of merriment.

"Isis liked me just fine before I met Meredith. Isis is a true woman; she is the goddess of the flirt. A woman to the core. The Egyptian legends say Isis is the goddess that taught woman how to tame man. She enjoys trying to tame any man that she takes a liking to. It upsets her when one gets away." He finished with a shrug.

"She got mad because you chose Chandra's mother over her?" Chase asked, incredulous. Fredrick nodded. "She tried to kill you over another woman?" Chase was grinning; he knew he probably shouldn't be, but he found it a bit comical. A goddess getting jealous over a mortal, it seemed kinda silly.

"Yes, she did. She thought that if anyone was going to give me the Chosen Child, it would be her, a goddess, not some simple mortal woman. She never understood that I cared nothing about creating the Chosen Child. I love Meredith more than anything in the world, that's all that ever mattered. Come on, now, let's get back to bed; it's going to be a hell of a long day of waiting tomorrow."

Chase nodded. He looked back into the darkness. His thoughts returned to what Isis had said about his letting go of what had happened to him. Chandra had said as much when they'd argued. He had to talk about it, or it would fester, and he would explode one day. Not the exact words Isis had used, but could Chandra have been right in a way? Would his holding it all in make it interfere with his powers so much that he would in fact *explode literally*?

He walked back to the tent and crawled into his sleeping bag, his thoughts in turmoil. Theryn had messed with his mind so much, he wasn't sure what was his own anymore. He rolled over and stared at Chandra's back. He wanted to grab her and pull her close, hold on to her forever. He forced himself not to reach for her, closed his eyes and slept instead.

CHAPTER 12

Tortured

I slept badly again. Whoever or whatever is the god of dreams seemed determined to torture me.

I stood in a field. I recognized it immediately as the field where Queebo had saved Luag's clan from the wyvern all those years ago. Only now daylight shown a feeble light, slowly fading, as the sun made it's decent through the sky.

A different battle raged all around me now, wyvern and dragons. Humans as well. Flames and smoke. I heard roars of anger and pain. I held a sword in my left hand; it was slick, covered in blood. The clothes I wore were strange to me, ancient, from another time. A yell made me turn. A man was running toward me, his sword raised to strike me down. Instinctively, I raised mine and parried his blow. The strike radiated down my arm; he was much stronger than I was and I wasn't sure if I could beat him, despite my skill with a sword. I knew I was skilled, knew I could fight well with the sword I held clutched in my hand.

His second blow sent me to my knees. I groaned, dropped, and rolled out of his reach. He let out a battle cry and dropped another blow, missing me. He misjudged his reach, misjudged me and my skill, and overbalanced, falling to his knees, leaving his back exposed. I didn't hesitate. I swung, striking him in the back before he could rise or twist beyond my reach. Blood flowed, and he didn't rise again. I stood panting, a stitch in my side. I looked around. The battle continued; so many dead, yet it continued.

Would it ever end?

"Elandra! Elandra! Girl, answer me!" A man ran up behind me and grabbed my arm, spinning me around. It was my father. He hugged me, and then began dragging me by the hand across the bloodied field.

"Elandra, I told you not to come here, girl! I don't know why you ignore me! Come; hurry, before anything happens to you. If they spot you, it would be a disaster!" I wanted to ask him who Elandra was. I was Chandra; didn't he recognize me? He dragged me off the field and into a nearby hut.

"You could have been killed! Look at you, covered in blood, carrying a sword! A woman with a sword! I have never understood your penchant for battle!" His voice softened with his next words. "Honestly, Elandra, what in heaven's name did you think you were doing?" He reached out a hand and gently brushed a bit of dirt from my cheek with a small smile and a shake of his head. I stared at him; it was my father, but it wasn't; he was a lot younger. He seemed different somehow, more carefree, despite the fact he was yelling at me about fighting in the battle.

"Well, what do you have to say for yourself?" I just stared at him. What could I say? I had no clue. I wasn't who he thought I was. This was the strangest dream I'd ever had. The door suddenly burst open, and several men came pouring through. They carried weapons and looked eager for battle. But why were they in here instead of out on the battlefield?

"There she is—grab her! She's the one!" I raised my sword and fought for all I was worth. I had a feeling this was the end of the line. My dad was throwing spells at the men, which was the last thing I saw before something hit me hard on the back of the head. When next I woke, I was in a cave. I groaned and sat up.

"Ahh, nice of you to join me, my dear child." I looked around, and I wished I hadn't awoke. I was staring straight at Theryn. He sat in an oversized golden throne atop a dais. He smiled an evil smile down at me. He was even larger up close than when I had seen him across the field in the vision I had had of Queebo's battle alongside Luag. I wanted to rant and rave at him for what he'd done to Chase, but somehow I knew he would have no idea of whom I spoke. I scrambled to my feet, my hand going for my sword, which was missing from its scabbard at my waist.

"My servants took the liberty of removing your sword, my dear. You won't have need of it here. Now, Elandra, I believe it is, why don't you tell me everything that Fredrick has taught you."

I backed away from him, my mind racing. Fredrick hadn't taught me anything. I had very little power. It was a lie, all of it a lie. My parents hadn't been great sorcerers; they had lied to get Fredrick to take me from them, and now they were dead. He cared greatly for me, but he also felt responsible for me because of their lie. I looked up at Theryn; now I was going to die, and Fredrick would never be the same. He would be shattered by my death.

My eyes widened. All of this information came at me in a rush. I remembered my dad saying the fever could be a false indicator. Elandra's fever had been a false indicator. But it hadn't been her fault; it had been her parents' fault. They had lied to my father. Theryn was still smiling at me, or Elandra, rather. I backed further away from the dark beast before me.

"You aren't leaving, my dear, are you? We are just getting to know each other. Now I want to know everything about you." Theryn's voice was falsely sweet when he spoke. He leaned forward, still smiling, showing a wyvern's pointed-toothed grin. Elandra screamed in pure terror as Theryn broke into her mind and saw everything she knew.

I felt her pain, her horror when he entered her mind.

I can't compare it with anything I have ever felt before, simply because there is nothing to compare with that kind of torture. It was the most horrific thing I have ever felt, and I never want to experience it again.

It is comparable with nothing. I can only imagine it to be the brink of the worst kind of death imaginable. For I'm certain that moments after Theryn pierced Elandra's mind, the torment it caused killed her.

Chase sat up. He was wide-awake, not sure, at first what had woke him. Then Chandra screamed again, her back arched like she was in pain, her screams ripping through the tiny confines of the tent. She writhed on the floor, looking as if someone had electrified her entire body. He grabbed her, pulling her into his lap, speaking to her as he did so.

"Chandra, what's wrong? Wake up! Chandra!" He cradled her in his arms, afraid she was hurt, but finding no source for her discomfort. Her body had been stiff when he'd first pulled her to him, her muscles tensed and bunched.

She blinked opened her eyes and looked up at him, her eyes wide and fearful. Suddenly, she burst into tears and buried her face in his chest, relaxing against him and burrowing closer. Seeking comfort and warmth, she was shivering. Stunned, he held her close and rocked her gently, murmuring nonsense to her.

Chase wasn't sure what had frightened her so badly. He didn't want to let her go; it felt too good just to hold her. On impulse, he leaned forward and kissed the top of her head gently. He was suddenly glad Fredrick had gone out with Echo and Hertha early this morning to go have a look around. Tightening his arms around Chandra, he was glad to have been the one to be there for her when she woke frightened. He wanted to protect her. She was his to keep safe.

When I woke in Chase's arms and looked into his face, I remembered Elandra's pain when Theryn had looked into her mind. Now I knew what Chase had suffered for two long years. The pain of remembering her suffering caused me to burst into tears. It had killed Elandra; in that all-too-brief moment that Theryn had intruded into her mind, it had killed her.

Why her? Yet Chase had endured it for two years. I cried harder. He held me gently, talking nonsense and rocking me in his arms. When he kissed my hair, I snuggled closer to him. It felt nice to be so close to him. I knew that soon the real world would intrude. He would remember his dislike of me; he would push me away. My heart would fracture a bit more, moving ever outward like the spidery cracks in a window pane, until there was nowhere left for it to spread; then it would shatter into a million tiny pieces.

Fractured. Shattered. Broken. No way to repair those tiny fragments.

I sniffled and hiccupped. I had gotten him all wet; I realized he wasn't wearing a shirt. I sighed, pressing my cheek against his warm skin. He felt very good.

I should get off his lap, I thought to myself, *before something happens that really shouldn't,* but I didn't move. He chuckled then. Great, now he was laughing at me. Things hadn't improved, yet I still didn't move away from him. Despite his laughter a moment ago, his voice was serious when he spoke.

"Are you all right, Chandra?" He sounded genuinely interested in my well-being.

"I'm fine. It was just a bad dream."

"That was one hell of a bad dream. You looked like someone was torturing you, Chandra. Trust me; I know what that looks like." I looked up at him. He wasn't kidding. I couldn't bring myself to tell him about the dream. I figured that maybe he would think I was making it up so I could say that I understood what he had gone through. I couldn't bear to make him angry at me again, I didn't want to see that look on his face ever again.

"I'm fine, Chase, really. It was just a nightmare," I assured him. He was still frowning. I smiled up into his face as best I could to try to reassure him. I leaned forward and gave him a peck on the cheek, just because I couldn't bear not to do it. Being so close to him was messing with my mind. I wanted to stay close to him. I knew I couldn't, though.

"Thank you for being there, Chase," I whispered awkwardly as I climbed off his lap, embarrassed now because of his lack of a shirt. I managed not to look at him; I didn't want to get caught staring. He nodded, but didn't say anything. He left the tent so I could change. Dad came back with Echo and Hertha a few hours later. They hadn't been able to find anything interesting. Wherever Isis had hidden the dragons, she had hidden them well. Chase had told me about the meeting with Isis while we had waited for Dad to get back. The short time we spent alone was a bit awkward after my awakening in his arms. Chase made it somewhat more comfortable by telling me all about Isis, even making me laugh a bit when he told me about Isis being jealous of my mother. Now that my dad was back, I focused on magic.

"What about that new spell you were going to teach us last night, Dad?"

He frowned and looked at Chase. I wondered what that was about.

"Dad, come on, we have all afternoon," I whined. Chase stood up and turned away. I reached up and grabbed his wrist. "Oh, no, you don't. No ditching class for you."

He looked at my dad, and then back at me. "Sorry, Chandra, I'm not allowed in class anymore." I looked at my dad. He turned away and walked over to where Echo and Hertha were, engaging them in quiet conversation, leaving Chase and I alone.

"Chase, you want to tell me what's going on? What happened last night? Why won't my dad teach you anymore?"

He frowned down at me, looking at my hand on his wrist. I blushed and dropped his wrist.

"Sorry," I mumbled.

"It's not your dad's fault, okay. It's mine. I'm just not any good at this magic stuff. Drop it, Chandra, you'll be the Chosen, and that's that. Happy?"

I blinked at him. What was that supposed to mean? "Wait, wait, what do you mean? I've seen you do magic, Chase. You're just as good as I am, maybe better. Don't give me that crap. You can't push some excuse on me about not being good enough. Tell me the truth."

He plunged his hand through his hair and turned away. "Just drop it, Chandra."

"Chase, look, whatever it is, we can all work on it together. Listen, we won't abandon you. You're part of this family now, whether you want to be or not." I walked around and stood in front of him. He stared into my eyes.

"I can't do it, Chandra. I can't let it go, what Theryn did to me. I can't. It's interfering with my powers. I blacked out last night while doing the shielding spell. What happens if I black out in the middle of a battle? What if it gets someone killed?" he hesitated a moment before plunging on. "What if it gets *you* killed?" He raked his hand through his hair again, leaving a disaster of riotous curls in his wake. That's what was worrying him, *me?* He was worried about hurting me. I could only stare blankly at him as he plowed forward.

"I couldn't live with myself, Chandra, if that happened. I couldn't let it happen. I can't stay here, with you; it's too dangerous. I'm too dangerous. You were right, one day I'm gonna explode. I don't want you around when I do. Theryn screwed with my head. I can't control my temper anymore. You saw what happened when you pushed me to talk; I lost it. I don't want to hurt you," he finished quietly.

I continued to stare at him, dumbfounded. He was telling me he was leaving. Rather than talk about what had happened to him, he was going to leave. Just like that, go away and leave me. Tear my heart out and take it with him. Didn't he understand that I would die if he left? I was being overly dramatic, maybe, but that's what it felt like.

"Chase, you can't just leave; the wyvern will find you. When you turn eighteen, you'll have your full powers. They can find you easily, either way. Theryn will know how to find you. You have to be careful. I can't … I mean, how will you hide? I'll worry about you all the time," I finished lamely. I stared down at my toes. He put a finger under my chin and tipped my face up.

"You would worry about me?" he asked quietly, searching my face for something, I wasn't sure what. I nodded, and he smiled.

"Why?"

How could I answer that without telling him exactly how I felt? I shuffled my feet a bit before looking up into those blue-gray eyes of his. They were focused and intense.

I shrugged. "I care about you, Chase. A lot."

He nodded slowly and gave me that smile I loved so very much, the dimple showing in his cheek. "Well, I guess I can't have you worrying about me, can I? That would only cause me to worry about you worrying about me. So I suppose I'll have to stay and keep an eye on you, won't I?"

I grinned and threw my arms around him. He hugged me back. He had just made me the happiest girl in the world; I wondered if he knew that, even if he had given me a roundabout answer about his caring about me.

"Thank you, Chase. You have to do one more thing for me, though."

He frowned, looking wary now. "I'm not sure I should agree to anything without some sort of explanation first."

"Chase, if you want to be able to use your powers, you know what you have to do."

He groaned and walked over to sit by the fire. I followed and sat next to him.

"Chase, it's not going to be easy, but if you're going to get past it, you need to talk about it. You could never go back to your family unless you do. It would put them in too much danger, having you on the edge all the time."

He looked sideways at me and sighed. I knew he thought there was no chance of his ever going back home. I gave up my last bit of persuasion that I thought I might have and told him the dream about Elandra.

"It killed her, Chase; as soon as he looked into her mind, the pain of it killed her. I think that if she had lived, it probably would have driven her insane. She was a strong woman, but ..." I couldn't finish. The memory of Elandra's pain was still much too fresh in my mind.

Chase was staring into the remains of the campfire. "Why did I survive and she didn't?"

I shook my head; that was something I couldn't answer for him.

"Probably because her powers were nothing compared with yours, Chase."

We both turned and looked at my dad. We hadn't been aware that he'd heard what we were talking about.

"Dad, I—"

He raised his hand and stopped me. "It's okay, Chandra. For whatever reason, you saw what you saw. I'm not here to question the way your powers work. Elandra was brought to me by her parents; they said they thought she was the Chosen." He shook his head. "I thought she was, too, for a while. Her fever was amazing. Not as high as either of you, but it was close. It didn't take long to figure out how wrong that assumption was—her being the Chosen, that is. Her parents were charlatans. Neither were great sorcerers; minor wasn't even an adequate word for them. Elandra, however, was an extraordinary girl." He smiled.

"She was bright, and she loved to learn everything. She was horribly inept at magic, however. That became clear almost immediately. She could barely perform minor spells. She took up swordsmanship. She was excellent at it. I didn't think she could ever be a match for a much larger man; she proved me wrong many times over. I worried about her constantly, anyway, despite her skill. She was like a daughter to me. I'd been alone for so long, it was nice to have someone else around. When they took her …" He shook his head sadly, not finishing that thought.

"The next time I went into battle against the wyvern, Theryn made it a point to seek me out. He and I had become somewhat like adversaries. I knew he led the wyvern, though I never knew his name. He knew that I sought the Chosen. When we met that day, he laughed at me. Talked about how quickly she'd died. Told me Merlin's prophecy was a lie, a bedtime story for children. I ran from the battlefield that day. I swore I would never fight the wyvern again. It wasn't worth the losses. I met Queebo and her clan two weeks later. I had not been fighting with any particular clan before that, even though I fought on the side of the dragons. I've been with Queebo ever since, save for the time I spent with you and your mother, Chandra." He finished quietly.

I looked at my father. Elandra had been his first daughter. He'd cared for her as her parents never had. Theryn had taken her away from him. I wanted to kill that monster; he didn't deserve to live after all the pain he'd caused to the people I loved. I wanted his death very badly, needed to kill him. When I met him on the battlefield, I would make sure he suffered for all he'd done. I hugged my dad; he pushed me away and frowned down at me.

"Don't think like that, Chandra, please. I won't lose you to Theryn, as well."

Chase looked between the two of us. "Did I miss something?"

I grinned over at him, knowing he couldn't *hear* the words in my mind that my father had. "You always miss something, Chase." I tapped the side of my head with a finger. "Unless you clear out those cobwebs of yours, you'll keep missing it, too."

He laughed and lunged at me. I took off running. It didn't take him long to catch me. Grabbing me around the waist, he flung me up over his shoulder.

"Oh, yeah, looks like I didn't miss anything that time." He slapped me on the rear end. I was laughing so hard, I couldn't reply. He swung me down and set me on my feet.

"Funny, Magic Boy. I was talking about your little shield you've wrapped around your brain. It means you can't hear me when I send out thoughts."

He cocked his head to the side. "What are you talking about?"

I stopped laughing. "Chase, your mind—you're shielding it from everyone, protecting it. You won't let anyone in. It's why you can't hear my thoughts, and everyone else can."

"Chandra, how do you know Chase is shielding his mind from us?" my dad asked.

I blushed. "Luag said he was doing it. So every once in a while, after he told me, I tried to send Chase a few thoughts, and when he didn't react, I knew Luag was telling the truth."

My dad looked angry with me. "You didn't think this was important enough to tell anyone?"

I shuffled my feet and didn't look at my dad. Yeah, I had, but since I had been upset, I didn't open my mouth.

Dad threw his arms in the air. "Well, that explains why you passed out during the shielding spell—two shields fighting each other," He turned to Chase. "That explains Isis, too—what she told you about interference."

Chase nodded, though he had simply thought it was his feelings, his emotions that were interfering.

"How do I stop it?"

Dad shook his head. "I don't know, Chase. I haven't dealt with this before." He glowered. "We're going to have to ask Isis, tonight, for some suggestions."

I didn't think he liked the idea of asking her for help very much.

CHAPTER 13

We Lose Our First Battle

Isis showed up at sundown, as promised. She was just as Chase had described her: beautiful, glowing blue, and mostly transparent. She swept into the canyon as if it were her royal palace.

"I have returned, Freddy, as I said I would. I don't suppose you have changed your mind about this foolish plan of yours?"

"No, Isis, our plan still remains the same," he answered almost tiredly. She nodded and turned to lead the way out of the canyon, when her gaze fell on me.

"Ah, you are Freddy's daughter." It wasn't a question. "I was correct, you are beautiful."

I blushed at her assessment of my person. I'd never thought of myself as even passably pretty. To have a goddess tell you you're beautiful was pleasant, to say the least.

"Hello, I'm Chandra. It's nice to meet you, ma'am."

She smiled kindly and looked at my father. "It would seem everyone is pleased to see me but you, Freddy."

Dad looked harassed. "Let's just get this over with, Isis."

She shrugged her delicate shoulders. "As you wish, Freddy dear."

His expression darkened. "Isis, will you stop calling me that ridiculous name?"

She only grinned at him. Chase stepped in before World War III started.

"Isis, about what you said last night. How do I stop the interference with my powers?"

"I already told you that, dear boy. Let the pain go, and you will be free."

Chase scowled at her. I looked at Isis; that seemed like a very simple answer to the problem. The goddess laughed a light tinkling sound that reminded me of these Chinese rain chimes my mom used to have.

"If you think it will be easy for him to let go of the pain and anger he holds close, my dear, then you will never fully understand it."

I thought back to my nightmare about Elandra and the pain she had suffered when Theryn had looked into her mind, and I shivered. Chase would have a long road to travel in order to recover from what he had suffered at Theryn's claws. Isis nodded solemnly as if she understood my thoughts.

"Come, we must go. Menkaura awaits our arrival." Isis didn't need any assistance to fly; she glided through the air gracefully. The cave where the Egyptian clan resided was barely a mile down the canyon, well hidden by Isis' magic. We entered and landed among the Egyptian clan of dragons. They seemed much less eager to meet with us than the Scottish clan had been. I could only guess Isis had a bit to do with their attitude. They were so few; I could see only six dragons. I could understand why Isis was so protective of her dragons. The leader came forward and stood next to Isis.

"Good evening, I am Menkaura. Isis has told us of your mission here." Menkaura was a deep navy blue. He reminded me of a politician, extremely distinguished and ready to tell you exactly what you wanted to hear, so that you would go away as quickly as possible. I saw a smile from Isis; apparently, no matter how well I guarded my thoughts, I couldn't hide them from her. A smaller gray dragon appeared at Menkaura's side and whispered something to him. Menkaura nodded, and the dragon withdrew.

"Usi tells me that all is well, you were not followed." Isis gave him a disgruntled look. Menkaura took no notice of Isis' displeasure.

Apparently, Menkaura didn't trust Isis to make sure they were safe. Yes, he was a politician; he distrusted everyone, even his protector. All that his navy-blue hide needed was a few pinstripes to complete the look. I smirked over that thought. I saw the corners of Isis' lips lift in a small smile, and she inclined her head to me. I looked down at my toes as my dad stepped forward to speak.

"Thank you for agreeing to see us, Menkaura. I'm Fredrick Strandon, my daughter, Chandra, Chase Ivers, Echo and Hertha. We come from Queebo's clan in America. We believe the wyvern will soon make their final stand to dominate the dragon clans, and the war will again begin in earnest. We ask that you join us in the fight against them," he said, giving the same speech he had to Scots dragons.

Menkaura frowned at us. "The wyvern have grown too strong to fight. Our only hope now is to remain hidden. If you think what few of us who are left could ever hope to defeat them, you are mistaken, *sorcerer.*"

Dad frowned at the leader of the Egyptian clan. It was clear that Isis had poisoned their minds.

"Do you not believe in Merlin's prophecy, Menkaura?"

The dragon leader laughed at my father. "That is a fairy tale; no child will ever be born that will defeat the wyvern. I am sorry, sorcerer, but my clan will not join this foolish effort."

"You would reject Merlin's prophecy so easily, Menkaura? What if either Chandra or Chase was the one, they both have shown remarkable powers already, and they're not even of age yet."

Menkaura smiled and shook his head.

"I am sorry, sorcerer. For years, many thought they found *the one* that would defeat the wyvern. I am tired of empty promises. I will no longer risk the lives of my brothers and sisters on them."

I wanted to scream at him. He was condemning his clan to a life in darkness, to live here in hiding. They would rather hide in this cave than have some measure of freedom. Isis had done this to them, poisoned their minds against fighting for freedom. I glared at her. Some goddess she was. Suddenly, I realized how ugly she truly was. Isis straightened her back and glared right back at me.

"You've no right to judge me, girl," she said flatly.

"You protect them well, Isis," I sneered at her. I turned to Menkaura. "Live here in darkness for eternity, then. Condemn your brothers and sisters to a life in the shadows. When you hear your cousins screaming in pain, fighting for their freedom, remember that you chose your prison in here. They chose to fight for freedom out there." I jabbed a finger toward the entrance of the cave. I turned away and climbed on Hertha's back. Chase climbed up behind me, his arms slipping around my waist, pulling me close. I didn't look back at Menkaura. I couldn't. I'd made it clear what I'd thought of his unwillingness to fight, his cowardice.

We left the Egyptian dragons behind. Pain heavy in my chest, we'd lost one for our side. I never would've figured any of the dragons would reject our offer to join the cause to fight for their freedom from the wyvern. We headed for China next. I leaned back against Chase. He rested his chin on top of my head, his hands linked around my waist. I guessed that he knew I was upset; he didn't speak just held me close. I was glad that we'd made up and I hoped we could be closer now. I didn't want my nightmare from Scotland to come true. I didn't want Chase to choose the path that would take him back to Theryn. I wasn't sure I could bear the perfect-haired Chase making a comeback. I loved the tousle-haired one too much.

Fredrick watched Chase and Chandra together, a frown creasing his brow. He wasn't sure he was happy about them settling their disagreement. They seemed unusually attached to each other. They had just met, yet they clung to one another like a lifeline; it worried him.

His mind drifted to the prophecy, ideas creeping into his brain. More worries needling at him. Ideas he didn't want to begin to consider were forming in his mind. He looked back at them again. If Theryn found out the truth, he would kill both teens instantly, without hesitation. He wished he could talk to Queebo about his suspicions. The old queen would understand his worries. His suspicions worried him, more so than the upcoming war did.

The war was just the beginning.

He had a sinking feeling that Chandra and Chase together would be the end.

CHAPTER 14

Flames In The Desert

Astorm hit us part of the way to China, and we had to set down and make camp in the middle of Pakistan. Not my idea of a dream vacation spot. I tried to hang on to my earlier excitement about all the traveling as we landed.

We had to find a cave to hide in; one that was not only big enough to hide both the dragons and us, but that preferably wasn't already occupied by some group of terrorists or soldiers of some sort. Dad made sure to break out the Tupperware and do some protection spells so our camp wouldn't be found by anyone or anything. It was looking like it was going to be a long night. Echo and Hertha decided to stay inside the cave, not daring even to go out to hunt. I was glad when they made the decision to stay in, I would've worried the whole time if they'd gone out.

Dad and Chase, however, decided to venture out. Dad figured as long as we were here, he and Chase should poke around and see if there might be any dragons hanging about the area. Dad decided to bring along weapons, just as a precaution, something I hadn't even known he'd packed. Nothing as modern as guns; no, sorcerers didn't use guns. He had a sword. Chase didn't know how to use a sword, so he had to make do with a knife, which he grimaced over. I knew exactly why he didn't want to carry the knife. They didn't want to risk openly using magic and drawing any attention.

I paced the floor the entire time they were gone. When they finally returned, they looked like they been in some sort of street fight and ended up on the losing side.

"Good lord, what happened?" My eyes were wide as I surveyed their battered and bruised bodies. Dad flopped down onto the floor, panting. His shirt was shredded and hanging in tatters, and he had a large gash on his head, as well as a bloodied lip. Chase didn't look any better. He had somehow lost his shirt altogether. This was the first time I had ever seen him without a shirt—not counting the time I had awakened in his arms after my nightmare, since I had tried very hard not to stare at his bare chest then. Beneath the blood, that was covering his bare skin; I noticed the nasty set of scars that ran along his chest.

"Chase, what happened?" I doused a cloth with water and handed it to him. I got another for my dad's head. Echo and Hertha were both anxiously waiting to find out what had happened. They'd moved forward from their spot at the back of the cave when both men had returned. My dad sat up as I began dabbing at the cut on his head. He spoke while I washed the blood from the wound on his head.

"We ran into some soldiers about a mile out. They didn't buy our story that we were lost. We tried telling them we were Americans, and we'd gotten separated from a tour group. They didn't want to hear it. Apparently, they thought we were American spies; when they found the weapons, it didn't help their impression of us much."

I gasped and asked, "Were they terrorists?"

"That's what we think; we didn't exactly get to ask them their names, Chandra. They took us to their camp—not exactly a hop, skip, and a jump from here—and kindly introduced us to their leader. *A lovely man.*" His tone said otherwise. "After interrogating us," he gestured to their injuries. I guessed the guy's idea of interrogation included some torture. He probably would've gotten along famously with Theryn, I thought.

Dad sighed and closed his eyes for a moment before continuing. "They locked us in a cell. As soon as it was quiet, I took it upon myself to unlock the door and get us the hell out of there."

Chase took control of the story. "They weren't too pleased with our escape. Somehow, they managed to track us into the desert. They took a few shots at us," Chase gave me a big grin. "I evened the odds up a bit. I figured in the dark, they wouldn't know the difference between a sorcerer and a rocket launcher, so I tossed a few fireballs at them," he said with a shrug.

Dad grimaced. "Yes, unfortunately for us, his aim is wonderful," Dad said with an added eye roll. "He took out the Jeep they were riding in. Blew the thing sky high. I'm afraid before long, the entire Pakistani army will be combing the desert for whoever killed those guys. We might be stuck here until they give up. We can't fly until the storm passes further on anyway." He winced as I dabbed at the cut on his head, and then frowned. "I guess we had better get some rest," he muttered as I continued to dab at the cut on his head. "I need to put an aversion spell on the cave. We don't want anyone getting extra curious and poking around too close to the entrance."

It was my turn to frown. "Wouldn't that have been good to do in the first place?" I asked.

"I really didn't think we needed it in the middle of the desert. I thought we were fine just hiding the entrance," he said indignantly. I sighed and went to look through the packs for a first aid kit. Dad beat me to the punch, performing healing spells on himself and Chase. He still wouldn't let me use my healing powers unless absolutely necessary. He didn't want me to tax my strength. I rolled my eyes at him. Chase sat down and leaned against the wall with a groan. I handed him a new shirt.

"Thanks," he said as I sat down next to him.

"Did Theryn give you those?" I asked, pointing to the scars on his chest. He sighed, looking down, a twisted smile curling his lips. He pulled the shirt on over his head, hiding the scars from sight. I wondered if he would talk about them. He took a deep breath and blew it out.

"Yeah, about a month after he captured me. Right after the first time I tried to escape."

My eyes widened. I had never known he'd tried to escape. He smiled and reached out, putting his hand on my cheek.

"I didn't hide in the corner the whole time bemoaning my fate, Chandra. At first, I fought like hell to get out of there. That first time, I got about three feet out of the cave before they caught me. That's the farthest I ever got." Pulling his hand from my face, leaning his head back against the wall, he kept talking.

"Theryn was so angry; I thought he was going to kill me for sure. The guards dragged me in front of him and tossed me on the ground at his feet. He was in a good rage. I stood up and faced him; I refused to kneel. That just made him angrier; he wanted my complete obedience. I figured if he wasn't going to let me go, then let him kill me. I didn't want him in my head anymore. When I saw his claws coming at me, I thought for sure it was finally over, that I was finally going to die. All I felt in that moment was relief that it was going to end. His claws tore through my chest; the pain was excruciating."

He looked thoughtful for a minute. "I really did think I was going to die. Something else happened when he touched me; it seemed to hurt him as much as it hurt me. It was like he couldn't bear to touch me and he never touched me again if he didn't have to. I'm not sure what happened, but it shook him. It also ticked him off, made him more determined than ever to break me, to show me that he was in control." Chase's smile was no more a smile than his earlier one had been when I'd asked him about the scars in the first place. "That's when he began making changes." His voice was bitter.

I frowned at him. "Changes? What do you mean?"

Chase gave a humorless laugh. "Look at me, Chandra. I'm not the same as when you met me that first night. Remember at the restaurant?"

I blushed when I remembered that night. How attracted to him I had been, despite what he had ended up doing to me. His eyes were focused on some distant point in the past while he spoke.

"Theryn's idea of a sick joke. He thought I was less than perfect. I lacked discipline. So he made me into his vision of perfection. Perfect. Perfect hair, perfect clothes. Perfect everything. His perfect little soldier. I had to obey his every order. I had no choice." Chase closed his eyes.

I leaned my head against his shoulder. I could only imagine how that had made him feel on the inside, being forced to dress as someone else, act as someone else. All the while having that beast inside your head telling you what to do and how to do it. A noise made us look up. Dad was standing there, looking uncomfortable.

"I think we should get some sleep now. There's no telling when we might have the chance again, that army could show up at any time. The spells might or might not hold. It all depends on how determined they are to find us. If they hang around for long, we might have to start taking turns keeping watch."

We nodded, and everyone crawled into their sleeping bags. I rolled over and looked at Chase. He smiled, I smiled back and reached out a hand; he caught it and kissed my palm. I shivered and smiled wider, closing my eyes and going to sleep. Our hands still linked.

If I thought my happiness over being on good terms with Chase would keep the nightmares away, I was dead wrong.

The God of Nightmares seemed determined to tell me something.

Another time, another battle. More blood, more death and pain, more war. I was weary of it. I spun, quickly, raising the sword in my hand, swinging it downward. Slicing and killing.

More blood.

More death.

The dragon beneath me swerved and flew downward, heading for a wyvern that had attacked a woman trying to flee the village we were defending.

"No, you don't, you filthy scum!" I shouted at the monster. I sliced again, and the wyvern ceased to be. A scream made me swing around. The woman I'd just saved was running flat-out for her life. I looked up, searching out the reason for her fear and desperate flight. Theryn was flying straight for her. We turned, but I knew we would be too late to save her and the babe in her arms.

Not again, my mind screamed! Too many innocents dead. I aimed and threw the sword I carried; it bounced harmlessly off Theryn's thick hide, unnoticed by the beast. He ripped the child from its mother's arms.

He flew off into the clouds, turned red by the setting sun, his army following in his wake. They had what they had come for; there was no reason to continue the fight.

We landed. The woman ran at me screaming, pounding my chest with her fists.

"You were supposed to protect us, Calan McIvers! My babe is gone! He. Is. Gone!" She wept bitter tears; giving up the punishment of my chest, she collapsed against me and just cried. I stood motionless. She was right: I'd failed. I knew there was nothing I could do to bring her child back. I didn't know who Calan was. Apparently, for the purpose of this vision, I was Calan. I looked around. So many accusing faces staring at me. I turned away, watching as the woman's husband pulled her into his arms and held her. I moved away from the accusing stares, walking through the village. I couldn't protect them. I had to leave. As I moved away through the empty streets, a voice spoke up.

"There will be others; there will always be others. If you give up and leave, they will have no one left at all to protect them, Calan. They need someone." I turned and saw the last person I would have expected: my father.

"Fredrick, I canna fight any longer. Too many innocents have died." He shook his head at my father. I didn't know who this man was that I was seeing through, but he knew my dad. So I knew this was important. I settled back to watch, seeing things through Calan's eyes.

"I know how you feel, Calan. I felt the same once, too. One day, the Chosen will come, and when that time is upon us, we must fight all the harder. We can't give up; we can't fail. As many as are taken, we must continue to fight."

Calan nodded slowly at him. "All right, Fredrick, if you can keep going after all you have lost, then I can as well." He looked back toward the battlefield. "But Brenna won't forgive me easily for letting Angus be taken."

My father nodded. "No, they never do, but he wasn't the one, Calan."

Calan nodded yet again, knowing he spoke the truth.

When I woke, sunlight was streaming in through the cave entrance, and my dad was standing near the entry looking out. It was a relief not to wake up from one of my dreams screaming in terror. I felt deep sadness for what had been lost, though: a child too young to have died. Chase was still asleep. I pulled my hand from his, wondering happily how we could have slept without moving our hands. I went to my dad's side.

"Dad?"

"Hmmm?" he said, turning slowly to face me.

I mustered my courage. I knew that what I had seen must be important, just as seeing Elandra had been.

"Who was Calan McIvers?"

He looked at me, wide-eyed.

"Where did you hear that name?"

I looked down self-consciously and rubbed at my arm. Then I told him about the dream. He turned fully, moving away from the cave entrance a bit, and sat down. I sat next to him.

"I haven't thought about Calan in years. He was a good friend. I miss him." He looked toward Chase and smiled. "Chase reminds me a bit of Calan sometimes. Calan had a habit of dragging his hand through his hair like Chase does." Dad chuckled a bit. "When you told me his last name, then when I saw him, I have to confess I thought maybe he could be Calan's boy. When he told us he was adopted—" he shrugged. "I figured the similarities in the last name and his looks were just a coincidence. Being adopted, though … maybe it's just wishful thinking on my part. He looks so much like Calan, though; he has Calan's eyes. When I saw Chase, it was almost like seeing him again. I had hoped—" Dad shook his head, clearing out the memories of his old friend.

"Calan and I fought together for a while," He sighed. "He almost left Scotland that day. Brenna was Calan's sister. She and her husband thought her son could be the Chosen. I didn't think it was possible. Brenna had no powers; neither did her husband. Just because Calan had them, Brenna hoped her son would someday. That's what brought Theryn after the boy—rumors. Calan decided to stay, and he continued to fight the wyvern in Scotland. I left with Queebo's clan when they decided to move to America. I haven't seen Calan in years. I don't even know what happened to him after I left Scotland."

I wrapped my arms around his arm, hugging it, laying my head against his shoulder. "You could ask Luag; maybe he would know."

Dad nodded. "That's an idea."

He dropped a kiss on my forehead. I had another question that I had wanted to ask.

"Dad, the men who took Elandra away—who were they?"

"Servants of the wyvern. They worked for them, worshipped them. Whichever. Some thought the wyvern were gods. Others were simply greedy and followed the gold they were paid. Either way, both made our lives difficult. We often didn't know who they were until it was much too late. Like with Elandra. I knew some of those men, worked alongside them. It was devastating to many when they found out who the betrayers were. It tore many families apart."

We heard a noise outside. Dad put a finger to his lips, and we both crept back to the entrance. Soldiers were creeping around outside the entrance to the cave. Dad's spells kept the entrance hidden. We hoped it would work well enough to keep these men disinterested in the cave. The two soldiers sat down in a shady spot. I poked Dad in the arm. He looked at me; I pointed to the men. They were American, not Pakistani. Not that that was going to make me jump out of the cave yelling, "Hey guys how are you?" We just eavesdropped on what they were saying.

"I don't know why we have to go looking for the guys who killed him anyway; whoever it was did us a favor, man." His buddy nodded. They both had some choice words about whoever the commander of the terrorists had been.

"Seems to me we should be thanking whoever those two guys were rather than hunting 'em down. Stupid Pakistani government, calling 'em fugitives. We all know they ain't fugitives. They're damn heroes. That Pakistani official has been working with the terrorists for years. We know it, they know it—hell, half the world knows it! If I found those guys, I'd escort 'em to the border, and the Pakistani government can kiss my behind." The two guys finished their cigarettes and headed back out into the desert sun. Dad and I frowned at each other.

"Apparently you and Chase killed someone important."

He sighed. "Important to who, is the question."

"Who cares," I answered.

Dad rolled his eyes. "At least we know for sure we didn't kill any innocent civilians. I think as soon as it's dark, we need to fly the coop."

I grinned at him; we weren't exactly flying chickens. He shook his head but smiled back at me. When night finally fell, we packed up, leaving Pakistan and the long prison term awaiting us if we were caught behind us. We were going to stick to killing wyvern from now on—at least, that was the plan.

We were back on track, heading for China. I prayed to whoever would listen to please, please let us find some friendly dragons in China. The storm had moved on by now, well past China, so we had clear skies ahead of us. I looked down in the darkness. I couldn't see much, just the passing lights of cities below us, interspersed with areas of darkness. I knew that Dad's spells kept us hidden from sight, but I still worried that Theryn would find us.

Magic couldn't hide us from him. Not when he had magic of his own.

CHAPTER 15

Post-it Notes Are Deadly

Near dawn, we set down on the top of a snowy mountain. There is one advantage to having a body temperature of a hundred and ten degrees: Cold weather isn't that big a deal. We set up camp as Echo and Hertha set off to find their breakfast; they were hungry after the long night in Pakistan. I looked around; it was peaceful and stunningly beautiful on top of the mountain. Dad was shading his eyes, looking out over the mountains.

"These mountains are some of the most beautiful in China. Zhari Mountain, the birthplace of Buddhism, there are many spiritual tourists that come here looking for peace. I think if the dragons would settle on any mountain, they would pick this one; it has a lot of spiritual meaning in China," he explained as we finished setting up the camp.

I shrugged as I looked over the mountains; a hot spot for spiritual tourists didn't sound like a great place for a clan of dragons to settle down to me. Chase burst out laughing. My dad and I turned around and stared at him. He turned bright red.

"Sorry, I just, um ..." He looked totally embarrassed. He glanced to me for help. It suddenly dawned on me why he'd laughed—he'd *heard* what I was thinking! He wasn't laughing at my father—he was laughing at what I had been thinking! I ran over and jumped on him, hugging him, practically knocking him flat. I was so excited, I yelled right in his face.

"You heard me, didn't you?!"

He smiled down at me. We stood there staring into each other's eyes. I'm not exactly sure what would've happened next, because my dad cleared his throat, totally ruining the moment. We jumped away from each other, embarrassed to have acted however we had in front of my dad. Chase ran his hand through his hair.

"Uh, yeah, I heard you." He gave me a brilliant smile, flashing white teeth.

Dad just shook his head at the two of us. "That's good, Chase. Let's hope you can keep that extra shield of yours out of the way from now on."

He nodded at my father. "Does this mean we can practice?"

I nodded in eager agreement at my dad, putting my hands up in front of me in a prayer like gesture. He rolled his eyes and shook his head. I figured he was asking, *Why me?*

"Okay, fine, but let's eat and get some sleep first, please?"

We both agreed.

Chase and I had a good chuckle over how Dad had set up the sleeping bags when we got a look inside the tent a few minutes later. I was guessing he wasn't comfortable with how close Chase and I were getting. He'd put his sleeping bag in between mine and Chase's. I shook my head; it wasn't like I was a child anymore. I would be eighteen in less than a year; Chase would be, too. Besides, I certainly wasn't going to go crawling into Chase's sleeping bag with my dad sleeping less than five feet away! Dad was just being silly, but of course, we let it be. Why start an argument with a guy who could vaporize you?

I yawned and snuggled down into my sleeping bag; after the last few nights, I really needed some sleep. So as I settled in, I begged, pleaded, bargained, and basically beseeched those nightmare gods to go away and please leave me be for just one day.

I was pleased to wake up, as the sun was making its decent toward the western horizon, nightmare free. I stretched and got out of my sleeping bag. I couldn't wait to find out what Dad was going to teach us today. Chase was already outside, practicing the shielding spell with Dad, now that he didn't have that extra shield hanging around his brain.

I sat down next to where Dad stood and watched. Dad grinned down at me.

"Chase is giving you a run for your money, sweetheart. He's up to four and a half minutes." Just as he said that, Chase's shield collapsed. Chase was grinning like a fool. I guessed he was happy to have beaten me at something.

"Congrats, Magic Boy! See, I told you that you were good at this magic stuff!" He was still grinning as he pelted me with a snowball. I laughed and grabbed some snow, throwing it back at him. I heard Dad groan; I picked up a fistful of snow and lobbed it at his head.

"Oh, that's it, kid, now you're asking for it!" That's the last thing I remembered; next thing I knew, Chase and I were snow people. Seriously, he had made us into snow people. I laughed and broke free of the snow. Chase was doing the same.

"How did you do that?" I asked him as I brushed the last of the snow from my hoodie. Dad was sitting on a rock, smiling at us. He didn't even look winded.

"Your lesson for today. *Desino dehinc* ... to stop time." He said it with a mischievous grin. I didn't need any encouragement for this lesson.

"Awesome! Show us!"

He laughed at me and uncrossed his arms. "This is a bit tougher to manage than your previous lessons; you have to really concentrate. Think the words, *desino dehinc*. There is no hand movements required for this spell; it's all in your mind. That's important. You control the whole spell; it will only last as long as you concentrate. Potentially, it could last years if you let it." He chuckled. "I don't know anyone with concentration that good, however."

Chase looked at me. A challenge showing in his eyes, and I thought, *Go ahead and try it, Magic Boy!* His grin widened.

I should've known I wouldn't have a chance against him. All he had to do was run his hand through that hair of his and flash me a smile, complete with dimple. I was lost right then and there. *I'm such a ditz!*

When time began for me again, I discovered that Chase had decided it would be funny to set me at the very edge of the mountain … I screamed and promptly fell off the edge. I thought I heard him yell my name, but I couldn't be sure; I was too busy muttering the transformation spell to listen closely. When I landed back up on top of the mountain, Chase was nowhere in sight, and Dad was laughing his head off. Tears streaming down his face, and he was clutching his stomach.

"Where is he, Dad?"

He pointed behind me toward the edge of the mountain. I turned around and looked where he had pointed; a large seagull was just sailing over the edge and landing. I fell over laughing.

"A seagull? You were going to save me as a seagull?" I gasped for breath, barely getting the words out, now laughing as hard as my father was. Chase transformed back as he landed.

"Chandra! Jeez … when you fell … it was the first thing I thought of! You scared me to death. I'm sorry; I never thought you would fall!" He stopped his ranting and gave me a disgruntled look. "Ya know, most normal people would've been startled and stumbled a few steps backward, *away* from the edge! No, you have to be different, don't you?" He grabbed me and hugged me so tight I thought he was going to crack some ribs.

I pulled away from him. "It's okay, Chase, really. I'm fine … see? How do you think I survived the last time you chucked me over a cliff?" I reassured him wryly.

He frowned at me. "Don't remind me, okay? I hated that. Theryn was enjoying that whole situation. I almost got free that night, you know? When I saw your dad come out of the restaurant, I fought hard against Theryn. I wanted to tell your dad what happened to you. Theryn won that fight; he forced me to run away. I wasn't sure if you'd survived the fall. The next time I saw you, I was so relieved. Theryn wasn't, though."

I gave him a hug and sighed. Our relationship was going to be difficult, that was for sure. At the very least, our conversations were going to be odd. I could see us in the future like, "*Oh, honey, remember the time you stabbed me at Yankee Stadium?*"

"Oh, yeah! Good times, good times!" Yep, it was going to be strange all right. Chase smiled and hugged me back, picking up my thoughts.

"Yeah, great, what are we going to tell our grandkids about the first time we met? Oh yes, I remember the first time I met your grandma, I tossed her over a cliff!"

I laughed till I couldn't breathe. "Well, if we survive long enough to have grandkids, knowing this family, it probably won't be the strangest story they ever hear!"

Dad joined in the laughter, although I could tell it was forced. I wasn't sure if it was because Chase and I were talking about our relationship continuing into the future, or my mentioning us actually surviving long enough to continue it, or both. Dad was the first one to sober up.

"Okay, you two, we need to practice some more before it gets dark."

We both nodded. I would've rather sat and snuggled with Chase by the campfire; however, I knew what Dad would think of that idea, so I kept my thoughts to myself. Almost—I shared them with Chase. I got another hug for that. When I saw the look on Dad's face, I knew it didn't matter that I'd kept my thoughts to myself; his feelings were plain to see. He wasn't happy about me and Chase and the direction of our relationship. We used the last of the daylight to practice. After night fell, we waited for Hertha and Echo to return, and then we set out to find the dragons. We used Chase's super magic-finding abilities again. It took a while before he found even a trace of magic. It wasn't a very large bit, though, which made Dad nervous.

We stood outside the cave entrance that Chase had found. Dad frowning and looking distinctly nervous.

"I just don't think it's big enough to be a whole clan of dragons."

Chase was inclined to agree with my father. He was getting better at sensing things. He still couldn't tell exactly what they were yet, but he had a sense of knowing how large they were, as well as a general sense of whether they were good or evil. This time, though, whatever it was just wasn't large enough for him to tell exactly what was going on with the magic.

"Dad, come on, how are we going to know what it is if we don't go check it out?" I was anxious to find the dragons. After our failure in Egypt, I really wanted the Chinese dragons to join us. I turned and started walking into the cave. Chase latched on to my arm and jerked me to a stop.

"Chandra, your dad's right, we don't know what's in there. It could be dangerous."

I shook off his arm and kept walking. "We need to find the dragons; either you're coming or you're not."

I heard him groan, but he was soon keeping pace with me. Dad was on his other side, holding a flashlight, for some things, magic just was not a substitute, I thought as the beam from the flashlight bobbed across the cave walls.

"Chandra, this really isn't a good idea. I have a bad feeling about what's in here." Chase looked around nervously at the darkened cave walls as he spoke.

I wasn't sure whether I disagreed with him or not; it was just that we didn't have any other leads at the moment. Dad suddenly threw out an arm and halted our progress as we rounded a slight curve. Chase may be the sensitive; my dad had the experience, however. "Turn around now … we need to go back."

I guessed he had tossed out one of those spells he used to seek out whatever magical creature was hanging about. I frowned at him and opened my mouth to ask why—too late. Something came at us out of the darkness. Whatever it was it didn't move quickly—stumbled, was more like it. I had a sudden vision of those old monster movies they used to show really late at night on cable. The thing moved like a guy in a cheap mummy suit in a low-budget monster movie. We all dodged quickly out of its way. Unfortunately, that meant moving away from the cave entrance and farther into the cave itself as the thing lunged and stumbled at us.

"Dad, what is that thing?" He had moved across the room from me now, rummaging through his backpack. "Dad!?!" What was he looking for, his damn Tupperware? I backed away from the mummy thing. In the blackness of the cave, I moved even farther away from the entrance, which was now around that small bend we had rounded. I couldn't see much. The only light in the cave was the little pool where Dad sat with the flashlight.

"Whatever you do, Chandra, don't let it touch you!" he yelled, not looking up from his backpack.

"That was pretty much my plan, Dad! I don't want that thing anywhere near me!" I dodged again and stepped back, trying to keep an eye on the thing in the darkness. I stumbled on a rock; my ankle twisted beneath me, and I went down to the floor. I tried to scramble back to my feet. "Ow dammit!"

"Chandra! Are you okay?"

Chase was shouting at me from somewhere in the darkness. No, I wasn't okay! I'd twisted my ankle. I was crawling away from that thing as fast as I could. The rocks on the floor were cutting into my hands. All I could think at that point was that it was a good thing the monster didn't move very fast. Suddenly, Chase was there, picking me up and swinging me into his arms, backing away from that thing. I conjured up a fireball and flung it at the creature. It hit it and did nothing to slow down its already leisurely pace.

"Dad, a little help here!" I shouted. I really wondered what he was doing; he appeared to be sitting cross-legged on the floor, writing frantically on a small pad of paper. Great, what was he doing, writing out his will? That was encouraging! Chase was still backing away from the creature. Soon, there was nowhere for us to go; a wall of rock was at our backs. Chase ducked as the thing reached for us. He stumbled sideways over a pile of rocks and dropped me; I went rolling across the floor.

"Chandra!" I heard him scream.

I groaned, stunned. I'd hit my head on something when I fell, probably a rock. I could feel a trail of blood working its way down my temple. I heard the creature shuffling toward me, but I didn't have enough wits to gather myself and move. I lay there dazed, waiting for whatever would happen when that thing touched me.

"Chandra, where are you?"

I wanted to call out to Chase. I really did, but my brain was all fuzzy around the edges. I couldn't seem to think straight. Inside my head, I screamed at him that I was right here, couldn't he see me? Where was my dad? Why wasn't he stopping that thing? He had to know what to do, didn't he? My head felt heavy, and my vision was blurred. I heard the shuffling gait of the creature getting closer; any minute, it would find me. Then what? Where were Chase and my dad? Why wasn't anyone coming to help me? And what on earth had my father been writing on that little pad of paper?

Just then, I noticed something looming in the darkness above me.

I wanted to scream; the thing was horrifying to look at. It leaned over me; its face was white, leached of blood. It was a corpse rotting and long dead, with arms reaching out, ready to grab me with decomposing fingers; its clothes were rags hanging off its rotting body. Eyes blank—no life to speak of in those half-rotted eyes. I closed my eyes, prepared for whatever horrible fate was in store for me. A deep bone-numbing coldness enveloped the air around me. Cold, I was so cold now. Involuntarily, my head twitched, and my nose scrunched up; the smell was gruesome. Honestly, it was worse than the time Mom and I got into a fight about cleaning Legend's litter box. We both stubbornly refused to clean it, for like maybe a month; it was really gross. Legend must have thought so, too; she took to using the flowerbed in the backyard for a litter box, which ticked Mom off so bad she finally cleaned the thing.

Bile rose in my throat. I was going to die; I just knew it. What would happen when the creature's cold, dead hand touched me? Would it hurt? How could it not? That thing was so horrible just to look at. Its touch must be equally as horrid to endure.

I waited in vain for my fate; the touch never came. Blackness enveloped my fog-filled brain. I welcomed its oblivion to block out the touch of that dead, rotted corpse.

"Chandra ... Chandra? Can you hear me? She's not waking up. Are you sure the healing spell worked?"

"Give her time, Chase. She hit her head pretty hard."

I could hear both their voices as if from a great distance. I groaned.

"Chandra ... thank God! How do you feel?"

I opened my eyes and looked straight into Chase's face. He was hovering over me.

"Chase, back off and give her some room to breathe, will you?"

He sat back after my father's stern scolding.

"What happened? What was that ... thing?" My voice sounded too high, scared and thin. I looked to my dad for the answer.

"Jiang Shi, the hopping corpse."

I stared at him. "You're kidding, right? A hopping corpse? Is that a joke?"

"I'm afraid not. They're very real."

I groaned again as I propped myself up on an elbow. "And what exactly is this ... this hopping thing?"

"The Chinese believe that when a person dies and their soul is prevented from leaving the body, it's trapped inside, unable to move on to the afterlife. The body can then reanimate and become exactly what you saw. Jiang Shi, one touch can kill you instantly. The only way to stop them is to release the soul from the body with a spell written on a piece of paper. You have to stick it to their forehead. Not exactly easy to do without touching the thing," he explained.

I stared at him; I didn't know what to say. We'd gone from color-coded Tupperware to killing a monster by sticking a Post-it Note to its forehead. This whole sorcerer thing was getting stranger by the minute. I flopped back down and closed my eyes. This day was just too much. So that's what he'd been doing with the pad of paper, writing down the spell to stick to the creature's forehead. What was next? Using a knitting needle to stake a vampire or your grandma's favorite silver tea service to kill a werewolf, I didn't dare ask.

"Chandra, we have to get going. We need to find the dragons."

I groaned; my head still felt all fuzzy, even though Dad had healed it. "Okay, fine, let's go, then."

Chase helped me up, and we climbed on board Hertha. It took another hour before Chase finally located something big enough to be the dragons; at least by then my head was clear. We avoided anything smaller, just to be safe. The cave was high up on a sheer cliff; no one with half a brain would've tried to climb to it. We flew in and hoped to get a warm welcome—that didn't include flames.

We landed in the middle of a large cavern and were immediately surrounded by seven dragons, including the dragons' leaders. All were eager to meet us. They had, strangely enough, been expecting our arrival.

"All of you please let our guests be; give them some room now."

I looked up to see a bright white dragon coming toward us. A black dragon—the site of it shocked me—followed her closely; I'd thought Theryn had been the only black dragon, before he had been turned into a wyvern, that is. As they drew closer, I saw that the black dragon wasn't truly black; he was a very deep gray color.

"Good evening. We have been awaiting your arrival, my friends."

I stared at the two dragons; they were very different, yet they seemed to go together. Almost like they couldn't be separated, no matter how hard you tried. The white dragon smiled down at me.

"That is the truth, Chandra. My brother and I are one and the same, two pieces of a whole. I am Yin, my brother Yang. We are the leaders of this clan. We welcome you to China."

"How did you know we were coming?" I asked, in awe of the two dragons.

Yin chuckled. "We know many things, my dear. The wyvern grow stronger every day. We have been waiting for the day that you would arrive to tell us it was time to fight. We knew that day would arrive eventually."

I understood now. They hadn't known *we* would arrive, just that someone would arrive to tell them it was time to fight.

Yin nodded. "So now the time has come to fight; the wyvern's rise to power must be halted." She looked to her brother. "What say you now, my brother?"

He had a scowl on his face. "I do not like this, Yin. We do not know these sorcerers. How do we know they do not work for the wyvern, that this is not a trap to lure us out of the safety of our home?"

I thought of the Egyptian dragons. That's how they'd thought—suspicion and only of safety. Isis had made them scared of the outside world.

Yang was frowning at Chase. "This one has the taint of the wyvern on him. I don't trust them, sister."

Chase grimaced. His fight to be free from Theryn was a sore subject; I didn't think he wanted to argue with the dragons about it. I stepped up to Yin, wanting to cut off her brother before he turned the entire clan against us and our cause.

"Yin, if I may?" I held up a hand toward her snout. She lowered her head and looked to her brother. He lowered his head as well, moving closer to me. I placed a hand on both dragons. I had to show them what I knew: everything about Theryn, Queebo's battle alongside Luag, Elandra's death, Calan's loss of his sister's son, and, in the end, something of Chase's own battle to become free of Theryn. All of it. They had a choice to make fight or hide. It wasn't a decision I could make for them. When it was done, I stepped back, leaving them to talk. To decide.

Chase draped his arm over my shoulder. "You okay?" He whispered. I only nodded, not trusting myself to speak. My emotions were a bit high after seeing everything over again. He gave me a squeeze and dropped a kiss on the top of my head. I peeked at my dad and saw him frowning at us. I looked away from him, blinking my eyes to keep the tears at bay. Why couldn't he just get over it already? I could do a lot worse than Chase.

Yin stepped forward and spoke. "My brother is still torn about the decision. We must discuss it further. I am sorry. We will make our decision in the morning, my friends."

Yin and Yang both agreed we should stay the night and rest. Dad agreed, after the fight with the Post-it Note monster, he thought I could use the rest. After all, we had to wait for the decision. I grimaced when he put his sleeping bag in the middle again. Chase was talking with the dragons. He figured if he was going to fight alongside them, that he should get to know them, especially after Yang's comment about his being "tainted." I looked back at my dad.

"Dad, this is getting a bit ridiculous, don't you think?" I hissed at him.

"What is, Chandra?"

"Oh, don't act all innocent, Dad! You don't like the fact that I like Chase. Admit it!"

He frowned and looked over to where Chase stood talking with the dragons. "Fine, no, I don't. The fact is, Chandra, I looked into the boy's mind; you didn't. Theryn may be gone, but he left his mark there. There's a black spot on Chase's mind, a spot I can't identify. It worries me. He could be dangerous. Theryn could've set a spell in there, a booby trap of some sort, for all I know." I stared at him. When had he planned on telling us this? Never? Was he going to let Chase walk around forever with a ticking time bomb in his head? He rubbed his hand over his face.

"Chandra, I don't know what it is, okay? It might be damage from Theryn occupying his mind for all I know! I'm not going to worry Chase over something I can't explain."

"No, but you'll try to ruin my life over it! That you have no problem with, do you?" I sagged. "Dad, I love Chase, whether you want me to or not. It's too late to stop it; it's already happened."

"I'm sorry, Chandra, but as long as I'm here, I'll try to keep you two as far apart as possible. I just think it's safer."

"Safer for who, Dad? Me or you?" I stormed off before he could answer. I wanted to go to Chase. I found Yin instead, almost as if she'd been waiting for me.

"Your father tries to protect you. Do not blame him, Chandra. He is doing what he thinks is best."

I wiped at the tears on my face. "What if he's wrong? What if it's not what's best?" My heart ached; it wasn't fair. Why did my life have to be like this? Why couldn't I be a normal teenager with normal problems, like zits and boys? Well, I did have the boy part. Yin smiled down at me.

"Fathers may not always know what is right and what is wrong, my dear. They will only try to do their best for their children. Especially their little girls. You must understand that. He is only doing what he thinks is right for his little girl. It may not be the right answer in the end, but right now, he doesn't see a better path."

I grumbled. Why did she have to make sense? Yin chuckled again.

"It is all right, my dear. He is your father; he will understand in the end." I wasn't sure if that was true or not, but I nodded. I walked slowly back to where we'd put down our sleeping bags. Feeling a bit sad, if I was the Chosen I was meant to fight and save the dragons. It was something I wanted to do; I had come to care deeply for them all. Yet, it was a vast responsibility. I was still just seventeen. There were days when I wanted to just be a kid, when I still felt like a kid, but I wasn't anymore, not really. I was right there, right on the edge between childhood and becoming an adult. I pushed out a long sigh. It was a balance that couldn't be held forever, I would have to step away from childhood eventually.

When I reached the sleeping bags, I saw that Dad was doing a great impression of someone who was asleep; however, I could tell he was faking it. He was too stiff and his breathing wasn't even. Chase was still up, sitting on his sleeping bag, leaning against the wall; he had a pad of paper out. When I approached, he looked up and smiled at me; his face fell when he saw me. I guess he could tell I was upset.

"Hey, what's wrong, Chans?"

I gave him a tiny grin when I heard his little nick name for me. *Chans. Cute, Magic Boy.* I shook my head at him, sending him a clear message that with my dad there, it wasn't the right time to talk about what had upset me. He nodded, showing he had understood. I sat down next to him, resting my head on his shoulder. I looked down at the pad in his lap; he'd been drawing. He was really good; I didn't know he was an artist. He'd drawn a picture of the dragons gathered, ready to go out for the evening hunt.

"That's really good, Chase. I didn't know you could draw."

He lifted a shoulder in a shrug, dismissing my assessment of his artistic abilities. "I always liked to sketch a lot when I was a kid. I never really thought about it much back then. I just needed something to pass the time right now—either that or go insane." He grinned at me. "I've already gone that route once, with Theryn in my head; I don't think I want to do it again."

I shook my head at him. *Not funny, Chase. Don't even joke about that. Especially in front of* him. I glared at my dad's back; Chase sighed and said nothing.

"You should think about becoming an artist; you're really good," I said softly, wanting to reassure him after my harsh words a moment ago.

"You sure you're not just saying that to butter me up?" There was a teasing glint in his eyes and a smirk on his lips.

I smiled up at him. "Hmmm, maybe, is it working, Magic Boy?" Just when I thought I would finally, finally get to kiss him …

"Will you two stop with the talk already? Some of us are trying to sleep over here!"

I dropped my forehead onto Chase's shoulder. I really wanted to smack my dad.

"Good-night, Chandra!"

I frowned at his back. *Really, so that's it, then? Good-night, Chandra? Thanks, Dad!* I turned back to Chase, leaned forward, and gave him a kiss on the lips—nothing fancy, just a quick peck, but I made sure my dad caught every one of my thoughts so he knew exactly what I did and exactly what else I would *like* to do. In very vivid detail. Then I stood and went, reluctantly, to my sleeping bag on the other side of my dad. I ignored his scowl, turning away from him. I hoped I could have another stretch of nightmare-free sleep. I clutched that thought close as I drifted off.

"Chandra, come on, get up." My dad's voice broke into my dreams just before dawn … a very pleasant dream of Chase and those wonderful things I would have loved to do after the kissing. I yawned and rolled myself out of my sleeping bag, rubbing sleep from my eyes. I watched as my dad wandered away to talk with Yin and Yang. I began gathering my things together; I thought about my rather wonderful dream as I did.

"You keep thinking like that, and your dad is never going to speak to either of us ever again." I blushed and turned to face Chase. He smiled and wrapped his arms around my waist, pulling me close.

"Please tell me you were the only one who *heard* that!" I looked around; no one else was looking in our direction. He grinned down at me.

"I don't think anyone else *heard* you. Guess it was meant for my … *ears* only," Chase replied with a grin and a chuckle.

"I guess so." I smiled, until I saw my dad coming when I looked around Chase's shoulder. "Here comes the big, bad sorcerer," I whispered. Chase laughed and stepped away from me. I was back to feeling miserable, only now I was fighting with my dad instead of Chase.

"Come on, you two, it's time to hear their decision." The look he gave us both said that he wasn't happy with either of us. We nodded at him and walked over to where Yin and Yang stood. Yang still had a disgruntled look on his face. I wondered if that was his natural look. Yin had her usual peaceful expression in place as she addressed us.

"We have waited many long years for the war with the wyvern to end, for the culmination of Merlin's prophecy." She glanced first at me, and then Chase. "Now these travelers have finally come and shown us that the time has come to fight! We will join the battle again; the wyvern must be defeated!"

I sagged with relief. They were going to come. They would join the fight.

I leaned back against Chase once we were sitting atop Hertha; he gave me a squeeze. I knew Yin had been right—Dad was just trying to do what he thought was right for me. That didn't mean I had to like it, but I could at least understand it.

As we took off, I turned to wave good-bye to the Chinese dragons. I sighed. One more stop left: Australia. Then back home and our training would begin in earnest.

How long before the real war started?

How long would Theryn wait before he tried to crush us all?

CHAPTER 16

We Find Truth

I thought a lot while we flew south toward Australia. I had a theory about my sudden lack of nightmares. I had realized the two nights that I hadn't had nightmares or visions, whatever they were, had been the two nights that I'd slept next to my dad instead of near Chase. It worried me. If my theory held up, then why was Chase the cause of my dreams? Was it that black spot in his mind? Or a simple coincidence? I needed to talk to Chase without my dad around, which was going to be a problem. I decided that I would have to involve Hertha; I focused my thoughts and sent Hertha a message. I needed her help. If she and Echo could get Dad out of the way for a while, I could talk to Chase, alone. I needed to see what Chase thought about my theory. She looked back at me and nodded. I hoped Dad wouldn't find out; he would be angry, but I needed Chase's help testing out my theory.

We finally landed late in the evening; darkness surrounded us. I was so tired; all I wanted to do was sleep. We wouldn't be able to look for the dragons tonight; it was much too late. We set up camp and crashed. I didn't even bother to argue with Dad about the sleeping bag placement. I would have to test my dream theory another time. I fell asleep immediately.

I dreamed, but it was pleasant, serene. Chase and I were sitting together laughing, chatting, nothing wrong in the world. The day was perfect; the sun shone down on us. I couldn't have asked for a more wonderful day.

I should've known it couldn't last; my new life could never be that perfect.

The scenery changed so rapidly, I barely had time to register it. Suddenly, it was dark. People were all around me; we were crouched in a trench of some sort, waiting for something to happen. I wasn't sure what, but it was important. A voice came out of the darkness, so close it made me jump.

"They're up there, all right, the whole lot of 'em. Our spies were right, Calan." The big man next to me nodded. I realized that this time I wasn't Calan, but then who was I?

Calan turned to me. "Molly, I want you to stay here. I couldna bear it if something happened to you, lass." He was speaking to me; I was Molly. His wife? Daughter? I probed Molly's brain for information. Wife, for sure.

"No, Calan, where you go, I go," I spoke to him. He gave me a pained expression but nodded his assent, turned, and spoke to the entire group assembled around us.

"Okay, we move now. The beasties won't be expecting us."

Oh, but they were. The spies Calan entrusted were not just his; they were Theryn's as well. Most of Calan's men were slaughtered instantly, before they even made it into Theryn's lair. Calan bellowed in anger over that final betrayal; it was too much for him. He took Molly and fled Scotland, vowing never to fight again.

Calan was still alive somewhere. I clung to that thought as I saw Theryn flying after them, anger over their escape clear in his coal-black eyes.

I woke screaming.

I fought at first until I realized it was Chase holding on to me and not Theryn come to get me.

"Chans, it's okay. Shush, sweetheart. Chans!"

"Sorry, sorry, Chase, I thought …" I dropped my arms and sagged against him.

"What in the name of God is going on?"

I looked up at my dad. "I had another nightmare, Dad, that's all. No biggie." He had his hands fisted on his hips, and he looked like he wanted to turn Chase into a bug and squash him. "Dad, I'm fine, honest."

"Chandra, I don't think that's why he's upset."

I turned to Chase, wondering what he was talking about. Chase released me and stood; for the first time, I saw what was making my dad angry. Chase had moved his sleeping bag right next to mine, cramming it in between me and the wall of the tent. Confused, I looked at him.

"Chase, why would …"

"Hertha told me about your theory, so after everyone fell asleep, I … uh … I moved my sleeping bag. I guess it was true." He didn't look happy about that; he picked up his stuff and moved it back across the tent on the other side of my dad. Not bothering to get inside his sleeping bag, he dropped down on top of it and flung an arm over his eyes, shutting us out. He was obviously upset about being the cause of my dreams.

"Would someone like to let me in on the big secret?"

I groaned and put my pillow over my head, falling backward, not wanting to answer my father.

"No," I mumbled from beneath my pillow

"Chandra, *now!*"

I came out from under my pillow and sat up again. "Fine, Chase is the cause of my dreams. There, happy? When he doesn't sleep by me, no visions, when he does, visions. Get it?" I stared at my dad, daring him to say something. He looked at Chase, then me.

"What did you see this time?" He said it with a resigned sigh.

I told him about Molly and Calan, the attack, and them fleeing Scotland. That I just knew, somehow, they had to be somewhere out there, that they were still alive.

Chase sat up and stared at me. "*What?!*"

I blinked at him and repeated what I'd just said.

"No … it can't be … *no!*" He stood and quickly left the tent. Dad and I looked at each other, and then followed him out.

He was pacing and frantically dragging his hand through his hair, mumbling to himself.

"Chase, you wanna share with the group?" I said as he paced past me. He stopped and looked at me.

"It can't be. It's gotta be a coincidence, right?" He started pacing again as soon as he had finished speaking. His hair was standing on end, a complete mess; he'd dragged his hand through it so many times.

"CHASE! Will you stop! What is it?"

He took a deep breath and turned to me. "Chandra, my dad's name is Calan and my mom's name is Molly."

I stared at him. No, it couldn't be. If it was, then … Theryn … if he found out. I looked at my dad. He'd been right: Chase *was* Calan's son.

"Dad … what do we do?" I asked a little anxiously. He was staring at Chase—just standing there—like he'd found a long lost friend.

"DAD, SNAP OUT OF IT!"

He shook his head, looking over at me. "Sorry. We need to find the clan here, and then we'll have to find Calan and Molly and get them to Queebo's. If Theryn discovers that Chase isn't adopted, they'll be in danger."

Chase started pacing again. I didn't know how to comfort him. He had just found out that the parents he'd thought weren't his real parents *were* his real parents.

Talk about confusing.

"Wait, Chase, what about your brother and sister, if you're not adopted, what about them?"

He shook his head. "I don't know. I'm the only one who even looks anything like my parents. Shelly and Jason are both blond." I could imagine how out of place Chase must've looked between his two blond-headed siblings with his jet-black hair.

"Dad, the vision I just had, both Molly and Calan, were you know." I gestured lamely; what I had seen of the fight was minimal, it had been a very short-lived fight since Theryn has been expecting them. However, both Calan and Molly had fought with magic. He only nodded at me, staring after Chase where he continued to pace. Since both Molly and Calan were of magical blood, I could only imagine how powerful Chase's magic might possibly be when he finally got his full powers. He could very well be the Chosen instead of me.

"It doesn't mean anything; you could still be the one. You both have unusual powers. You could still be the Chosen, Chandra." My father finally said quietly. Chase had paced himself off several feet by now. I gestured toward Chase helplessly. Dad's shoulders sagged; he nodded in resignation and motioned toward Chase. I hugged him and ran to Chase, wrapped my arms around his waist, hugged him; he hugged me back, resting his chin on top of my head.

"Chans, what do I do? We have to finish what we stared here, but my family … what if Theryn finds out? How do I protect them?" I stood on tiptoes and kissed his neck.

"Chase, your mom and dad can handle themselves. I wouldn't worry about them. We can find the Australian dragons, and then go get your family. Everything will be okay." I couldn't be sure if what I was telling him was true. I knew his parents could handle themselves; I'd seen it.

Dad packed up the camp while Chase and I sat and talked. Dad seemed to have finally accepted that Chase and I were going to be together. I wondered if the fact that Calan was Chase's dad had anything to do with it.

Fredrick stood for a minute and watched Chandra and Chase together; he felt defeated and turned away. He hadn't told Chandra the whole truth about Merlin's prophecy. He'd never truly trusted Merlin; the old coot tended to twist things to suit his purposes. He looked back at the kids, their heads close together, talking softly. He sighed; Meredith would think it was wonderful that Chandra had fallen in love. He grimaced, she was too young for that sort of thing; she had her whole life ahead of her, if the wyvern didn't get in the way. He still worried over the spot in Chase's mind as well.

He went and started packing things up. They had dragons to search for; as long as they were up, they might as well be on their way. He thought of the prophecy again. It made more sense now, he supposed, if you considered Chase as part of the equation. He remembered the day he'd first heard Merlin's prophecy. His father had told the whole of it to him. He hadn't paid much attention to the thing before that day.

The words were inscribed on his brain; he would never forget them.

A child will be born of magic blood, a chosen child with powers beyond those we can imagine. This child will save all of dragon-kind and destroy the wyvern. Beware, those who would seek this child for their own fortune, for there is more to it than the words I first spoke. The magic is powerful, yes, it is true, but its secret I cannot reveal. A half of a whole, a piece of a part, two make one. In the darkness first, then the light, a child lost whose home is right. When this riddle you solve, the power of the wyvern will dissolve.

He understood it now. Chase was the answer to the riddle. The other half of the whole. He made Chandra whole; he was her other piece. He'd been in the dark when he was Theryn's prisoner; now he was in the light, free. Chase had thought he was adopted, lost, but he was in the right place all along. The riddle was solved. There wasn't a Chosen Child—there were two. Chandra and Chase together made the Chosen possible. It was a riddle, all right. Chandra may have been meant to be the Chosen, but without Chase, it wouldn't be possible. Chase was the key to unlocking the potential for the prophecy. Without him completing Chandra, the whole thing meant nothing. Fredrick ground his teeth. Merlin's prophecy—*bah*, more like a trick. Now that Chase and Chandra were together, they could dissolve the power of the wyvern. He knew it wouldn't be so easy to defeat the wyvern. He finished clearing the camp, and then went to get the kids—it was time to get going.

CHAPTER 17

Viva Las Vegas

All three of us were pretty quiet as we searched for the last clan—we had a lot to think about.

Chase was trying to locate the dragons, while keeping his mind off of his family. I knew he was still worried about them. I wished I could make him feel better about everything. While Chase was giving directions to my dad, I watched as the sun came up over the horizon and lit up the landscape below.

I was trying to keep from worrying about Chase, worrying about his family. And my dad? I couldn't tell you what was on his mind, I wasn't privy to his thoughts, but whatever they were they had to be deep. His brow was deeply furrowed and he kept mumbling things to himself and shaking his head.

Chase kept redirecting the dragons until we finally left the coast of Australia all together and headed to the little island of Tasmania. I grinned as I pictured the *Looney Toons* guy. It's a beautiful island, though. I'd always wanted to visit Australia, my room had always been plastered with posters and magazine articles about both Australia and Tasmania. I knew for a fact that Tasmania was one-quarter national parks. I supposed that it would be a decent place for the dragons; at least the land couldn't be developed inside a national park.

Chase found a likely cave relatively near one of the coastlines. He sensed something he thought was more likely to be qualified as a clan of dragons.

We entered the cave, flying in through a tunnel entrance, which was much shorter than any of the others we'd encountered thus far.

The smallest clan of dragons, containing only five dragons, greeted us but they were the most carefree by far. Their leader was Garoo, a rust-colored, jovial dragon.

"G'day, mates, welcome! What brings ya to our little island paradise?" Dad stood there blinking at Garoo. I giggled. He wasn't exactly what one might expect a dragon leader to be; he certainly didn't behave like a dragon leader. Garoo looked past my father to where I stood.

"Pray tell, little Sheila, what exactly should the expected behavior of a dragon leader be?" I ran down the list of dragons that I knew in my mind, discarding Menkaura right away as he skipped through. Honestly, he was just to annoying even to consider. Garoo chuckled and shouted across the cave to a red-orange dragon. "Hey Maka, you remember that time we tied those empty tin cans to Menkaura's tail?"

The red-orange dragon came forward, laughing uncontrollably. "Yeah, that was bonzer, Garoo! I really miss that stuffy bloke."

I couldn't help it I laughed out loud. These dragons didn't strike me as the serious type.

Garoo gave me a huge toothy grin. "I like you, little Sheila."

I smiled back at him; as soon as I could stop laughing, I spoke. "Thank you, Garoo. I like you, too." Dad sent me a cool look. I stuck my tongue out at him, causing Garoo to laugh some more. Dad stepped forward and spoke up.

"Garoo, we came here on a mission. We're seeking out whatever clans we can find; we believe that the wyvern are preparing for the final battle against the dragons."

Garoo considered my dad for a moment. His gaze flicked over to Chase, pinning him in place with a piercing dragon stare. "What about you, bloke? You've been awfully quiet."

Garoo seemed like he rather enjoyed putting everyone on the spot. Chase reddened when Garoo put him in the spotlight;

however, he spoke up immediately. "Fredrick is right, the wyvern are preparing for a large-scale battle. Theryn has developed a spell to speed the hatching of the wyvern eggs. He hasn't mastered a spell to catch up their mental development, however. They tend to be … uh, a little immature on occasion."

Dad looked distressed at Chase's revelation. It was the first time Chase had spoken so openly about his time with the wyvern. I was glad he finally seemed able to speak about it some. Garoo sat more upright, his face grim.

"All right mates, I think the wyvern have been 'round too long anyway. It's 'bout time they cark it."

Chase blinked at Garoo's words, and then looked at me. I shrugged. Garoo smirked. He seemed amused by our confusion.

"Translation for our American friends, cark it—shuffle off this mortal coil, pushin' up the daisies, kick the bucket, the eternal stare, bought the farm, bit the big one, dead as a doornail, worm food, quit this world, snuffed it, been liquidated."

My father rolled his eyes. "Thank you. I think we get it, Garoo. Cark it means die." Dad obviously didn't find Garoo as humorous as I did.

Garoo winked at me. "No problem, mate, anytime. Now tell us where, and we'll be there, ready to fight."

Dad sagged with relief. Garoo was a happy-go-lucky dragon, but I could see he was serious when it came to talk about fighting the wyvern.

He invited us to stay for the day to rest and eat. We agreed to stay until nightfall. Dad asked Garoo to carry a message back to Queebo at the Grand Canyon. We would need assistance once we found Chase's family. Echo and Hertha wouldn't be able to carry us all back home to the Grand Canyon. When it was time to sleep, Chase thought it best if I got a good night's—or day's—rest. He slept apart from me. I wondered if we would ever be able to sleep near each other without me having a whacked-out vision.

When it came time to leave, we bid farewell to Garoo and his clan. We would see them again when we returned to the Grand

Canyon. First, we had to find Chase's family in order to get them to safety.

We left Australia behind, heading for Chase's home in Nevada, with the hope that his family hadn't left there, praying they had stayed put, waiting for him to return home. I was shocked to find out that Chase and I had lived only about an hour apart from each other. In the same state all along, but we never knew it; so close yet so far apart. While Chase's parents had chosen Las Vegas to settle in, my mother had chosen little, out-of-the-way, no-wheres-ville Boulder City. I had to admit it, I was jealous. Chase shrugged it off.

"Chans, trust me, Vegas is no big deal. It kinda sucks, especially if you're a teenager. There's, like, nothing to do. Practically everything there is for adults." He shrugged.

"Trust *me,* Chase, Vegas is probably *waaay* more interesting than Boulder City any day!"

He held up his hands in surrender. "Okay, fine, you win. I give up!"

"At least you know when to surrender, Magic Boy!"

Our good-natured arguing continued throughout the rest of the flight. Dad wanted to fly straight through till we reached Nevada; the dragons agreed. Chase had sensed something he couldn't identify following in our wake. Dad feared it could be Theryn or his nasty minions.

As it was we had lost four months already in travel time, even with Dad's spells to assist us. I couldn't believe that much time had passed. We were all getting pretty tired by the time Nevada came into sight. I voted for a long nap. I was outvoted; such is my luck. They were all anxious to find Calan and Molly and get home.

Chase wanted to know his family was all right. Dad wanted to see his old friend again. When we arrived, Hertha and Echo flew off to meet the others that Queebo had sent to aid in our return home at the spot they had designated.

Chase stood nervously at the end of the walkway that led up to his family's front door. He hadn't been here in over two years.

"Chase, just go ring the bell. If they're not here, we can just say sorry, wrong house."

He gave me a pained look. "I just … I don't know what to say to them if they are still here."

"How about, *Hey, I'm home. Sorry it took so long, but the wyvern got me.*"

He smiled at me, hugged me, and took a deep breath. We all walked up the walkway together. I ended up having to ring the bell. I figured if I didn't do it, we would've stood there all night.

The woman who answered the door was short, with bright red hair and brilliant green eyes. She wasn't exactly plump, yet she wasn't slim, either. She was earthy, real.

It was Molly. I knew her the minute I saw her, even though I hadn't actually ever seen her face. She threw herself at Chase, hugging him and dragging him in through the open door.

"Chase! My baby! You're home! Calan! Get in here! Chase is here! He's home! My baby is home!" She screamed, while hugging him and sobbing. I wondered how she'd recognized Chase on sight. I mean, okay, it had only been two years. Could he really not have changed that much? Then I remembered my dad saying how much Chase reminded him of Calan.

"Mom … Mom, calm down … I'm fine … Mom, you're choking me!" I could tell Chase wanted to hug his mom just as tightly as she was hugging him, maybe cry, too; he was trying hard not to. I didn't know if it was because we were there or because he didn't want to encourage his mom.

It made me feel that we were intruding on a very private moment. I was just wondering if maybe we should wait outside when I saw Calan come through the doorway from the adjacent room. His eyes widened when he saw Chase standing there. Then his eyes lit on my dad, standing just behind Chase and to his left a bit. He barreled through Chase and Molly to get to my dad.

"FREDRICK! YOU TOOK MY SON! AND YOU DARE TO HAVE THE NERVE TO SHOW YOUR FACE IN MY HOME!" I screamed when Calan hit my dad at a run. He was a big guy; like linebacker big, or a pro wrestler. He had to be like six-foot-three, at least. He had the muscles to back up the build, too. He threw Dad through the wall. *Through* the wall. Plaster and debris rained down as they disappeared into the room on the other side of the now-ruined wall. I had to wonder if he backed up that tackle with magic.

"*Dad!*" Chase bellowed at his father. I screamed and jumped over the debris, trying to find where they had landed. Chase was faster; he beat me there. Chase was still calling out to his dad.

"Dad, stop it! Fredrick didn't take me! Dad, it wasn't Fredrick! It was the wyvern!"

Calan stopped with his fist raised, ready to punch my dad in the face. I ran to my dad, sobbing.

"What did you say, son?" Calan stood slowly and went to Chase.

"Fredrick saved me, Dad, he didn't take me; it was the wyvern. You should've warned me, Dad. Given me some clue, so I would've been prepared. I was prisoner for two years."

Calan turned away from Chase, toward us. I was crying; my dad was covered with injuries and blood. Calan was a lot stronger than my dad; his size alone gave him the advantage. My dad hadn't fought back; he wouldn't fight his friend, no matter the provocation. He had several broken bones. Calan had gotten in a few good punches before Chase could stop him. Calan reached for my arm to pull me up. I shook his hand off. Anger and worry for my dad made my voice shake.

"Don't touch me! Leave me alone! He's hurt! I have to help him!"

Calan looked to Chase for help, unsure what to do with the hysterical teenage girl before him. Chase came to my side, crouching down next to me, putting his hands on my shoulders to get my attention.

"Chans, it's okay. We can help him."

I looked at Chase. I knew I could heal my father, but I was too upset at the moment to concentrate. I let Chase lead me away. Calan lifted my dad and carried him into the living room, gently laying him on the sofa. Molly hovered over my dad, doing the healing spells needed to fix the damage done by her husband.

Chase and I stood back and watched; he held me in his arms. I was still upset by what had happened. Calan waited for Molly to finish, and then he went to sit by my father.

"Fredrick, I'm sorry. You dinna deserve that."

Dad gave a shaky nod. I noticed that Calan's brogue only came out when he was emotional, and only in bits and pieces here and there. I supposed he tried hard to leave it behind. The accent would only help to give him away.

"It's okay, Calan. I suppose I would've reacted much the same if Chandra had been taken. Though, I doubt I would've been able to do as much damage to you." They both shared a chuckle. Calan took a deep breath and looked at my dad.

"It's good to see you, my friend. I must confess; I had no idea you were even still around." He clapped my dad on the back as he sat up beside Calan. Dad winced but smiled.

"I thought much the same of you, Calan." Dad looked to where Chase and I stood together, and he sighed.

"Calan much has happened. We need to get you and your family out of here immediately, *all* of you. I have so much to tell you."

Calan frowned at my father. "Fredrick, that's going to take some time to do, Shelly is at college, Jason has a basketball game this evening."

"Calan, dear, it won't take long at all, you know Shelly's been prepared for this since Chase was taken. All I have to do is call her; she'll be here in no time at all, and Jason should be home any minute now."

Calan shifted his frown to Molly. "That girl has always been too bright for her own good."

Chase spoke up then. "Wait, Shelly *knows*?"

Calan gave a deep sigh and a nod. "The girl has the Sight. No magical abilities to speak of, but she always knew what you were, Chase. What we all were. It's one of the reasons we adopted her."

Chase frowned at his father. "And Jason?"

Calan chuckled. "Nope, Jason is just, Jason. Let's just say, your mother was feeling maternal. So there's Jason for you."

Molly whacked her husband on the arm. "Calan Ivers, take that back this instant! Jason is as much our son as Chase is! He's part of this family!"

Calan grinned as he stood and grabbed Molly around the waist, hauling her into his arms, giving her a kiss, and then releasing her. She stepped back, patting at her hair and flushing a red to match her hair. It was easy to see that Chase's parents loved each other very much.

"I'll go call Shelly," Molly said before whisking off to the kitchen; we could hear her dialing the phone. Calan eyed the two of us, still standing close together.

"So, Chase, are you going to introduce me to your friend?"

Chase turned red, pulling his fingers through his hair. "Dad, this is Chandra, Fredrick's daughter," I frowned up at him. He slid his hand through his hair again. "My, uh, girlfriend." He seemed extraordinarily nervous about telling his father I was his girlfriend. I gave Calan a big fat grin.

"It's nice to meet you, sir."

He raised an eyebrow and looked at my dad, who shrugged. "I told you a lot had happened, Calan."

Before Calan could say anything, we heard the sound of the front door opening, followed by a loud slam. A voice sounded from the front hall.

"I'm home! Hey, what happened to the wall? Oh, man, why's it always my room that gets messed up?!"

Chase laughed. He looked down at me, a big grin on his face. "That's Jason."

Jason came through the archway into the living room. He was the opposite of Chase. Although he would have some height someday, at fifteen, he was much shorter than his brother, though he matched me at five-foot-four. His hair was a dusky blond, short and spiked. His eyes were a bright shining blue, pure, clean, and perfect. He would definitely be a good-looking guy, if you could get past the smart-ass attitude.

"Dad, what happened to my room? Aww man … Chase?! Is that you? Jeez, you got tall! And huge!" Jason did have a point; Chase was on the large side. He would be just as big as Calan if he gained any more muscle.

"Yeah, runt, it's me. How ya been, kiddo?"

Jason ran at his brother, full speed. Chase dropped his arm from around me and caught his brother in a hug.

"Jeez, Chase, where'd you go? Mom was pissed! She wouldn't let me out of the house by myself for, like, ever! And Shelly cried for like months! It was the worst!" As he stepped away from Chase, Jason spotted me. He stared. I had the distinct impression he was trying to figure out what I looked like without clothes on. I crossed my arms over my chest. "Hey, who's the babe?"

Chase burst out laughing. "The 'babe' is my girlfriend, so paws off, runt."

Jason looked disappointed, but then he grinned. "She got a sister?"

Chase rolled his eyes and shook his head at Jason. Calan chuckled at his sons.

"Jason, come with me. I need to tell you a few things, and we need to pack; we're going on a trip."

I watched father and younger son leave the room. "Please tell me you were nothing like him when you were fifteen!" I said, throwing a look at Chase.

"Hey, I taught him everything he knows!"

I slapped him across the chest and went to sit by my dad on the couch. Molly came back out of the kitchen.

"Did I hear Jason out here?"

Chase nodded at his mother. "Dad took him to what was left of his room to explain and pack."

"Shelly is on her way. She was already packed, ready to go. She said it would only take her a few minutes to get here. I hope she doesn't go and get a speeding ticket racing over here. She was excited to hear you were back, Chase."

Chase looked nervous about seeing his sister again. Their fight was the reason he was taken. If they hadn't fought, he never would've been out walking on the ridge. He walked over and plopped down next to me, throwing his arm over my shoulders. I rested my head against him.

Molly prattled on about anything and everything, telling us all about Shelly's college courses. How she hadn't picked a major because she was just so sure Chase would show up any time, and they would have to leave anyway, so why bother? She talked about how she'd kept Chase's room exactly how he'd left it. Chase laughed.

"Mom, I was fifteen. I seriously doubt any of my clothes will still fit me. I've grown just a bit, as you can see."

She shrugged. "Well, all your things are still there, dear, if you want to get anything before we leave."

Chase smiled excitedly, jumping up to go to his room. I tagged along. I wanted to see what fifteen-year-old Chase had been into.

No surprises: It was a typical fifteen-year-old boy's room, posters of rock bands and some swimsuit models. The only differences were his drawings on the wall.

"Did you draw these?"

He looked up from the desk drawers he was rummaging through. "Yeah, when I was twelve, I think. I drew the other ones on the wall over there, too." He thrust his chin in the direction of the drawings on the opposite wall. My eyes widened. He really was a good artist, even when he was younger.

"They're great, Chase."

He shrugged. He was very casual about his drawing abilities. He gathered up a bunch of art stuff and packed it into an old backpack. I saw him toss some other things from a dresser drawer in, too, but I was too interested in his drawings to pay much attention to exactly what it was he was packing. He looked around the room with a small smile.

"I missed this room a lot while I was stuck in that cage at Theryn's."

I hugged him. I would bet it wasn't just the room he had missed, but the house and everything and everyone in it.

We went back to the living room, Molly was still telling stories to my dad. Chase grimaced when he heard her telling my dad about the time he and Shelly had convinced Jason that there was an evil creature living in the hall closet. Jason hadn't gone near the closet for a whole five months.

Suddenly, Jason came hurtling back into the room. "Chase, is it true? Are you really a sorcerer? Can you do magic? Hey, can you turn Brad Mennins into a cockroach? He's such a jerk!"

I started laughing. Chase grinned at his little brother.

"No, Jason, I can't turn Brad into anything. I'm still training. Not that I would turn him into anything, if I could."

"Aww ... come on. He's the biggest—I mean it—*the biggest jerk* ever! He held Mark down the other day and shaved a D into his hair; he said it was for Dork. Poor Mark had to go get his whole head shaved!"

I was dying laughing. I couldn't help it; the kid was funny. Chase rolled his eyes.

"Jason, Mark will live; his hair will grow back. Besides, Brad is an idiot; he'll probably work at some fast food joint the rest of his life."

Jason folded his arms over his chest and gave Chase a look that said, *That's the same thing Dad said.* The front door opened and slammed shut once again, and Shelly breezed into the room.

Shelly Ivers was not what I had expected. She was the girl every other teenage girl loathed, feared, and yet wanted to be. She was the perky blonde captain of the cheer squad you can't help but hate and yet yearned to be exactly like in your weaker moments.

She was tiny—I mean it, *tiny*, about four-foot-eleven, if that. Thin as a swimsuit model. Her hair was a wonderful coppery blond color filled with a mixture of sun-blended highlights, and her eyes—good lord, any other woman would kill for her eyes. Maybe a few guys would, too. They weren't exactly blue; they were sorta aquamarine, water-around-the-Great-Barrier-Reef blue, if that makes any sense at all.

She squealed when she saw Chase and grabbed his face in her hands, squishing his cheeks like someone's eighty-year-old grandmother would. I'm not even sure exactly how she even managed to reach his cheeks, as short as she was. Despite her very perky cheerleader-ish voice, when she spoke, you just knew this was not some dumb blond standing before you.

"Chase! Oh, thank goodness you're safe! I've been beating myself up since you went missing!" She was alternating between hugging the life out of him and holding him back so she could look at him. When she hugged him and he hugged her back, I felt the great big evil green jealously monster try to rip its way out through my chest. I knew to Chase, Shelly would and could only ever be his big sister, even though they weren't technically related. That didn't stop me from being jealous of her. She was just so gorgeous; it was hard *not* to be jealous of her.

"Shell, it's okay, don't worry. It took both of us to argue. It wasn't your fault."

Her shoulders sagged as she dropped into a chair. "No, Chase, it was all me. I started the fights because I knew, and I was so jealous." She gave him a sad look. "I knew what you were going to be one day. What I couldn't ever be and it made me mad. I let it get to me. I was being a dumb kid. Can you ever forgive me?"

Chase frowned at her. "Shelly, what do you mean?"

She took a deep breath, like she was preparing to tell something she'd been keeping a secret for a very long time. "I knew you were going to have powers from the first day I laid eyes on you, Chase. I knew that Mom and Dad were sorcerers. As I got older, I realized that even though I could see these things—that was the only thing that was special about me, and I didn't think it was that big a deal." She shrugged.

Chase smiled and hugged her. "It's okay, Shelly, I think I probably would've felt the same way, though I would've been a lot meaner than you were."

She laughed and hugged him. As she released him, she leaned back and studied him. "Your aura is, like … wow, Chase, way brighter than it used to be. Did you get your full powers already?"

"Some, but I'll get my full powers when I turn eighteen."

She grinned at him. "Well, what are we waiting for, then? Let's get going!"

I stood up as Shelly did. Her eyes swung over to my dad and me when my movement drew her attention. She gasped and froze in the process of standing up. I looked down at myself—what was wrong with me?

"Wow!"

I looked at her and blinked. Wow? She was saying wow about me. Had she looked into a mirror lately?

"Chase, who's she? Her aura is ... like, *wow* ... I mean, yours is like ... but hers ... blows yours out of the water!"

I looked at Chase. He shrugged and turned to his dad, who had just come back into the room with several suitcases. Calan gave a small chuckle.

"Shelly has figured out that a sorcerer's aura is a great way to measure powers. Apparently, Chandra's is brighter than yours, Chase."

I gave Chase a smug grin. *Take that, Magic Boy.* He lunged at me, and I dodged him, running; he chased me around the living room. Still grinning, I transformed into a canary to make my escape.

"Not fair, Chans! Get down here so I can catch you!"

I fluttered to the floor and changed back. "You lose!" I stuck my tongue out at him. I turned around to find his whole family grinning at me. I blushed.

Dad cleared his throat. "I think it's time we left, everyone."

We piled into Molly Ivers' minivan and drove to a nearby park with an immense soccer field. The dragons melted out of the darkness.

"Awesome!" Jason said in a breathless voice. Leave it to Jason to state the obvious. It took some time to secure everyone's luggage, but we were soon on our way.

Dad on Echo, Chase and me on Hertha, Calan and Jason were on the emerald Mocte. Finally, Molly and Shelly rode Galanah, the violet dragon.

It wasn't that far back home to the Grand Canyon, but with Jason screaming out "how totally awesome" this was every five seconds, it seemed a lot longer.

We were about halfway home when the wyvern appeared out of the cloud cover. Chase swore because he hadn't sensed them. With the distraction of his family along, and his brother flinging questions at him, I could guess why he hadn't sensed them.

"Chandra, Chase, help cover Jason and Shelly!"

We nodded at my dad. Jason and Shelly had no powers to speak of, so they couldn't protect themselves. The wyvern didn't stick around long to fight. Once they figured out they were up against more than just my dad and two novice sorcerers, they fled. Having Calan and Molly with us turned out to be a great surprise for the four wyvern.

I'd been looking forward to getting back to the peace and quiet of our cavern home. It had become anything but peaceful and quiet in our absence. With four clans of dragons now living there, it was getting a little crowded, even with its colossal size.

Queebo was glad to see Calan alive and well. She was happy to meet the rest of his family, too, including Chase.

Queebo seemed especially interested in Chase. I didn't know why; she and Dad seemed to share some sort of understanding. I saw a look pass between them as I introduced Chase to her.

Later as I headed off to my room, I walked right into a three-way argument between Chase and our fathers.

"I don't care what either one of you think! It's up to Chandra anyway! We're both almost eighteen so it doesn't matter!" I stopped dead, staring at the three of them. Chase turned to me, relief clear in his eyes.

"Chandra, will you please explain to them that your dreams are important?"

I turned bright red. They were obviously discussing where Chase was going to sleep.

"Dad, you know Chase is right. Every vision I've had has taught us something, even if it was only a small thing."

He folded his arms over his chest, scowling at me. Calan had a similar look for Chase. Calan was most certainly the more intimidating of the two.

"Besides, Chase has a point; in less than a year, we'll both be eighteen. We aren't exactly kids anymore."

They were both still scowling. I glanced at Chase, hoping for some help.

"I'm sleeping in Chandra's room, and that's it."

Well, that wasn't exactly the help I had hoped for. He grabbed my hand and tugged me away toward my room. I sent an apologetic look over my shoulder at both our dads as Chase towed me into my room.

"Are you sure that was a good idea, Chase?"

"Chans, if you don't want me to sleep near you, then just say so."

"Chase, that's not what I meant. I'm just not sure making enemies of our dads is a good idea."

He wrapped his arms around me and grinned. "They'll get over it, eventually."

I smiled. He was right, but I knew they wouldn't like it. "So, Magic Boy, where exactly *were* you planning on sleeping?"

He laughed and kissed the tip of my nose. "I think in order to keep the peace, we'll find me a nice little bed of my own to move in here. I don't want to push our dads too close to the edge."

"Smart idea, Magic Boy."

That's exactly what we did. Chase found a bed back in Mom's room of extra furnishings and put it on the far side of the room. The dads had decided we could move it closer, foot by foot, if I didn't have any dreams, until Chase was close enough for me to have a vision. The two of us had reluctantly agreed just to make the dads happy.

To my disappointment, moving Chase closer wasn't necessary. I dreamed just fine, even with him across the room from me. Though I would've preferred the comfort of having him closer—a lot closer.

Especially after what I saw that first night.

CHAPTER 18

I Become The Nightmare

Uncontrollable rage—anger unlike anything I'd ever felt before in my life. Whoever I was in this vision was very, very angry. I didn't like it. I struggled with the hatred; it was all consuming. I was flying; that's all I had to tell me who I was at the moment. I hadn't a single clue other than that. I swooped lower toward a stream to drink the cool, clear water. I stopped and glanced at my reflection; anger screamed through my brain again. I shrank from the reflection, tried to tear myself from the vision.

No! It couldn't be. Not this—I didn't want to see this! Wake up already! I didn't wake up. I was resigned to the fact, that I was, for whatever reason, Theryn. Okay, that's it, I was definitely *not* going to refer to myself as Theryn—nope, no way! I was separating myself from that monster right off the bat!

I understood the rage now, Theryn; no wonder. I felt the anger, the hatred over what he was, what he had become. Was this just after he'd been turned into the wyvern? Theryn took flight again, soaring over the earth. A sudden scream from the landscape below alerted him to the fact that he was flying much too low. Some villagers had spotted him, even in the darkness. They panicked at the sight of the strange, terrifying beast flying over their tiny village. His rage renewed, brighter, and more horrifying, than before. Renewed anger over what he had become. Over what had been done to him. I saw it in his mind, the little sorcerer and the spell that had turned him into this beast. His resentment and the raw fury burned brightly inside him.

I knew what he was going to do. I shrank back and tried to hide, I couldn't hide from the terror I saw, not while I occupied Theryn's brain and saw through his eyes. He destroyed the entire village, killed everyone. Ripping and tearing, destroying everything and everyone. Using his new form exceedingly well, finding it easy to use the new weapons provided by his new body to destroy those around him. So much blood and carnage; I shuddered, trying to tear myself from the vision.

Why did I have to see this? I already knew he was a monster. Why show this to me?

After the carnage he'd wrought was over, he stood back and surveyed the outcome of his temper. The destruction was total, the carnage gruesome, the village a blood-soaked maze of debris. He still remembered what he had been though; he couldn't hide from that, couldn't forget *who* he had been. It tore at his heart and mind to have done such destruction to those who had once trusted him so, who had looked to him for guidance and protection, for wisdom. For leadership. He flew off and hid in the mountains, away from everyone, everything. Away from the destruction that he had brought to pass. He had planned to stay there till he died, alone in his misery.

His shame.

If it hadn't been for *her*, he would have succeeded in his attempt at suicide.

I recognized her on sight. The sorceress from the clearing in that memory I had seen in Queebo's mind. I wished I could tell Theryn she was evil, but this was something that had already happened. I couldn't change it, as much as I wished to.

Her name was Esemer. She acted like she was his friend, like she was there to help him, care for him. She befriended him and nursed him back to health. She stayed there with him in the mountains, never once betraying her true nature. She was patient with him, despite her desperation to win him to her cause. Then, finally one day, she began her plans to take over, to defeat the dragons.

First, she had to take over Theryn. The only way she could do that was to make him forget, forget who he had been, what he had been.

"I can make the pain go away, Theryn," Her voice was soft, cajoling. "I know a spell. I can make you forget it all. It's very simple." Her hands stroked his large head between those great horns of his softly, as she spoke. Reassuring him that she was his friend and that she cared for him, was only trying to ease his pain. It took her weeks to talk Theryn into it. Despite her eagerness to destroy the dragons, she was patient; she took her time breaking him down, convincing him to take her offer. When finally, his pain was too much to bear anymore, he agreed. When the spell was complete, Theryn was a blank slate; all he remembered was that Esemer was his dear friend and that she cared deeply for him. Beyond that, he knew nothing, remembered nothing of his past, who he had been, what he had been before he was Wyvern.

He belonged to her now. She twisted his mind, dragged him down, and made him evil. He now believed that both the dragons and all of mankind were his enemies. Now he wanted the dragons dead as badly as she did. He wanted to kill them all and enslave mankind. It was horrible to watch the two of them planning it all.

More horrible still to watch Esemer use her magic to begin to birth more of his kind. They weren't exact copies of Theryn; they were smaller than he. And not pitch-black; they were a sickly gray color. Nor could they speak English as he did, though Theryn could understand them perfectly. They were still wyvern, standing on two legs as he did, with the bat-like wings and hand-like extensions at the end and, of course, the poisonous tail barb. Inside Theryn's head, I shuddered in revulsion.

Once again, I woke screaming in Chase's arms.

"Chans, honey, it's okay."

I calmed as soon as I heard his voice.

"We have got to stop meeting like this, Magic Boy," I joked.

"Yep, people are gonna start talking." He quipped as he rubbed a hand up and down my back. I really liked the fact that he was continuing to sleep with no shirt on, despite the angry dads sleeping just down the hall from us. I snuggled closer to the warmth of his skin, enjoying the feel of having him so close.

Just then, aforementioned angry dads appeared in the entry to my room, both of them looking none too pleased that Chase was sitting on my bed, holding me in his arms. He sighed, kissed me, just to annoy them, and then got up and went to sit on his bed across the room. He crossed his arms and glared at our dads while I told them about my dream.

Neither was happy about what I'd seen. It did give us new insight into Theryn's mind, however. He'd known who he was after the change, he never would've taken this path if not for Esemer.

They stayed for a while discussing whether or not they thought it was possible for Theryn to be turned back to our side again. My father thought it was much too risky even to try to turn Theryn back. We were better off wiping out the wyvern all together. I shuddered; getting into Theryn's mind was way down on my list of options. Just when I thought I would die of boredom, they finally left, giving us both stern looks on the way out. As soon as they were gone, Chase was back on my bed, I snuggled up to him with a sigh.

"You sure you're okay, Chans? Seeing through Theryn's eyes wouldn't be my first choice of a happy vision. Maybe your dad was right; I shouldn't sleep in here," he said sadly.

I sat up and gave him a pleading look. "*Chaaase,* no! Don't say that! I like having you here." I lay back down. "Besides, it annoys *them.*"

He chuckled, kissing the top of my head. "If the dreams start to bother you, though, I want to know. If they scare you, please tell me."

"I will, Chase, I promise. Now be quiet, Magic Boy, so I can go back to sleep."

His chest rumbled with laughter under my ear. I smiled. My sleep wasn't disturbed again that night; apparently, one vision a night was my limit. I slept peacefully in Chase's arms for the rest of the night. It was a very pleasant way to sleep.

Unfortunately, we were awakened the next morning in a very unpleasant fashion when Calan discovered us in the same bed.

"CHASE MALCOLM IVERS, GET UP THIS INSTANT!"

We both jumped up and out of bed, slightly disoriented, not exactly sure what was wrong. Calan was frowning at us, his face red, hands on his hips.

"Just what do you think you're doing, boy?" His voice was stern.

Chase stared at him. "Up until a minute ago, Dad, sleeping!"

Calan apparently didn't find that funny; his face got redder. "Don't play games with me, boy! We let you get away with sleeping in here for one reason and one reason only! Because of Chandra's visions—not so you two could get all cozy!"

It was Chase's turn to get angry. I could see his temper flare. I knew he had one as bad as his father; I'd seen it before. *Scots,* I thought, rolling my eyes. I sat back down on the bed, not wanting to get between them, figuring it was better if I stayed out of this argument.

"And I told you, there's nothing you can do about it! Chandra and I are almost eighteen! We could get married as soon as we turn eighteen if we wanted to, and there's not a thing you can say about it! So just stay out of our business, Dad!"

I blinked and stared at his back. *Whoa, married? We haven't even discussed that, Magic Boy … slow down a minute.*

He turned and looked at me. I got the feeling from the look he gave me, he'd just yelled out the first thing that had come to mind. However, when I thought about being married to Chase, it didn't sound like a bad thing at all—it sounded kinda wonderful. Apparently, Calan didn't agree.

"MARRIED? MARRIED?! THERE IS NO WAY IN HELL EITHER FREDRICK OR I WOULD EVER ALLOW THAT TO HAPPEN!"

Chase rounded on his dad, yelling loudly. "ALLOW IT! YOU WOULDN'T HAVE A CHOICE! EIGHTEEN, DAD, REMEMBER. WE WOULD BOTH BE ADULTS!"

"We'll see about that, Chase! We'll just see about that!" Calan's voice lowered to a barley controlled snarl. He looked first at Chase, and then me, his glare as cold as a glacier. He turned and stormed out of the room. I flopped back on the bed. Chase was staring at the door his father had just disappeared through.

"I think we're in big trouble." He came and sat next to me.

I groaned. "That, Magic Boy, is an understatement if I ever heard one. Why on earth did you have to go and mention marriage to him?"

He gave me a lopsided grin. "I guess somewhere in the back of my mind, I knew it would piss him off the most." I rolled my eyes. He looked somewhat disappointed. "Why, you wouldn't want to marry me, Chans?"

I smiled and shook my head at him. "Not just to piss off our dads, Chase, no."

"Aha, but if I were to get down on one knee and do it all proper-like, you would say yes?" he asked hopefully.

I blushed. "Yes, Magic Boy, if you did it the right way, with all the right words, I would say yes."

He smiled, jumped up, and sprinted across the room. He went rummaging in the backpack he had brought from his house, and then came back. He got down on one knee. I felt tears rush into my eyes. *Oh, no, Magic Boy, you didn't.* His grin was simply idiotic and adorable.

"Chandra, I know … well, I know that we haven't known each other that long and all … but I think the minute I saw you … God, I sound like an idiot," he muttered and swept a hand through his hair. I giggled.

"You sound perfect, Magic Boy." My voice caught, and my throat felt all closed up.

He cleared his throat, "Chans, I love you more than anything; will you please marry me?" He held out a small black velvet box. Inside was the most beautiful ring I'd ever seen. It was old, very old. Gold with an oval-cut amethyst set in the center instead of a diamond. The band had a sort of twisted pattern to it, so it looked as if it were hugging the amethyst. Smaller, round-cut diamonds were set into the bands that hugged the amethyst in the center.

Tears slid down my cheeks. I couldn't speak, I just nodded, thinking, *Yes, Chase, yes, I will.* He slid the ring on my finger; it fit perfectly. He smiled.

"It was my grandmother's ring. Do you like it?"

I nodded and threw my arms around his neck, hugging him. We shared our first real kiss. It was special, wonderful and, dare I say it, magical. Corny, romantic, and straight out of a sappy romance novel. It was all of that—and ruined when my dad walked into the room.

Our day seemed destined to be a bad one.

"CHANDRA MARIE STRANDON!" He had obviously talked to Calan.

I groaned and let my head fall to Chase's chest, his wonderfully muscular, perfect, bare chest.

"Chandra!" came my father's warning tone from behind me; he had heard my unguarded thought.

Chase stood and took a deep breath. "Sir, I'm sorry, but you and my father are just going to have to get used to the fact that Chandra and I are adults now and start treating us that way. You can't stop us from being together, not now." He glanced back at me briefly before looking at my father again. "I've just ask Chandra to marry me, and she's accepted. Neither one of us want to hear any more talk about us having separate rooms."

My dad's gaze swung over to meet my eyes. I held up the hand with the ring on it, turning my eyes away from his.

"It's true, Dad."

He spluttered, turned, and left. I heard him screaming my mother's name, and then Calan and Molly's names as well. Chase came over and sat back down.

"Maybe it's time we joined everyone else for the day."

I nodded in agreement. I had a feeling it was going to be an extra long day.

I was right. Shelly was excited; she immediately appointed herself a bridesmaid and the talk of dresses, flowers, and wedding dates began. Jason congratulated his brother; he grumbled that he would never have any chance at ever dating me now. I didn't have the heart to tell him he never had a chance in the first place.

Both of our mothers, while professing in front of the dads that we were indeed too young to get married, seemed overjoyed about planning a wedding, all the same. We both knew that our wedding was going to be a while off, possibly years, depending on how long the war with the wyvern lasted.

When we finally got a minute alone, Chase spoke up about the wedding date. "Chans, maybe we should just do it soon—maybe even now, before the war starts. So we can spend as much time together as possible, you know, just in case."

I frowned; I didn't want to think about the *just in case* scenarios. He hugged me close.

"I know, I don't want to think about the *just in case* part, either, sweetheart, but maybe we have to."

It would seem I couldn't hide my thoughts from him. I told him I would think about it. We decided to spend the day away from magic practice for once. The dragons had all found out about Chase's drawing abilities, much to his discomfort. They had all decided that the greatest treasure they could possess at the moment was a drawing of themselves done by Chase. I sat and leaned back against one of the dragon's nests, watching Chase, surrounded by a group of dragons.

As I watched, he reached back and smacked Mocte on the nose with his pencil as the dragon leaned in and started critiquing the drawing he was doing of Mocte's mate, Amireth.

"Chase seems quite popular. I do think they are all acting like children, however."

I laughed and looked up at Queebo. "Only because Chase has already done your drawing."

She lay down next to me, smiling. "Perhaps that is so, my dear. Has your father talked to the both of you yet?"

"Queebo, my father won't talk to either of us, unless it has to do with lessons." I waggled the ring on my finger at her.

She chuckled and gave me a knowing look. "Well, I told him this morning he must, but I suppose I will have to do it, then." She shook her head. "That man is stubborn; I will give him that. It is time you both were told the prophecy."

"Queebo, my dad already told it to me, the first night I got here."

She shook her head. "No, Chandra, he only told you part of it. It's time you heard the whole thing." She took a deep breath and repeated the entire prophecy. I stared at her wide-eyed when she had finished.

"Whoa, that's a mouthful. What does it mean, exactly?"

"No one knew, until now. Your father figured it out when he saw the two of you together. There never was a Chosen Child, not really. Together, you and Chase make up the Chosen. Your powers work together. It was destined to be, Chandra. One cannot exist without the other. You see, you are each half of the other's whole. Chase was the one in the darkness, now in the light. Lost, but not really. Do you understand? The two of you together will defeat the wyvern's power, defeat the wyvern utterly."

I nodded, looking toward Chase; he was laughing at something Mocte had said. I wondered what he would say when I told him about the prophecy.

Maybe he was right—maybe it would be better if we got married right away, *just in case*. I suddenly felt as if the whole weight of the world were on my shoulders.

That night, Chase and I decided to heck with separate beds— the dads could fume silently if they wanted to. Chase figured if we were going to get married anyway, we might as well share a bed. My dad hit the roof when he saw Chase removing his bed from our room.

"Where do you think you're going with that, young man?" His look was stern, his arms folded across his chest.

I groaned. "Dad, if Chase and I are going to get married, what difference does it make?"

He kept his eyes on Chase when he answered. "You're not married yet, Chandra."

"*Daaad!*"

"Chans, let it be. Fredrick, Chandra and I are going to be sleeping in the same bed, that's it. We aren't going to be, uh …" Chase turned red. He didn't seem able to complete his thought.

Chase and I had discussed our wedding plans, and we decided to go the old-fashioned route, and consummating of, uh, stuff, would wait until we were married. I blushed now, too. Having this conversation with my dad wasn't high on my list of things I most wanted to do.

"Dad, Chase and I have decided to wait for ... um ... you know ... *that* until after we're married."

Dad was still frowning at us. I sighed and hid my face in my hands; God, this was embarrassing. "Dad, no baby-making stuff, get it? You know, no, um ... S-E-X."

He still looked as if he didn't believe us, but he grunted and walked away.

"God that was the most embarrassing conversation ever." I was sure my cheeks were flaming red.

Chase laughed. "Yeah, it was up there on the list."

I wondered how Calan would take the news when my dad told him. Chase winced when he caught my thoughts.

"I'd rather not think about that right now, Chans thanks!"

I smirked. *You're welcome, Magic Boy!*

We got his bed out of the room. Chase was so happy, he couldn't stop grinning. The moms had helped us find a larger bed back in the storage area, so we removed my old bed as well and replaced it. The moms seemed happy to help us with whatever we needed, as long as the dads weren't around to see it. I was glad when everything was finally done. I flopped back on the new queen-sized bed and sighed. The new bed was pushed up against the wall off to the right as you walked into the room. Chase grinned down at me.

"Well, finally done, ready for bed?" He gave me an evil grin and waggled his eyebrows at me.

I burst out laughing. "You know, Magic Boy, you need serious work on that evil grin. Theryn would be disappointed in you." He lunged at me; I made a halfhearted attempt at escape. Chase trapped me, holding me down playfully.

"So, now what? I win, you're my prisoner."

I smiled up at him. "Well now, I don't know ... hmmm ... will you let me go if I give you a kiss, Mr. Evil Sorcerer?"

"Nope, sorry, never." I giggled at him. Chase was smiling, his dimple showing. Slowly, he leaned down and touched his lips to mine. We were in the middle of one of those wonderfully passionate kisses, my mind a total fog, when his dad cleared his throat from the doorway. Chase looked up at his father. Calan looked distinctly uncomfortable. Chase arched an eyebrow at his father.

"Dad?"

His dad dragged a hand through his hair. "Sorry, son … uh … I just wanted to … let you and Chandra know that … uh … . Fredrick and I … were … uh …"

"Spit it out, Dad."

His dad ran his hand through his hair again. I smiled when I saw that unconscious gesture. Chase had definitely gotten that trait from his dad, all right. Chase frowned down at me. I guessed he had caught that thought and didn't like me comparing him with his father right at that moment. Calan rushed out his words, obviously uncomfortable seeing his son in an intimate position with his girlfriend. I wondered why. After all, it had made him angry before. Why would he be uncomfortable now instead of screaming at us? Dads were so weird!

"We wanted to teach the two of you something new later tonight. Set your alarm for midnight. Meet us out on the ledge."

"All right, Dad. See, was that so hard?" Chase said with a little smirk. His dad frowned, turned quickly, and left. I grinned up at Chase. He sighed heavily, staring down at me for a minute. He looked disappointed that we had been interrupted.

"I guess we had better get some sleep, then."

We got up reluctantly. Chase left the room so I could change. Another of our agreements: no seeing each other in the buff until after we were married, sort of to avoid temptation and all. I was particularly glad about this arrangement, because I still wasn't sure how Chase was going to feel about the scar on my chest. I was self-conscious about it, not because it was ugly, but because it might remind him of when Theryn had been in his head.

Chase came back a few minutes later; he had gone and changed into a pair of sweatpants and a T-shirt. As soon as he came into the room, he dragged the shirt off over his head and flung it on the floor. I smiled; he was so accommodating, knowing how much I loved that bare chest of his. I'm such a girl. I snuggled up to him and laid my head on his chest, listening to his heartbeat. We fell asleep just like that. I figured it was worth whatever horrible vision I had just to be that close to him.

Maybe I was wrong ...

CHAPTER 19

Dream Shared

I knew this place … it was the rim of the canyon. But I was still
me—at least, I think I thought I was. I looked down at myself. I
was wearing my pajamas. Weird, I'd never had a vision like this
before. I'd always been someone in the vision, except for that first
one I'd had when I had touched Queebo. I looked around; it was
dark and quiet. The ridge was empty; it must be very late. I heard
footsteps then. I looked toward the sound. I gasped and put my
hand over my mouth.

Oh no, it couldn't be.

A hand fell on my shoulder, and I jumped. I turned around to
see who it was.

"Chase? How?"

He shook his head, shrugging his shoulders. He was staring at
the boy walking down the rim of the canyon toward us.

I looked back toward the boy. I knew him, yet I didn't. It was
fifteen-year-old Chase, leaving his family's hotel room in anger. We
followed him down to the rim of the canyon. He didn't see us, or
couldn't. He was walking, head down, hands in the pockets of his
jeans. I wished I could yell at him to go back. I gave my Chase a
pained look. He reached out and grabbed my hand, squeezing it.
We knew what was going to happen, yet it was still a shock when
the wyvern's huge form melted out of the darkness behind fifteen-
year-old Chase and scooped him up, carrying him away. We were
swept along with the wyvern and the other Chase. He was terrified;
his eyes huge, his mouth open in a soundless scream.

I looked at my Chase; he wasn't looking at himself. Instead, he was scanning the ground. I realized he was memorizing the route to Theryn's lair. We would finally know where it was.

Chase couldn't remember; he had been too terrified that night to notice where the wyvern was taking him. Even after, Theryn had done something to keep him from remembering where the lair was, despite the fact that Chase had been in and out of it many times since his arrival. Chase just couldn't seem to remember where it was.

All too soon, they were headed down to a cave. The wyvern dropped Chase, none to gently, to the ground. He skinned his knees and scraped his hands. The wyvern dragged him upright and shoved him forward, down a narrow tunnel. I looked to my Chase.

"To Theryn's throne room," he whispered. I nodded, showing that I understood.

It looked much like the throne room Elandra had been in, same throne, same sized dais, just a different cave, different country. Fifteen-year-old Chase refused to kneel. The wyvern that had brought him forced him to his knees in front of Theryn. Theryn gave the younger Chase a disdainful look and spoke to the wyvern that had brought him.

"Good, you found him again. Where?"

The wyvern spoke in a guttural language of barks and grunts. Theryn was the only wyvern that spoke English. We could only assume it was because he'd been a dragon before he was a wyvern. His counterparts were simply mere shadows of Theryn, imperfect carbon copies. Theryn then turned his penetrating gaze to Chase.

"Well, boy, we finally meet face-to-face. What's your name?"

Chase stared at Theryn, silent.

"Speak, boy! I assume you can speak; you are not ignorant!"

Chase straightened his spine stiffening. "No, I'm not. I can talk, I choose not to. I don't talk to strange *things* that kidnap me in the middle of the night."

I had to admit he was brave. I wouldn't have spoken to Theryn like that; I would've been scared stiff. My Chase squeezed my hand, understanding my thoughts. Theryn stood and began to pace around fifteen-year-old Chase—a looming shadow of doom, pacing around him, trying to intimidate him.

"I wouldn't be so cocky, *boy*. Do you think your powers are a match for mine, then? Has your father or mother taught you so much, *boy*? Are you truly the Chosen? Is that why you are so confident, *boy*?"

Fifteen-year-old Chase was frowning, confused by Theryn's words. "What are you talking about? What powers?"

Theryn laughed a cold, mocking laugh. "Don't play stupid, boy. I can see the magic in you. You are a sorcerer born."

Chase laughed now. "A sorcerer? You're kidding, right? There's no such thing as magic. And my parents—I don't think so, not them. As far as being *a sorcerer born*, Mr. Creepy Wings, I don't know who gave birth to me. My parents didn't care enough to keep me around. They gave me up as soon as they could." He shrugged as if it didn't matter to him who his real parents were. Theryn frowned fiercely at Chase.

"You lie, boy! I can see your magic! I will find the truth for myself." He stared Chase down, his eyes locked on the boy in front of him who refused to cower in his presence, and then roared in anger. He waved his hand-like wing tip at the guard, who hauled Chase up and dragged him off. I looked up at my Chase. He was still watching the scene in front of him as he spoke.

"I think that was the first time he tried to look into my mind. He failed. It took him four days to get in." When he looked down at me, I saw the pain in his eyes.

When we looked back up, the scene before us had changed. Chase was back before Theryn, standing tall, refusing to kneel until forced to do so by the guards. My Chase was frowning now, as if trying to figure out the scene before him. He suddenly nodded and turned to me.

"This is four days later. He tried every day to talk to me, to get me to admit I was a sorcerer, I kept telling him I wasn't. This is the day he managed to get into my head." His voice was filled with pain once more with the remembrance of what had transpired while he was Theryn's captive. We watched the scene unfold.

"Good morning, Chase. You know; if you would just tell me what I want to know, the torture would end. It's very simple, boy." I could see Chase was becoming angry. Theryn could, too. He was pushing Chase on purpose. I frowned, wondering why the younger Chase couldn't see it.

"Honestly, boy, it's so simple, really. I just want information. If you provided it, I would end the pain." I saw that the younger Chase's hands had clenched into fists at his sides. I doubted he believed what Theryn said.

"Since you refuse to tell me anything of your parents, tell me of Chandra Strandon. Have you seen her or her father? Fredrick wouldn't be far off if he knew of your existence; the man is a nuisance. I would crush him if I could find him. He has made it his life's work to find the Chosen before I do."

Young Chase looked up at Theryn, anger bright in his eyes. "I don't know anything," he spoke through clenched teeth, a muscle in his jaw ticking.

Theryn gave a low, dark chuckle. "Oh, I doubt that, my dear boy. I intend to find out everything you know in time. You can't block me forever. I have ways of making you speak what is hidden way back in the dark recesses of your mind. Secrets you think you've hidden away, I can find."

The boy before him didn't look scared by his threats. Quite the opposite—he was angry. The guards could no longer hold him; he threw off the claws that held his shoulders and rose to his feet to stand before Theryn, his whole body vibrating with the anger he could no longer contain. Even at fifteen, Chase had been tall and muscular.

"I don't know about any damn Chosen. I don't know about any sorcerers. I have never heard of Fredrick Strandon or his daughter! I am not a sorcerer! My real parents cared so damn much about me, they dumped me on the steps of a church when I was five days old, like a piece of trash! You can take your questions and ram them down your throat! I'm done listening to them! I'm finished speaking to you!" His voice had been controlled fury until the end, when he lost complete control of the anger, screaming right in

Theryn's face. If the guards hadn't grabbed his arms, he probably would have thrown himself at Theryn. My Chase winced at the part about his parents dumping him on the church steps; he knew now that was a lie.

Theryn wasn't at all angry about Chase's outburst. No, quite the opposite—he had an evil, satisfied, sadistic, little grin on his face. Even I shrank back from it, hiding my face in my Chase's shoulder.

Younger Chase dropped to his knees on the floor, clutching his head in his hands, bowing forward until his forehead touched the cool stone of the cave floor. I knew Theryn was in his mind. Theryn laughed; I shivered violently. Chase put his arm around my shoulders. I looked up to see that his eyes were once again filled with the familiar pain. I knew this must be far worse for him to see than for me. He now understood exactly how Theryn had forced his way into his mind.

When he had lost control, let his temper rule him, Theryn was able to enter his mind. It was his anger that let Theryn in.

The scene shimmered and changed yet again, to show fifteen-year-old Chase sitting in his cage, his back against the bars. A wyvern guard stood just outside, stiff and silent, never looking at the prisoner inside the metal bars.

Suddenly, another wyvern came and spoke quietly to the first; they glanced at Chase, and then left. Chase sat up, instantly alert, and crept to the cage door. Somehow, he managed to open it. He looked left, and then right and sprinted down the narrow passage ahead of him.

This was the first time he had tried to escape, when Theryn had struck him. I was pretty sure I didn't want to see this. He was out the entrance in minutes. He was sure he'd made it; he was free! In an instant, he was flat on his back, a wyvern sitting on his chest. A second wyvern appeared out of the darkness, they hauled him back inside to Theryn's throne room.

Theryn was sitting on his throne, tapping a claw on the arm of his golden throne. It was almost as if he'd expected this. I gasped and looked up at my Chase. Our eyes locked. He spoke quietly, suddenly realizing what it meant.

"It was a test. He wanted to see if I would try to escape. I should've known I got out much too easily that night."

Theryn's eyes glowed with rage, fiercer than what I'd felt when I'd been inside his body in the vision I had had of him. He stood now, towering over Chase; the two guards that had brought him back had forced him to kneel, holding him there so he couldn't stand.

"I warned you, *boy*, you belong to me now! I will not have disobedience from you! You *will* obey my orders!"

Chase struggled against the guards, surging to his feet. "I don't belong to you, Theryn. I never will!" He raged, ending by spitting in Theryn's face. Theryn raised a clawed hand. Chase's eyes closed, turning his face away from Theryn as his claws tore across Chase's chest.

Blood oozed out from the slashes across his chest as Theryn's claws ripped through his flesh. Chase screamed and fell to the floor, but Theryn—Theryn fell back, stumbling away from Chase, screaming as if his whole body were on fire.

He yelled at the guards to remove Chase. He stumbled to the back of the cave and plunged his curved, claw-like hand into a small pool of water, washing the blood from it. Only when Chase's blood was washed from his claws did he find relief. Theryn stood back from the water.

Alone now in his chamber, he began to pace. We watched the great beast, confusion apparent in his ebony eyes. He looked up then; for the first time, we noticed the staff hung on the far wall. Esemer's broken staff; he'd kept it. He spoke to it now.

"Essie, what happened? If the boy is not the Chosen, why does his blood burn so terribly?" He shook his massive head. "I cannot touch him again; I will not risk it. I wish you were still here, my friend. I need your guidance." We were shocked that Theryn would have any attachment to anyone, a friendship even. It made him seem almost human. Almost.

Chase and I both woke when the alarm went off at midnight. We'd forgotten about the lesson Calan had told us about. We both felt drained; the vision had been hard to see. At least I had Chase with me; I doubted I would've been able to watch that alone. We struggled out of bed, groggy and disoriented. After we were dressed, we went to the ledge and were stunned to find out our lesson today wasn't going to be one in magic. The ledge looked like an old-fashioned battle arena, something out of a medieval jousting event or something very like it.

"What the …" we chorused in unison. Dad and Calan looked up at us; they'd been practicing with swords when we came out. Much to our embarrassment, they were both stripped to the waist, and both were all sweaty from their sword practicing. Not something you want to see, your dads shirtless and sweaty … ugh … gross!

"Took you two long enough; it's almost one already."

I groaned, great, another lecture. I was too tired for that. "Dad, can we do the lecture thing another time?"

Before we even considered letting them grind us into the dirt, Chase and I had to tell them about our shared vision. Neither was pleased about it, Calan, the least of all, because of what Theryn had put Chase through.

"Chase, I'm sorry, if we had told you something, anything, maybe none of that would've had to happen." Calan hugged Chase tightly.

"Dad, it's okay. It happened; it's over. We have to move on now. Let it go."

I knew that I had said those same words to him not so long ago. Calan nodded and turned away; I doubted he wanted Chase to see the tears in his eyes. My dad was still frowning over the vision; he finally shook his head, seeming to push the vision away for now.

"When the battle begins, it will be best if you both know a bit about practical self-defense as well as magical self-defense. It will help."

"Can't we just have an M16?"

Both dads frowned at Chase. My dad sighed.

"Chase, a gun won't work; we're talking ancient magic here. Modern weapons won't work against it." We groaned; sword fighting wasn't on the top of any teenager's list of things to learn.

Chase smirked at me, winked, and pulled his shirt off. I giggled. *Nice, Magic Boy, and totally not fair! No distractions allowed!* Now that I could direct my thoughts and keep them to one person, I could *speak* only to Chase when I wanted to. It had definite advantages. I smirked. Two could play the distraction game. I looked down at my jeans and sweatshirt.

"I think I need a wardrobe change. I'll be right back!" I dashed down the tunnel and back to our room, tossing things out of the drawers, hoping Mom had brought my workout things when she'd gone back to the house to pack. When I finally found them, I grinned wickedly, changed quickly, and ran back to the ledge, appearing triumphantly in my dinky sports bra and bike shorts. Dad probably would've gone through the roof if we'd been inside with a roof for him to go through. However, to my and both of the dads' surprise, it was Chase who was upset. I backed away from him, not sure why he was mad.

"Chase? What's wrong?"

"Go change, *now!*"

"Chase, seriously, why? What on earth is wrong with what I'm wearing? Practically every woman in the world wears something like this when they work out! Don't tell me you're going to be some caveman and try to tell me what to wear, because that's not gonna fly! I will wear what I want to, when I want to!"

He swept his hand through his hair and turned away. When he spoke, his voice was filled with pain.

"I'm begging you, Chandra, *please go change.*" I was confused. Why should I have to go change? What on earth was wrong with my clothes? My dad put his hand on my shoulder and spoke softly.

"Chandra, I don't think your choice of clothing has anything to do with why Chase wants you to change. I think it has to do more with ... with ... what he can ... uh ... *see.*"

I was still confused. If Chase loved me, why on earth should it bother him to see my body? I stiffened and looked down. I hadn't thought about it when I put the sports bra on. Oh, no. The scar. It was partially visible.

"Oh, Chase, I didn't mean … I'm sorry … I forgot about the scar." I went to him, touching his arm, but he didn't turn around. "Chase?"

He groaned, sounding like he was in extreme pain. "Just go change, Chans."

I wanted to cry. If he couldn't look at me now half dressed, what would happen later, when we were married and … I couldn't finish the thought; it was too painful. I turned and ran back to our room. The tears started before I was even off the ledge.

"Chase, you need to go to her, son. You can't leave it like that. She's not going to change and come back."

His shoulders slumped, his hand going automatically to his hair. He knew his dad was right. The pain he'd felt when he'd seen the scar on Chandra's chest had been immediate and horrifying. How was he going to deal with seeing that scar on her chest for the rest of their lives together? Seeing it and knowing that he was the one who had put it there? He looked at his dad, not sure what to do.

"Dad, how …" He held his hands up lamely.

"You love her, son?" his dad asked gently. Chase nodded mutely. "Then it will all work out in the end. Now, go talk to her; we can practice another time. Go on."

Chase turned around numbly and left.

I threw myself on the bed, sobbing uncontrollably. Chase would never love me enough to get past what had happened that day. He could never look at the scar on my chest and forget, never. It would stand between us as surely as if Theryn were still in his mind. Sobs tore through me. I curled up, trying to hide from the pain; there was no place to hide, nowhere, not ever.

Suddenly, I stood, dashing away the tears on my face. It wasn't Chase's fault—it was Theryn's fault. I grabbed my sweatshirt off the floor and pulled it over my head, coming to a decision. I ran back out into the dragon living room, calling for Hertha, the words repeating themselves in my mind over and over. *It was Theryn's fault, not Chase's.* I was determined now to put it right.

Hertha wasn't keen on my plan when I explained it to her, but when I told her I would go without her, if I had to, she finally agreed to take me.

Chase walked slowly back toward the room he and Chandra shared, taking his time, trying to figure out what he could say to Chandra to fix things. He wandered for a bit, thinking, not going directly to their room. How was he going to tell Chandra that everything was going to be all right after what had just happened? It would be—at least; he hoped it would, if he could figure out a way to tell her exactly how he felt. He loved her. He knew that. He just had to figure out a way to get beyond what had happened that day, get beyond what Theryn had forced him to do.

He spent the next forty-five minutes searching for her. He found his father and Fredrick sitting near Queebo's ledge, talking, sitting in chairs they had pilfered from the kitchen.

"Dad, I can't find Chandra anywhere. Something's wrong." He was frantic by now, afraid that she'd done something stupid while she was upset. Calan looked to Fredrick, who frowned and called for Echo.

"Echo, have you seen Chandra?"

"She and Hertha left some time ago; why do you ask?"

Chase froze, terror climbing through him. "No, she wouldn't. She couldn't be that stupid." He ran his hand through his hair, stopped, and then did it again, leaving it standing on end.

"Chase? She wouldn't what?"

He looked at Fredrick. "I think maybe I know where she went." He looked grim. Both Fredrick and his father looked expectantly at him. "I think she went after Theryn."

"She did *what?!*" Fredrick jumped up from where he'd been sitting, knocking his chair over.

"I'm not positive, but if she went anywhere while she was upset, that's where it would be. We know where his lair is after that vision we shared. She was upset because the scar disturbed me. It stands

to reason she would get angry at Theryn for what he did to me."
Chase was surprised he could be so logical with the possibility of
Chandra being so close to that monster. Calan stood now, too. He
could see the frantic edge that had crept over Fredrick.

"Fredrick, calm down. We need to plan before we go after her.
Rushing off will do the lass no good."

Fredrick nodded, but he wanted his baby back where she
belonged, right now. The thought of her in Theryn's clutches
sickened him. All he could picture was the fair-haired Elandra. He
couldn't lose another daughter to Theryn.

I didn't think; I just flew. Theryn would pay. He'd hurt everyone
I loved in some way or another. I was done with the suffering.

"Chandra, this plan is foolish! You do not know enough to fight
Theryn! He will destroy you!"

"Hush, Hertha! I'm the Chosen. It's in the *almighty prophecy,* isn't
it? I will destroy him and win the day. Why not now?" I muttered
bitterly. Hertha whimpered. She had never seen me so angry. To
tell the truth, I'd never seen me this angry. I pushed to the back of
my mind the fact that the prophecy proclaimed that Chase and I
were the Chosen *together,* so for me to have claimed I could win the
day alone was a bold-faced lie. And I knew it.

"Just follow the route I gave you. You don't have to stay."

She whimpered again. "Chandra, please reconsider!"

"*No,* Hertha! It ends today!" I snapped. She said no more. Just
flew quietly on till we reached the spot I'd directed her to. She set
me down a half a mile from Theryn's lair.

"Go, Hertha. I won't have you injured."

"*Chandra, please!*"

"*No,* Hertha, go!"

She nodded and flew off without another word. I began my
long walk to Theryn's lair, knowing I had to reach it before Hertha
made it back to the dragons' cave and told the others where I had
gone.

I prepared myself to battle the monster that had haunted my
dreams for far too long now.

CHAPTER 20

I Face The Nightmare

When the cave came into sight, I felt no relief. I wasn't glad to see it. I felt only dread at what I was going to face here. Theryn, the monster of my nightmares.

I walked right up to the entrance, surprising the guards that lurked just inside.

"Take me to Theryn, now."

They looked at each other, and then scrambled to follow my order. Neither touched me, just ushered me forward. I walked down the now-familiar route to Theryn's throne room. He gave a small start when the guards thrust me into the room.

"Ah, Chandra Strandon, you've come to me. How *interesting*."

I doubted he actually found it interesting. More like frustrating.

"Hello, Theryn."

"So, what brings you here, *child?*"

I knew Theryn would try what he had tried on Chase; he wanted to make me angry, make me lose control, so he could get into my head. After all, that's how he had gotten into Chase's head.

"You, Theryn, what else?" I answered as calmly as I could.

He grinned at me evilly. "I didn't think even you were stupid enough to face me alone. You must truly believe your powers to be awesome. Do you really think you are the Chosen, *girl?*" He stood and began to circle me, like some giant, leathery bird of prey. "So, where is our young friend Chase?" I stiffened but remained silent. "Come now, Chandra, don't you want to talk about Chase?"

I told myself to remain calm. I wondered how much he really knew about Chase and me.

"That's not why I came, Theryn. I came to end this, here, now, before it becomes necessary for any more bloodshed. There has been too much of that already."

He cackled. "Yes, too much bloodshed, too much death, too much war, Chandra. Do you want peace, then? Is that it?"

"I am not such a fool to believe you would offer peace, Theryn. I'm here to fight." Laughter, deep mocking laughter came from him. It reminded me too much of the mocking threats I'd gotten when he'd occupied Chase's mind. It sent chills through my entire body.

"Oh, you wish to fight me? A fight to the death, is it? Winner take all? If you win, the wyvern go away and leave the dragons alone? Is that it? And if I win, Chandra, what if I win?" His voice was deep and cold.

I gave him a grim smile. "Then I suppose you get your war, Theryn."

He threw his head back and cackled, showing white, pointed teeth—very sharp, glistening in the dim light of the cave. "Oh, yes, because your dear Chase would come avenge your death, wouldn't he?"

I stiffened. "Chase would fight in the war, I assume, but not to avenge anything. I'm not here to talk about Chase. He has nothing to do with my reasons for coming here." Which, of course, was a total lie; he had everything to do with why I was here. But Theryn need not know that. Theryn didn't look as if he believed my little speech.

"Such an honorable cause, sacrificing yourself so that your true love may live a little longer, my dear." Theryn's voice dripped honeyed sweetness, mocking my words.

Stay calm, stay calm, I told myself over and over. I gritted my teeth, trying not to react to his words. "I told you, Theryn, Chase is not the reason I'm here." Another laugh; he got right in my face this time and snarled his words.

"That ring on your finger says otherwise, *girl.*"

Self-consciously, I hid my hand behind my back. He shrieked with laughter, spittle flying from his lips to fleck my cheeks. I backed away from the scornful look in his eyes, concentrating hard on not lifting a hand to wipe the flecks of spittle from my face. I didn't want to give him the satisfaction of knowing it bothered me.

"And now I know exactly how to destroy the Chosen!"

I could hear the glee in his voice as he made that final declaration, his self-satisfaction in knowing he had somehow won this little battle of wits we were having. He motioned for the guards and spoke in the language of the wyvern. They grabbed my arms, hauling me away. I fought like a woman possessed. I had come to end this, and by God, I was going to!

"FACE ME YOU COWARD! FIGHT ME THERYN!!"

I fought the guards, but it was no use. The wyvern guards were much stronger than I was. Theryn continued to laugh. His voice followed me out of the room and down the passage.

"Oh, yes, Chandra, you have given me the perfect way to destroy you! When your one true love, Chase, arrives to rescue you, you will have the pleasure of watching him die! Right before your very eyes! And I will make the boy suffer for his betrayal when he escaped me; that you can count on, Chandra!"

I renewed my struggles against the guards, trying desperately to escape, all to no avail. Theryn's mocking laughter echoed down the passage, bouncing from rock to rock, sounding raw and loud in my ears when it hit. I kept shouting at him to face me and fight, even as the guards tossed me into the very cage Chase had been held captive in. I sobbed, collapsing to my knees on the cold ground, pain tearing through me. Chase—I had to warn him to stay away! I knew he would indeed come for me. My mind screamed. I had to make him hear me somehow; I knew I had to make him hear me.

Chase … Chase, you have … have to stay … away, don't come for me … please, it's a trap … please … Chase, stay away … Theryn will kill you … to destroy me.

I was crying so hard, it was difficult to concentrate on the words and focus on Chase. I knew I had to get the message to him, to warn him. I repeated the message over and over, until I finally fell into a dazed, exhausted sleep.

Chase was frantic to get to Chandra. He hunched over Mocte's emerald back, praying they wouldn't be too late to reach her. Suddenly, he sat upright, listening hard.

"Dad, Dad! I hear her—oh, Jesus, no! She's telling me not to come for her. Dad, what do I do?"

They landed so they could talk more easily.

"Chase, what did she say? Tell us exactly what you heard."

He nodded, tears running unchecked down his cheeks now as her words continued to run through his mind. He couldn't block it out. She seemed to be sending a continual message.

"She says not to come for her, that it's a trap. That Theryn will … he will …" He swallowed hard through the lump in his throat. "Kill me to destroy her."

Fredrick and Calan exchanged looks.

Chase was frantic; they had to save her from Theryn. "We can't leave her there! We have to go get her!" He could hear the terror in her voice. He couldn't abandon her.

"Chase, we canna go rushing in with no plan. Theryn *will* kill you." His dad said the words gently, putting a hand on his shoulder. He looked at his dad, knowing he was right and hating it. "Chase, you know it would destroy Chandra if she saw Theryn kill you. She would never survive it, son." His shoulders sagged in defeat, knowing his father spoke the truth. He agreed; they would return when they had a plan.

Silently, he swore he would get her out of there, no matter what it took.

CHAPTER 21

I Survive Hell ... Barely

I didn't know how much time had passed since I had come to Theryn's lair. I didn't bother to try to keep track. It would have been impossible with no sunlight anyway. My only company was my own tormented thoughts. I worried constantly that Theryn would appear to tell me that it was time to watch Chase die. I never knew if any of my constant messages to Chase got through. The way the guards were beginning to watch me, I had the feeling they thought I'd gone 'round the bend. And perhaps I had. The silence and my own thoughts were torture. Maybe that's how Theryn wanted it.

I couldn't blame them for thinking I had lost my mind. I'd changed, becoming silent, withdrawn. Mostly because I was constantly screaming silent messages to Chase. I'd stopped yelling for Theryn to stand and fight me after that first long day had passed; he wouldn't. I knew that now.

But the waiting was horrid. I couldn't stand it, not knowing when the end would come. *This is what Chase felt when he was here,* I thought. My fear grew day by day. How many days had passed now? Did it matter, really, as long as Chase was still safe?

He was, wasn't he? Had he come to look for me? Did he still care for me? Or was he still angry over our fight about how I'd been dressed that last day? That was too depressing a thought even to consider, so I shoved it to the back of my mind and locked it away. The days continued to roll by, each blending obscurely into the next, my thoughts going around and around in my mind like a silent little merry-go-round, torturing me with their continual painful little rotation around my mind.

Maybe I was going slowly insane. How exactly did one tell?

My pain swelled, deepened; surely, it couldn't grow anymore. Could it? Death would be welcomed now. I missed the comfort of Chase's presence. *Magic Boy, at least you're safe,* I told myself again and again.

Though, I would like to see him just once more before death claimed me. A small smile touched my lips. Just to watch him run his hand through his hair. See him smile; see that adorable dimple in his cheek. I shook my head. I couldn't wish for that. If Chase were here, Theryn could hurt him. I curled tightly into a ball, wanting to hide.

Sobs rent me in two. It was over; I knew the end had to be near now. Chase wasn't coming, either because he didn't care enough for me anymore to come, or because he'd heard my message and turned back. Whichever it was, I knew, Chosen or not, I was on my own now. That hurt more than anything I could imagine.

Except maybe Chase dying. Yes, the thought of Chase dying hurt much, much worse.

Chase was determined; the plan was set in place and final. Everything was in place; tonight they would get Chandra back.

A month had passed. He groaned; it had been so long since she'd gone to Theryn. Chase was impatient; he wanted her back. The dads had taken their time—too much, in his opinion—to plan. They didn't want any mistakes. This was too important.

Now that it was finally time to go, he was anxious to leave. He would finally have her back, and God willing, Theryn would be dead. He stood in the entrance to the cave, watching the sun sink slowly behind the horizon. He urged it to sink faster. Mocte stood by him, shifting impatiently. Both wanted to go, *now.*

When darkness was full upon them, the group left, ready to do whatever was necessary to get Chandra back, knowing some of them may not return. Chase had laid out the wyvern's lair as best he knew it. They had all the information they could; they were as prepared as they could be. Chase had spent this last month training, learning as much as he could so that he could help the best that he could. He would not let Chandra down. His face was set. Theryn would not get into his head again, not this time. He and Fredrick had discussed it. The only thing they had come up with was to allow Chase to put up his own defense. As Chandra had put it, wrap up his brain in his own little shield and protect it.

They only hoped it wouldn't interfere with any of his other magic. He wouldn't perform the shield spell, just to be safe, since they knew that might cause interference. They flew toward Theryn's lair, closer to Chandra, closer to whatever fate had in store for them.

I woke suddenly when the door to the cage creaked open. The guards hauled me up and dragged me out. No! It couldn't be; I'd told him to stay away! I screamed at Chase. He had to listen!

Chase, you have to go—you can't come here! Theryn will kill you! Please go! Please, for me, go! Go!

My heart ached. I didn't want to tell him to leave me, but I knew I had to. The guards dragged me down the passage to Theryn, forcing me to kneel before him. It was the first time I'd seen him since the night I had arrived here. He'd left me alone to suffer, to wallow in my own terror.

"Oh, my dear, you certainly can't see Chase looking like that; you're a mess. Well, I suppose a month in captivity will do that to a human."

A month? Had it really been that long? He stood and wandered over to stare up at the staff on the wall. I hated that staff and everything it represented. Theryn continued his speech. He must've thought a lot about what he would say when this moment finally arrived.

"Your dear, sweet love, Chase approaches." He gave a mirthless little chuckle. "He has brought the whole gang with him. It will be nice to see all my old friends again. Chase, Fredrick, Calan, and Molly."

I wanted to weep; not only had Chase come, but the whole family as well. What if they were all killed? I couldn't bear the thought of it.

Chase, no, please. You all have to leave! He knows you're coming! God, please, go back! He's going to kill you all! Go back! I kept my face as blank as I could. I didn't want Theryn to know; he couldn't find out I was sending them messages.

Chase grimaced when Chandra's voice first screamed into his mind. *Chase, you have to go—you can't come here! Theryn will kill you! Please go! Please, for me, go! Go!* He warned the others that Chandra was aware that he was coming. The second time her voice raced through his mind, he wanted to scream; she was frantic. He hoped Theryn couldn't see it. *Chase, no, please. You all have to leave! He knows you're coming! God, please, go back! He's going to kill you all! Go back!* Theryn knew that everyone was coming; so be it. He warned the others. They were ready. Theryn wouldn't know what was happening, despite what the beast would *think* he knew.

They were close now; he could no longer allow Chandra to speak to him. He had to shut off his mind as he and Fredrick had discussed. It was painful to shut himself off from her, even if she wouldn't know he was doing it. He squeezed his eyes shut as her voice cut off midsentence.

I kept my features plain, schooled them to look as bored as possible. It was hard knowing that Chase and the others were so close. Theryn kept me apprised of their progress.

"Come, Chandra, it's time to go meet your intended. Ahh ... I do wish we had time to improve upon your appearance. Oh, well, you will just have to go as you are!"

The guards came forward, latching on to my arms, dragging me back out and down the passage toward the entrance. Theryn had done something inside his lair to disable my powers. I wondered if I would be able to use them outside the cave. Theryn was smiling; he was too happy, which worried me. I balked when we made it to the entrance.

Oh, God, there were so many of them. So many. *Chase, there are too many of them. Please! Go back! Please! There are so many of them!* I stumbled forward, the guards the only thing holding me up now. Theryn smirked down at me.

"You finally see, Chandra, your side cannot win. My army outnumbers yours by quite a lot." He was almost giddy in his excitement. I wanted to retch. Chase, my poor Chase. He wouldn't have a chance; none of my family would. We had been naive to think we could win against something as evil as Theryn. We were children.

They came then, Chase, my dad, Calan, and Molly. The wyvern let them land. My mind was still silently screaming at them all to leave while they could. Chase didn't even look at me.

None of them did. They dismounted and walked slowly forward, a silent march to their death. That's what it was in my mind. Tears slipped slowly down my cheeks. Why weren't they listening to me? They had to go. Theryn would kill them! Chase led them forward; he stopped in front of Theryn. *Standing tall, brave till the end,* I thought.

"Let her go, Theryn. This is over."

Theryn burst out laughing. "You dare to make demands, *boy?* You are outnumbered! Surrender now and maybe I will spare you. We can work together, as we did before."

I could see the distaste plain on his face. Chase would never work with Theryn again.

"This is your last chance, Theryn. Do you submit?"

"You never did have a brain, *boy!* Kill them all!" Theryn bellowed the order to his troops. I screamed; I couldn't help it. They couldn't die! Not because of me!

Chase was ready for this; they'd practiced, over and over again. He knew that Theryn's army would outnumber them. Sheer gall was all they had on their side.

Theryn would let them land simply because he would think they were stupid. The wyvern leader was overconfident.

They made their demands. Theryn refused, as he knew the beast would.

He ordered them killed, as he knew Theryn would.

All expected, all planned for. Now, if only it kept going that way.

All hell broke loose as soon as the wyvern attacked. The guards shuffled Chandra back to the cave entrance, protecting her, keeping her as far from the battle and Chase as possible.

I lost sight of Chase almost immediately. I struggled against my captors. "Chase! Chase! Where are you?" No use; it was much too loud for him to hear me. I still couldn't use my magic.

They had hauled me back into the cave entrance. I kept my mind blank, free of any thoughts. I didn't want to distract any of my family during battle. There were so many wyvern; how could any of them hope to survive? I saw flashes of each of my family. Tears continued to flow freely down my face.

Then an odd thing happened—the guards went slack and slumped forward to the ground, dead, blood flowing from the stab wounds in their backs. I looked frantically around. Chase appeared suddenly at my side. I flung my arms around him, crying, trying to pull his face down to kiss him.

"Not now, Chandra, we have to get out of here!" His voice was harsh, flat. His eyes moved past me over the battle taking place behind us. I nodded, realizing that now wasn't the time for a heartfelt reunion, as badly as I wanted one. We made it three feet from the cave—ironic, I thought. Theryn loomed over us.

"I knew you would go right for the girl, Chase. You're so predictable, *boy!* You'll not escape me that easily!" Chase shoved me behind his back, raising his sword. Theryn lunged, not with his deadly sharp claws or his pointed teeth; he swung his tail around in a graceful arc, the barbed stinger flying with deadly accuracy. Chase fell, dead, as soon as the stinger struck his chest, piercing him through the heart. I knew the poison would've killed him almost instantly, if the strike to the heart hadn't. Theryn laughed, his great head thrown back with glee. I heard shouts all around me, sounding dim and far away, drowned out by the sudden loud ringing in my ears. I was frozen in place, staring down at Chase, just staring. Shock and disbelief kept me rooted to the spot.

Suddenly, Calan was there by my side, lifting me and carrying me away. I stared back at Chase's body lying on the ground—blood, so much blood. He can't be dead, though—he can't be, no! I pushed at Calan's arms, trying to get him to let me go. I had to go to Chase! I could save him, heal him! I had the power to fix him! We are the Chosen! He wasn't dead!

My dad ran through my line of vision, his arms out. He scooped up Chase's lifeless body, throwing him over his shoulder. His sword swung outward, slicing at Theryn. Theryn hissed, striking back at my dad; he was too fast, already out of reach. Echo was flying low by his side. As I watched, Dad jumped onto his back and Echo circled away from Theryn's reach.

Calan continued to run with me in his arms. Molly appeared at his side, pain etched on her face. She had a wound on her upper thigh, blood flowed down her leg, and she was limping badly. Would she be okay? I thought numbly. I watched as she stumbled, and then righted herself. We ran until the dragons appeared at our side. Soon, we were flying. It didn't matter, though; my reason for living was gone.

Chase was gone.

Queebo met us on the ledge when we returned. Her eyes were full of dread when she saw the lifeless body my dad carried in his arms.

"Oh, dear me, no." She shook her head. "Come, let us all go inside. Fredrick, tell me what happened." I listened dully as my dad began to tell her about the battle. Calan still held me, his hand moving slowly up and down my back in a soothing gesture. I didn't want to be soothed; I wanted Chase back. I was immune to anyone else's pain; I felt only my own deep, unending sorrow. I knew somewhere inside my mind that he and Molly had lost their son. Yet, even that didn't touch me.

Dully, from a distance, I heard my father's voice as he moved closer to the moment of Chase's death. I didn't want to hear it all over again, to hear my dad tell how Chase had died. I didn't need to hear it; I had witnessed it. I struggled out of Calan's arms and ran to my room—no, our room, Chase's and mine. I cried like my soul had been torn out. My heart was gone. Chase was gone. I couldn't make it real, no matter how many times I said it.

Chase was gone. Chase was gone.

The words repeated over and over, yet still they didn't seem real. How could he be gone? How? I sobbed harder, my chest hurting with the force of it.

My dad came to me some time later; I don't know how much later. He sat on the edge of the bed next to me. "Chandra, we need to talk." I shook my head, refusing to look at him. "Honey, there are things we need to discuss. Plans need to be made." I shoved myself upright, anger at him clear on my face.

"That's all you care about, your stupid war! Go make plans, then. I don't care, Dad! Leave me alone." I fell back, burying my face in the pillow, crying anew. I could hear the loud sigh he released.

"Chandra, I wasn't talking about the war. I was … I was … I meant … we have a funeral to arrange." I rolled away from him, curling up and crying harder, hugging the pillow to my chest. We were supposed to be planning our wedding, not his funeral! I felt the bed give as he stood.

"Chandra, when you're ready to talk to the rest of us, please come out. Calan wants you there." I tried to curl myself up further, clutching one of Chase's shirts to my chest as well as the pillow.

I spent days in our room, refusing to leave. Someone brought food; I never saw who, nor did I care to look. I ate very little, just enough to survive. I knew that eventually I would have to leave our room, face the world. It was out there—waiting. Theryn was waiting.

Legend was the only one who would put up with me; she stayed by my side despite my constant crying fits.

One thought kept me alive: Theryn had to pay for what he'd done. He had to die for taking Chase from me.

My need for revenge was greater than my need for my own death. That need for revenge is what forced me to choose to continue living rather than wallow in my own grief until death came for me as well. It was the one thought that got me up and out of our room.

It was now time to bring the war to Theryn. I was almost eighteen. I would train harder than ever. For Chase. I would kill Theryn. For Chase.

I would stand at the funeral, and I would look into that cherished face one final time, watch them lower the casket into the ground.

Then I would find the beast that had caused my sorrow and kill him.

This was not over.

Victoria lives in Las Vegas, Nevada with her husband, daughter, a corn chip lovin' cat named Max and a slightly neurotic dog named Bear. She's a Chicago transplant who only misses her husband's relatives and the Chicago style food, but can definitely live without the humidity, the mosquitoes, or the below freezing temperatures in the winter. Jeans and T-shirts are Victoria's usual style, she thinks black high top Converse go with everything. Even if they don't, she wouldn't care anyway. Victoria can usually be found either typing furiously at her computer, or with a book in her hand. She encourages her daughter to read regularly. Both love all books, though they specifically love the fantasy genre above all else. Reading and writing are not only a hobby of Victoria's; they define her life.

Drop her an email at victoriakaer@gmail.com. You can also follow Victoria on Facebook or on her website, www.authorvictoriakaer.com

Made in the USA
Charleston, SC
22 August 2016